TOUCHSTONE

'What's up, lad? Come on, out with it, tell us what's wrong.'

Reddened eyes staring from his white face, he spoke in a flat voice. 'I'm not weeping. It's the scholarship.' There was a catch in his voice. 'I haven't got it.' . . .

Violet, hearing the savage tone, felt afraid. 'What are you getting at, Lionel?' His eyes burned like red-hot coals. He ought to be in bed, she thought. His strange way of talking could indicate that he was feverish.

But his answer came coldly enough, each word sounding as though it had been hewn from crystal icicles. 'Your sister, Mother, the eminent Mrs Holroyd – she made certain that I would not go to college. She refused my scholarship, that's what I'm getting at. What price now brothers and sisters rejoicing at each other's success, eh?'

TOUCHSTONE

Aileen Armitage

Every good wish

Aileen Armitage

ARROW BOOKS

Arrow Books Limited
62–65 Chandos Place, London WC2N 4NW

An imprint of Century Hutchinson Limited

London Melbourne Sydney Auckland
Johannesburg and agencies throughout
the world

First published 1986

Printed and bound in Great Britain by
Anchor Brendon Limited, Tiptree, Essex

ISBN 0 09 940310 2

For Rosie,
who started me off on the Hawksmoor trail,
with love and thanks

Men have a touchstone whereby to try gold:
but gold is the touchstone whereby to try men.

Thomas Fuller: *The Holy and Profane State*

ONE: 1886

Over the grey slate roofs of Hawksmoor a fitful
October sun struggled to prolong the last flicker of
summer. Inside the James Stott Ward of Hawksmoor
Infirmary, Cedric Moorhouse struggled in a final
valiant effort to hang on to life.

Outside a tram clattered past, rumbling slowly up
the hill and out of town on its long journey up to
the Outlane moors. The woman seated beside the bed
clicked her tongue in annoyance. The gaunt figure lying
under the starched sheets did not move except to inhale
erratically and noisily.

A nurse entered, followed by a portly gentleman
wearing a clerical collar who stood uncertainly by the
door.

'Your husband has come to join you in your vigil,
Mrs Holroyd.' The nurse spoke quietly in deference
to the patient's extreme condition, but her manner
remained matter-of-fact as she brought forward
another chair.

The woman moved stiffly in her seat and eased back
the collar of her fur-edged jacket.

'I'm glad you came, Percy. It can't be long now.'

Husband and wife sat mute while the nurse felt her
patient's pulse and lifted one of his eyelids. The only
sound to disturb the afternoon stillness were the dying
man's stertorous breathing and the crackle of the
nurse's apron.

'Has he regained consciousness at all?' The vicar's

voice was timorous, almost apologetic. He had been in the presence of death many times, but never before at the passing of a man so feared and respected as his father-in-law. The nurse shook her head. 'I'm afraid not, Reverend Holroyd. It's possible he may rally before the end, but don't count on it.'

The nurse closed the door behind her. Percy Holroyd regarded his wife's averted profile apprehensively and held his tongue. This was a terrible ordeal for Charlotte but any words of consolation he might try to offer would surely go amiss. This was a Moorhouse drama, a moment in which only Charlotte and the old gentleman could participate; Percy must express his concern only by offering Charlotte his sympathetic presence.

She was staring out of the window, deep in her own thoughts, when the nurse returned some time later.

'Sister suggests you might like to go down to her office for a cup of tea, Mrs Holroyd,' she said quietly. 'She recognises you won't want to leave the hospital at such a time.'

Charlotte looked back sharply at the figure in the bed and hesitated before answering. 'Will you be sure to call me if there's any change?'

'Indeed I will. I'll stay beside him.'

Percy followed his wife out into the corridor and paced along beside her, their footsteps ringing out sacrilegiously on the stone floor and echoing along the tiled walls. Nearing Sister's office Charlotte paused.

'I've been thinking, Percy. Which printer was it that Miss Hardcastle used to print those funeral cards when her father died? They were so restrained and dignified.'

Percy was shocked but at the same time infinitely reassured. Whatever the crisis, Charlotte always remained true to her practical, capable self.

'Why, I can't recall, my dear. But she did promise to call to see me in the vestry tomorrow – I'll ask her then if you wish.' He was pleased in a way, for the daughter of the late Sir Ramsden Hardcastle would be flattered, and it was always politic to keep on the right side of one's benefactress. Indeed, if it had not been for her interest he would not now be vicar of St Mark's. Second only to Hawksmoor parish church, it was a comfortable and reasonably lucrative living.

'It's a pity you won't be able to conduct the funeral service,' Charlotte murmured. 'You could give a splendid eulogy, I'm sure. But it will have to be the vicar of the parish church, I'm afraid, Father having been such an outstanding figure in Hawksmoor, alderman and ex-mayor and all that. What a shame.'

Percy ventured to speak, encouraged by her implicit praise. 'I hope he recovers consciousness before the end, my dear, for your sake.'

She sighed. 'Yes, indeed. I hoped he might ask for Charles. Having no son of his own to follow him, he always adored our son. He never quite took to Berenice as much as he did to Charles.'

A thought struck Percy and foolishly he voiced it. 'It is possible if he wakes that he might ask for his other grandchildren as well.'

Charlotte darted him an angry frown. 'Other grandchildren? What are you talking of, Percy?'

'Why, Violet's little ones, Amy and Lionel. And come, to that, shouldn't you send word to your sister that her father is dying? It seems only Christian, my dear, whatever happened in the past.'

Charlotte seized him by the arm. 'Percy! You cannot have forgotten what happened! We never want to see or hear of Violet again! You would not have me bring her here to distress him now, surely?'

Percy Holroyd fluttered his hands. 'That was a long time ago, and I'm sure he would want to have her here at the end – I mean, with your dear mother being gone so long he would be content, I'm sure, to have both his children close by when the moment comes.' Seeing the icy glow in his wife's eyes, Percy stopped.

'Percy, Sister is waiting for us. I do not think you

meant to hurt, for you are a kindly man, and I forgive you. But, after all the shame and misery Violet brought to the family, is it right Father should endure the suffering her presence might bring?'

'It must be done, my dear. He is her father, after all! And you'll have to invite her to the funeral.'

Charlotte turned away, then, straightening her jacket, she tapped at the door of Sister's office and entered. Percy followed, deep in thought. Violet Mallinson, whatever her misdeeds, should not be kept in ignorance of her father's imminent death. Charlotte viewed her sister as a feckless, self-willed creature, a view she held so strongly that never, never could Percy Holroyd voice his own opinion that Violet was a creature more sinned against than sinning. Indeed, to anyone other than Charlotte, she might appear a woman of strength and courage who had battled on to protect her own in the face of enormous difficulty, a woman highly to be admired.

Over the clinking teacups Percy was aware of a murmured conversation between Sister and his wife.

'I am sure your family will be of tremendous support to you, Mrs Holroyd,' Sister was saying smoothly. 'You have been very courageous during all these hours of waiting, but it can't be long now.'

Charlotte smiled, a weak, brave little smile, and dabbed her eyes with a lace-edged handkerchief. At that moment there was a peremptory knock at the door and the nurse entered hurriedly, her face flushed.

'Mrs Holroyd – come quickly! You might just be in time!'

Charlotte leapt from her seat and hastened to the door. Percy half-rose, uncertain whether to follow. At the doorway Charlotte turned, her face drained of colour.

'Percy – you know where to find Violet?'

'Ah, I think so, my dear.'

'Then send for her.'

Percy could hear her hasty, clattering footsteps recede down the corridor as he picked up his hat, nodded to Sister and went out of the carbolic-soaked atmosphere of the hospital into the evening. Over the grey slate roofs the setting sun was spreading its last glow, and by the time he turned the corner into Northgate it had gone.

Violet Mallinson gazed down fondly at her night-gowned child, who was squatting on the hearthrug playing with her favourite rag doll. Putting aside the chemise she was making for her, cut down from one of her own, Violet leaned across to stroke the child's head.

'We have no choice, my darling. We have to go, all of us. I can't leave you and Lionel here alone.'

The child pouted, a frown deepening between her dark eyes, and she tossed her head. 'I hate funerals! I don't like seeing the wagon and a box in it, 'cause I know there's a dead person inside.'

'A hearse, Amy, not a wagon,' Violet corrected gently. 'But we have to go, I'm afraid. He's your grand-father, you know – my father.'

Amy looked up, the doll momentarily forgotten, and Violet could see in the child's eyes that she was trying hard to visualise her mother as a little girl like herself. After a moment the frown faded.

'I can't remember Grandfather very well,' she murmured, picking up the doll again and starting to swathe it in a strip of discarded calico. 'It's so long since he came. I remember Uncle Edwin, though – he used to bring me bon-bons,' she added brightly.

'Grandfather could be kind, too,' Violet replied thoughtfully. It had not always been easy for him, but he had turned out not to be as callous and uncaring as he once had seemed. For all his hatred of Tom Mallinson, he had come to her aid at last when she really needed it. Not until Tom's death, though.

11

'*Mean bastard, I'll dance on his bloody grave, I will, or me name's not Tom Mallinson.*'

Poor Father. Once so strong and indomitable, he had become a frail, querulous creature by the end, no longer the force to be reckoned with, the man who used to intimidate all.

'Shall I have a new dress?' Amy asked.

Violet smiled. Clearly the child had been contemplating the possible ways of turning an unpleasant obligation to her advantage, and mentally the mother reviewed her resources.

'I think not, sweetheart. Your dark blue merino will do perfectly – but I'll have to make a crêpe armband for you.'

The clock on the mantelshelf gave an asthmatic whir and began to strike. Violet threw up her hands.

'My goodness, eight o'clock already! Come, let me put the curlers in your hair for you, ready for bed.'

The child rose obediently and came to kneel by her mother, the rag doll still clutched in her hands. One could guess at her thoughts from her expressive little face, thought Violet, for it was seldom in repose. Her lips more than any other feature were the indicators of her drift of thought, briefly and prettily pouted as they were now, or nibbled or sucked in when she was agitated. And when she was thwarted she pouted a prolonged and petulant moue. But smiles of pleasure were never far from her face. Violet wondered what profound deliberation was producing the present hesitant little tongue-flick along Amy's lips.

'I've decided I want to be a lady when I grow up.'

Violet chuckled, twisting a rag into the lustrous dark hair. Just like her father's – Tom, of the soul-searching eyes and as lean as his daughter promised to be . . .

'Of course you will, silly. You can't grow up to be a man.'

'Ouch! You're tugging! No, I mean a real lady. Mr

12

Bradley the butcher said you were a lady, a real lady. That's what I want to be.'

'*There will be no eyebrows raised, I assure you, Mrs Mallinson. You will be accorded all the respect due to a lady such as yourself.*'

'Did you love Grandfather, Mother?'

'Of course, sweetheart.'

'Then why aren't you weeping?'

It was Amy's way to ask unanswerable questions. 'A lady mourns in private, not in public.' It was an evasive answer but the child seemed satisfied.

'Did you weep when my father died? I didn't. I was only a baby.'

Seven years ago, and still I think of you and miss you, Tom, you and your brooding presence. I miss Frederic too, for all he did to me. 'Of course, but that was a long time ago.'

'I think I'll weep when Bella dies,' the child remarked, twisting her head to hold up the doll. 'She's poorly, you know. I'm putting a bandage on.'

'Poor Bella. She'll be better soon. Oh, Amy, just look at your clean nightdress! You must have leaned over the grate – look, there's a nasty smudge of black lead on it.'

Scolding her lovingly, Violet took the child upstairs and put her to bed. 'Hush now, don't wake your brother – he's been fast asleep for ages.'

She looked fondly at the two little heads, one darkly entwined in rags, one fair, side by side on the pillow. Then, tiptoeing out, she went back downstairs to sit by the fire. It was ironic, she thought, that the first time Charlotte had contacted her in all these years it had to be to summon her to their father's funeral. Doubly ironic, since she knew Charlotte would sooner have cut off her right hand than get in touch with one so far below her in the social scale. Charlotte would recognise her only with stiff reserve when the time came, and discontinue the acquaintance as swiftly as she could. That was one thing that could be said for Charlotte – predictable to a fault, she never changed her ways. She was probably still the sanctimonious prig she had always been.

'*But you promised, Charlotte! You promised you wouldn't tell Father!*'

'*I didn't actually promise, Violet, not in so many words. I was only acting in your best interests since you seemed so set on this stupidity. Rushing off to elope with Father's apprentice, indeed! You need a steady, secure marriage like mine.*'

Steady and dull, married to someone like her Percy. Maybe it had been unwise to marry Tom but at least it had been a marriage born of love. Amy had been born out of that love. Lionel, now – Lionel was born of passion, passion such as she had never known could exist. Charlotte would be forever a stranger to such passion.

'*A modest woman seldom desires any sexual gratification. She submits to her husband only to please him.*'

Poor Charlotte. She had missed so much, and yet, what good had she herself gained from all her experience?

Sighing, Violet put away her scissors and needle in the wicker workbasket and began gathering up the threads and shreds of calico from the floor. As she straightened she heard the door open quietly.

'Mother, I can't sleep.' Amy's wistful little face was regarding her plaintively from the doorway. Violet tried to look cross.

'Why ever not, may I ask?'

'Bella is very poorly, Mother. I'm afraid she might die.' She held out the rag doll, entreaty in her dark eyes.

Violet took the doll. 'No, she won't die, darling. Grandfather died only because he was old. You'll see – Bella will be well by morning, especially if we give her a dose of our special medicine.'

14

The child watched while she mimed the action of pouring from a bottle and offering an invisible spoon to the painted lips, then the dark eyes looked up enquiringly. 'Is she all right now?'

'She will be by morning. Now go back to bed and don't worry.'

Poor child, thought Violet, as Amy slithered off her lap and left. Death, like darkness, was incomprehensible to a young mind and therefore to be feared. She reproached herself for the way she had broken the news to Amy. Though the child had appeared to accept it equably, it evidently disturbed her.

Thank heaven Amy had never known the circumstances surrounding her father's death. The mystery of Tom's disappearance that night seven years ago had never been satisfactorily explained.

The coals in the hearth slithered and settled with a crash. Violet stretched to ease the ache in her shoulders. She had been sitting sewing for far too long. It was time she put the flat-irons on the fire to heat up if she was to get the ironing done before it was time for bed. Amy and Lionel would both need clean smocks for school in the morning.

As she watched the droplet of spit hiss and slither across the hot, shiny surface of the iron, Violet thought again about Charlotte and recalled the last time she had seen her. It had been that night in Langdenholme, just after Tom's death, when Father sat surrounded by his guests, Charlotte amongst them. She recalled her own entrance, unexpected and in shabby contrast to the finely dressed diners seated around the candle-lit table.

'*You can feed this lot in style – now feed this*.'

Remorse still stabbed her to remember how she had dumped her tiny newborn baby in the centre of that table, but poverty and hunger had left no other choice.

No choice. Except to follow up the offer of the admiring gentleman who had witnessed it all. '*If ever*

*you are in London . . . I should be enchanted . . . It
takes courage to do what you did . . . '* Frederic
Newman. But for that night, Frederic would never
have come into her life – and Lionel . . .

Violet sighed deeply and straightened, rubbing a
hand down her aching back. The iron was cold and
the clock was showing half-past ten already. As she
prepared for bed the handsome, humour-lined face of
Frederic Newman still hovered before her inner eye.

*'Stay with me, Violet, mistress of my home, and my
heart.'*

Tears filling her eyes, Violet lit a candle from the
fire, put out the lamp and went slowly upstairs.

A grey mist hung low under the ancient yew trees of
Hawksmoor parish churchyard. Outside the lych-gate
coal-black horses stood patiently before a now-empty
hearse, their black plumes waving and their breath
rising in puffs of steam. One or two sightseers loitered
at the gate, having seen the brass-handled walnut coffin
carried in by black-hatted mutes, followed by finely-
dressed mourners.

'Who is it, then?' enquired one plump lady carrying
a basket.

'Mr Moorhouse,' replied another, composing her
face into an expression resembling sympathy.

'Who?'

'Moorhouse, tha knows. Him that were mayor a
while back.'

'Oh aye, him. Lovely flowers he's got, hasn't he?'

She nodded at the bouquets and wreaths now being
lifted down from the hearse and carried into the grave-
yard to where a freshly turned mound of earth indicated Moorhouse's last resting-place. Then, with a sigh
at being reminded of life's brevity, she carried on her
way up Kirkgate to the market place.

The other woman lingered long enough to hear the
faint strains of 'Abide With Me' and then, after a

16

pause, to see the straggle of black-garbed figures begin to issue from the church porch. Then, remembering she had still to buy fish for tea, she too hurried on up the hill.

Amy was bored. Funerals were nowhere near as exciting as birthday parties, she reflected, and her knees were sore from kneeling for so long. Singing the hymns was quite nice, but that lady wearing the shiny black necklace kept sobbing noisily and spoilt the sound. It was a relief to be going outside at last. She hugged Bella tightly inside her coat.

Lionel was making a funny noise as they emerged from the porch. 'What's the matter?' Mother asked.

'My tooth hurts,' he grizzled, 'and it's loose.'

'I'll pull it out for you when we get home. Like I did Amy's.' Mother's voice was low, soothing, and she pulled them both by the hand to stand well back, clear of all the other people, just as she had done when they entered church. All the other people seemed to be wearing far nicer clothes than themselves.

'With a piece of string tied to the doorhandle? Will it hurt?' asked Lionel.

'No. Now hush!' said Mother. 'People don't talk at funerals.'

'Will the tooth fairy bring me a penny for it, like she did for Amy?'

Mother sighed. 'I expect so. Now be quiet.' She looked very pale, thought Amy. Maybe she was cold.

The vicar stood by the big hole in the ground. Alongside it lay the coffin, with ropes underneath. The fat lady with the shiny necklace was still sobbing, but her face could not be seen behind the black veil. Next to her stood a big boy with shining fair hair, fidgeting with the cap in his hand.

Amy watched as men lifted the ropes and began lowering the coffin into the hole. How neatly the hole fitted the box; barely an inch to spare all round it.

She wondered whether they had measured the box beforehand to cut a hole so precisely.

'Ashes to ashes,' said the vicar, and someone handed a little silver trowel to the fat lady. With a strangled moan she threw a trowelful of soil down on to the coffin. It made a clunking sound. Mother made a faint sound but made no move from where they stood at the back of the group. Lionel was playing with his loose tooth. Amy shivered. It was cold out here and the vicar was droning on and sounded as if he would keep going for ages yet. She moved back a few paces, anxious to move, to run about and get warm. From here they looked such a miserable bunch of people. She turned and walked away quickly across the turf of the church-yard. No one would miss her, not while they were busy laying Grandfather to rest. Mother said he needed rest.

Poor Bella. She needed to be laid to rest too. Amy pulled the doll out from under her coat and looked, concern filling her little face, at the rag-shrouded figure in her hand. Poor Bella. She cradled the doll close to her cheek and walked soundlessly across the wet grass to the far corner of the churchyard, where a small grave lay open. Far from the mourners grouped around Grandfather's grave she knelt by the mound of freshly dug earth under the shadow of the great yew.

It took only moments to scoop out a hollow large enough to contain the tiny figure. Amy was busy pressing the damp soil into place over the little body when she became aware of someone beside her. She looked up, startled.

It was the big boy who seemed to be with the fat lady, and from this angle he seemed enormously tall, his cloth cap now covering his fair head. She frowned at him.

'What are you doing?' There was curiosity in his tone but a kind of gentleness as well. She could not bring herself to voice the dismay she felt at being disturbed in her private ritual.

'Nothing. Why have you left the others?'

He knelt down beside her, ignoring the damp earth on the trousers of his Norfolk suit. 'My sister was whining. I think Mother's crying upset her. What are you burying?'

Amy sighed. 'Bella.'

'Who's Bella? Your kitten?'

Reassured by his understanding tone, Amy confided in him. 'My dolly. She's been very sick, and now she's dead.'

'Oh!' His air of interest vanished. 'I like animals. I've got a pony, you know, and I'm to have a bigger one soon – Cracker's only twelve hands.'

Amy stared at him, disbelief giving way to scorn. 'You don't expect me to believe that – I'm not stupid, you know. Ponies don't have hands.'

He scrambled to his feet, laughing as he brushed the dirt from his knees. 'I was talking about her size, silly. Still, I suppose I should have known better than to expect a little girl to understand.'

Amy scrambled up, angered by his derision. She glared up at him. 'I'm not little, I'm seven. How old are you?'

'Ten – eleven at Christmas.' He smiled down at her with a patronising air, as if she couldn't help her deficiency in years, and Amy hated him.

'Go away, you horrid boy. I want to say my prayers for Bella, and I don't want you here. Go away!'

She dropped to her knees again, crouching on the cold earth and shaking. Over her clasped hands she could see his feet beside her, and wished he would go. At last he did, then after a moment she heard him come back and take a deep breath.

'Here,' he said quietly. 'You ought to have flowers.'

She watched him bend down and stick a single frost-seared rose into the earth. Anger flooded her. How dare he try to organise her funeral! Leaning forward, she seized the rose and winced as a thorn pierced her thumb, then flung it away as far as she could.

'I don't want your flowers! Go away!'

She buried her face in her hands and sucked the place where the thorn had penetrated. Nasty, hateful boy, she thought. Then she heard him sniff.

'Girls are stupid,' he pronounced. 'I wouldn't leave anything I cared about to rot in the ground like that. I wouldn't want the worms to eat it up.'

Amy unclasped her hands and looked up at his mocking face. 'It's you who's stupid, not me,' she retorted. 'Worms don't eat people.'

'Shows how much you know, then, because they do. Once their coffin rots, then the people rot, and the worms eat up all their skin and blood. Ugh! There's only bones left. Haven't you ever seen a skeleton?'

She stared at him in horror, unwilling to believe, then turned back to the mound of earth and began frantically to tear away the newly flattened soil until she retrieved the doll. Hugging its muddy figure close to her chest she flung one last malevolent look at the boy and ran back towards the mourners, tears burning her eyelids.

The group of black-clad figures was breaking up and melting away. Mother was still standing motionless, head bowed and one gloved hand holding Lionel's. As Amy approached she turned and smiled wanly. A plump gentleman broke away from a knot of people which included the fat lady and came across to where they stood.

'Violet, my dear,' he said softly.

Mother smiled again. 'Percy, how kind of you to recognise me.'

'I speak for Charlotte – she's much too overcome. She asks if you would care to come back to the funeral tea at Langdenholme.'

Mother shook her head. 'So kind, but I'd best get

20

the children home – this damp air is not good for Lionel's chest.'

The gentleman coughed and cleared his throat. It occurred to Amy that perhaps as he had his collar on back-to-front that might account for his difficulty. 'Well, after tea Mr Bickerstaffe will be reading Mr Moorhouse's will,' he said hesitantly, as if he was saying something impolite.

Mother took hold of Amy's hand and turned away from him. 'I'm sure if there's anything I should know, Mr Bickerstaffe will get in touch with me soon enough, thank you, Percy. Please give my regards to my sister.'

The plump gentleman hurried after them down the path towards the gate. The fat lady was already being helped into a black carriage, still weeping. The nasty boy and a girl about her own age stood nearby. Amy ignored them.

'I'm sure you will be mentioned,' the gentleman was muttering. 'Perhaps you should be there.'

Mother turned to face him. 'You are kind, Percy, and I appreciate it – and the effort it must have cost Charlotte to invite me. But I shall hear, if indeed there is anything to hear.'

His plump face creased into a smile. 'You were always a proud woman, Violet. I wish you well, indeed I do.'

Amy felt her mother's tug and as they walked away she noted that though Mother was still pale she held her head high as they walked out through the lych-gate into the cobbled street. Lionel suddenly broke the silence, holding something up in the air and crying out in triumph.

'My tooth's come out, all by itself! Will the tooth fairy still bring me a penny?'

Percy Holroyd watched without surprise the way his wife's manner changed visibly from grieving daughter to mistress of Langdenholme during the progress of the funeral tea. He hung back in the shadows, if shadows there could be in the brilliantly chandelier-lit drawing room of Langdenholme, and observed the grace with which she acknowledged the condolences of Halliday, Dawson and all the other councillors and dignitaries of Hawksmoor. She was splendid. Percy was content; life was good to him. He had only once made an astute move in his life, and that had absolved him from having to make any more. Marrying Charlotte had brought everything a man could desire; from being a humble curate he was now the proud possessor of his own comfortable living at St Mark's and presided over his family in the comfort and ornate elegance of Langdenholme. Well, to be truthful, it was Charlotte who did the presiding – but who was he to complain at the role to which he had been summoned?

And he owed it all to Charlotte. She was a determined woman, with a tenacity that would have done credit to the shrewdest of businessmen. That she undoubtedly inherited from her father, for old Moorhouse had been a force to be reckoned with in the old days. He had succeeded for a time in ousting Charlotte from Langdenholme, but she had been quick to seize her chance that time when Violet was forced to leave her child with him and go to London. Old Moorhouse had not been able to cope with a baby alone, and Charlotte had been delighted to oblige.

The will was still to be read, of course, but it was unlikely the old man would throw his elder daughter out of the home she had occupied for the last seven years. Lawyer Bickerstaffe was talking smoothly in the corner to Dawson, and his angular face showed no sign of being the bearer of bad news.

With murmured polite apologies and repetitions of sympathy the guests began to leave, aware that more important business was still to follow. When the last had departed, Charlotte invited Mr Bickerstaffe to her father's study. Seating himself in a high-backed chair,

Percy half-expected her to sit at her father's desk, but instead she motioned Bickerstaffe to sit there, and she sat opposite him, at a distance from her husband.

'Is Mrs Mallinson not able to join us?' the lawyer enquired, peering over his pince-nez. Charlotte's mouth set in a thin line but she made no answer.

'I fear not,' murmured Percy. He could see his wife's bosom heave and fall, the jet necklace glittering in the lamplight the only indicator of her thoughts.

Bickerstaffe pursed his thin lips. 'Then I'll begin. There's no need, I think, to read the will out in detail. I'll come instead to what concerns you.'

He picked up the document and peered at it through his pince-nez, running a spiky finger along the lines. The silence in the room was absolute.

'Ah yes. "*To my dear, devoted daughter Charlotte I leave my house and the bulk of my estate, after the bequests I have named, in the sure and certain knowledge that she will maintain it for the future inheritance of my grandson Charles. To my son-in-law Percy I leave my gold hunter watch and whatever other pieces Charlotte may deem suitable.*" There follows Mr Moorhouse's other bequests, smaller ones to servants and a more fitting one for Mrs Mallinson, plus an endowment to fund a scholarship at the new Technical College each year for a needy student. A handsome gesture, if I may say so.'

Percy could read the unspoken question in his wife's eyes and ventured to voice it for her. 'You say Violet is provided for, Mr Bickerstaffe?'

The lawyer's expression remained impassive. 'Ah, yes, an annuity which I shall divulge to the lady herself, and a number of shares.'

'Shares?' Charlotte's voice sounded like a small explosion.

'Of little or no value,' Bickerstaffe said smoothly. 'The company was flourishing at the time Mr Moorhouse made his will, but now, I learn it is trading very poorly, almost on the verge of bankruptcy, I'm told.'

'I see.' Percy could hear the mollified tone of his wife's voice. 'Is there any further mention of Charles – or Berenice?'

'No, but it is clear that your father intended them both to benefit through you, Mrs Holroyd, knowing you would care well for the estate.'

'To be sure. Then, if the business is completed, I'll ring for a bottle of Madeira,' she said in tones of great satisfaction. Percy watched her cross to pull the bell-rope, gliding like a stately galleon across the Turkey carpet. She was an impressive figure, there was no doubt of it, tightly laced and corseted into that well-fed pouter-pigeon shape. Black watered silk suited her giving an illusion of slimness to her ample curves but, truth to tell, he much preferred the generous amplitude of her body when, at last uncorseted for bed, she allowed her flesh to subside gently into the places nature had ordained it to be.

Long after the lawyer had gone and dinner was comfortably digested, Charlotte sat contentedly by the fire in the drawing room, playing with the rings on her plump fingers. 'Kind of Miss Hardcastle to send a floral tribute,' she remarked. Percy murmured agreement, not looking up from the paper.

'I think Father disposed of matters very thoughtfully, don't you, dear?' she went on. Percy looked up quickly, startled by the unaccustomed endearment. 'I mean, he ensured that his grandson would succeed to his due rights. Very thoughtful.'

'He made no mention of his other grandson, I noted,' Percy remarked, and then realised his blunder. He rattled on recklessly. 'I mean, I know Lionel is the youngest of the four grandchildren, but he is male too. I mean, I know he's not a Moorhouse, but then neither is . . .'

'Exactly,' snapped Charlotte. 'Lionel's a Mallinson, and therefore counts for nothing.'

'We're not even sure he's a Mallinson, born as he was after Violet had been away in London so long,' muttered Percy, anxious to make amends.

Charlotte glared. 'Please do not imply that my sister may be no better than she ought to be,' she said icily. 'I do not wish any such slur to be attached to my family name.'

'No, of course. I'm sorry, my dear. And I remember you told me her husband might not have died that night after all. Lionel could still be his child.'

Charlotte's composure had completely disappeared. 'I'm tired, Percy. Let's talk no more of all the silly gossip about the past – Violet is a widow and could have done quite well for herself if only she'd married Edwin Glover, as Father hoped she would, but she chose not to. If she finds life trying as a result, she's only herself to blame. She always was headstrong.'

'Quite.' Highly principled might be another's choice of adjective, but Percy knew better than to quibble.

'Not one of our sort,' Charlotte continued, 'although she was born and raised the same as I was. I shall not, of course, entertain her here.'

'No.'

'Nor recognise her children – whatever their parentage. Did you notice how badly behaved they were today? The boy had his finger in his mouth the whole time and the girl was chewing her lip. She ran off too, I noticed. No control whatsoever.'

'So did Charles – go off, I mean.'

'See what I mean? He was set a bad example by that wretched child. We must make certain that Charles and Berenice never come into contact with their working-class cousins – it could be very bad for them. And now let's go to bed.' She rose quickly and Percy knew that she intended no further discussion of the matter. It was settled. Neither Violet Mallinson nor her children would ever set foot in Langdenholme, so long as Charlotte was its mistress.

Alone by the fire after the children had gone to bed, Violet took out from the drawer the exercise book in which she confided her thoughts every night. She listened to the slow tick of the clock as she dipped the pen in the inkstand, then stared at the blank sheet reserved for today.

'What shall I tell you today, diary?' she murmured aloud. 'That I could weep no tears for my father though I loved him? That the graveyard served only to remind me of Tom and how we used to meet there in secret? I have to tell you, diary, for there is no one else to confide in – oh, I wish my precious Amy were grown up, for I know she would understand. Ah Amy, child of my heart, you looked so pale today, and talked so little. Not like you, little one. I fear it is your first taste of death, coming face to face with it for the first time, that has disturbed you. I should never have taken you. It is my fault.'

She sighed, dipped the pen in the ink and wrote:

'Today Amy asked why Uncle Edwin no longer calls to visit. I cannot bring myself to tell her the truth. Father was buried in the same grave with Mother.'

TWO: 1897

Amy hurried along the busy cobbled street towards Hawksmoor town centre, biting her lip as she heard the parish church clock strike seven. Lionel would probably have given up and gone home without her by now: he would hardly have stood shivering in the market place for nearly an hour, and him not yet earning enough to get a new jacket to replace the old threadbare one.

She quickened her pace as she passed darkened alleyways and steamy foodshops with their inviting odours of hot faggots and saveloys, trying to ignore the pangs of hunger in her stomach. She hadn't eaten since noon, when Mr Sidgwick allowed his assistants to take a half-hour break in turn to eat their sandwiches. He never allowed her and Cissie to take their break together. And to make matters worse they had been kept open late tonight by an indecisive customer unable to make up her mind about which pair of gloves to choose. Someone had to stay until the woman was satisfied. Amy saw Mr Sidgwick signalling to Cissie that she could leave, but she had had to stick it out.

'There, it was worth it, wasn't it?' Mr Sidgwick demanded when at last the woman had gone. 'She chose the kid ones in the end. I think she'll be very satisfied with them.'

Which was more than he would be, Amy vowed inwardly. An undecided customer might afford Mr Sidgwick a perfect opportunity to keep Amy behind alone, but thank God she had been able to plead an appointment with her brother. Her employer, small and balding and imperious, had excruciatingly bad breath when he came too close. If only she were trained for some other kind of work she would be glad never to see the inside of Sidgwick's Emporium again.

To her relief she saw Lionel's tall, lean figure still hunched under the gas lamp at the corner of Westgate. He did not smile as she approached. His dark eyes scowled at her.

'Where've you been till now? I'd almost given up.'

'Fussy woman couldn't make up her mind. Been waiting long?'

He shrugged thin shoulders. 'Long enough.' He turned and fell into step beside her, and Amy took his arm. She could feel by his tenseness that he was cold. 'Tram's just gone,' he remarked. 'Half an hour till the next. Might as well walk.'

She felt a surge of tenderness, seeing how pinched and starved he looked. 'Tell you what,' she said, squeezing his arm, 'let's go into the Pack Horse. I'll treat you to a hot toddy. We'll get the next tram.'

He paused, looking down at her with a frown, and then decided not to argue. He looked frail in the light from the steamed-up windows, younger than his seventeen years. As they turned into the warmth of the public house, where the sweet smell of ale mingled with the acrid aroma of smoke, he was coughing. They sat at a corner table and Amy felt concerned.

'Your chest troubling you again, Lionel?'

'Nay, it's nowt. Sooner I get away from that coal dust, the better.' He glanced over his shoulder, nodded and raised a finger to the man behind the bar. He came across to the table. Amy could see black-toed boots kicking up the hem of his long white apron.

'How do, lad. What can I get thee?'

'Hot toddy, for both of us.'

'Aye,' said the man, 'there's a right nip in the air tonight. Folks need summat to keep the cold out of their bones.' He trudged back behind the counter, nodding to himself.

Over the steaming mugs of toddy Amy watched Lionel's eyes, darting and restless, as he surveyed the room. His gaze lingered on the group of office workers laughing near the doorway. He grunted.

'They can laugh,' he commented, 'them in nice clothes, working in a warm office all day, and a decent wage packet to take home of a Friday. Not like us.'

Amy reached a hand across the table to touch his

28

arm. 'We could be better off if we really put our minds to it, Lionel. All we have to do is decide what we want, then work at making it happen.'

He sniffed. 'Easier said than done.'

She withdrew her arm crossly. 'Oh, come on now, Lionel. You never get anywhere if you talk like that. I know what I want, anyway.'

He put his mug down. 'You do? What?'

Amy drew her bag along the bench towards her and withdrew a sheet of paper which she handed to her brother. He looked at the many columns of closely written hieroglyphs, mystified.

'What's this, then? I can't make head nor tail of it.'

'It's Mr Pitman's Penny Plate. I sent away for it.'

'What for?'

'So I can learn to write shorthand, of course. I want to get a job in an office.'

He sniffled and handed the paper back to her. Amy saw with relief that colour was beginning to suffuse his cheeks again. 'Shorthand's not enough, Amy. You'll need to be able to type as well.'

'I know, silly. I've done something about that too.'

She reached into her bag again and withdrew a letter. Taking out a single folded sheet of paper she read it aloud to him.

'Dear Miss Mallinson. We thank you for your application for the post of assistant clerk in our office. In reply to your query we would advise you that the initial salary will be fifteen shillings per week, rising to fifty-five pounds per annum on completion of your training to our satisfaction. We would be obliged if you would present yourself for interview at this office on Friday coming at ten in the morning. Yours faithfully . . .'

Amy screwed up her nose. 'There's some scribbly

29

signature I can't read, per pro Wadsworth and Firth Limited. There, what do you think of that?'

Lionel sipped his toddy thoughtfully. 'Wadsworth and Firth? Where are they?'

'Down Princess Street. It's quite a big office. They do copy typing for lots of other businesses and they train you in typing while you work there. I'd have to do general dogsbody work at first, I expect, but it's one way to learn and earn at the same time. I couldn't ask Mother to find the money to send me to a commercial college. I think she'll be pleased, don't you?'

'You're getting fifteen shillings a week now, as senior assistant at Sidgwick's.'

'But this job's got prospects, don't you see? I want to get on in the world, not be forever scraping and saving like Mother. Surely you want to get on too, Lionel. Do you know what you'd like to do with your life?'

He set his mug down on the table and leaned across to her, and for the first time she saw a light leap into his dark eyes. 'Aye, I do. More than anything I'd like to work in textiles. I've read a lot about textiles and there's such a lot of new developments happening now in the woollen trade – new looms, new machines, marvellous new designs – it's all so fascinating, Amy. I'd give me eye teeth to have a hand in it.'

Amy chuckled. He was beginning to be infected with her own enthusiasm, and she was pleased. She pushed her seat back from the table and rose. 'Then that's settled. All we have to do now is find ways and means to contrive it. You must get into textiles – perhaps you could go to the Technical College. Maybe Mother could find the money for you.'

He drained off the last of the liquid in his mug and set it down. 'I doubt that. But I did hear from a lad at work that there's scholarships to be had for those who're hard-up. I could apply for one of them. I'd work like the very devil to get there, Amy.'

She smiled down at him. 'That's my lad – that's the way I like to hear you talk. Let's go and talk it over with Mother – she'll be getting fretful by now, keeping our dinners hot on the range. Come on, it's about time for the tram.'

As she preceded her brother towards the door she had to pass the group of office workers. Consciously she drew herself erect, with her nose just a little higher in the air than usual, aware of the young men's approving glances. *I'll be as good as you are soon*, she promised herself inwardly, *by heck I will*.

Violet listened intently to her daughter's excited chatter over supper that night. As she put the dishes into the sink, hearing Amy's flow of words, at the same time she was aware of her son's gawky unease as he seated himself by the fire. How different her two children were, she reflected. Amy so like herself at the same age, impetuous and eager for life to begin.

'Well, what do you think, Mother?' Amy demanded at last. Violet continued wiping plates and stacking them on the dresser for a few moments without answering. She was considering the proposals with judicious thought.

'Well, there certainly seems no harm in Lionel applying for a scholarship if he knows how to go about it,' she ventured at last.

'Oh, I do,' Lionel interrupted. 'Jack Sykes told me where to get the papers. I can see to it this week.'

'But as to you working in an office,' Violet went on, turning to her daughter, 'I'm not so sure about that. I've heard a lot of tales about how employers take advantage of the young girls who work in the office.'

'Oh now, Mother,' Amy protested, 'don't you think I know how to fend for myself? Mr Sidgwick's not always an easy customer, I can tell you.'

Violet regarded her sharply. 'Mr Sidgwick? You never told me . . . If I'd known . . .'

Amy jumped up from the table and busied herself putting the dishes away in the dresser. 'There's a lot I don't tell, Mother. There's no need. I can manage. But Mother, I really do want to work in an office – I want to dress smart like office girls do.'

'Smartly,' said Violet, laying emphasis on the last syllable. 'And you do dress nicely now.'

'It won't cost anything,' Amy persisted. 'I'll save up and buy new clothes for myself. And I'll start learning that Pitman shorthand tonight. I'm quick, you know. It'll take me no time at all to pick it up.'

Violet was sorting the knives and forks into the cutlery drawer. The girl certainly had initiative, she thought, you had to give her credit for that, and it would be a shame to dampen her enthusiasm. Oh, to have that eager fire of youth still throbbing in the veins, and not the chill feeling that life had somehow passed one by. But Amy was impetuous: eagerness was one thing, but sometimes the girl's ideas carried her into foolhardy ventures she later regretted. Not so Lionel – he was the deep, the cautious one.

'All schemes cost money,' she pointed out. 'If you're willing to finance yourself, well and good, but if there's money to be spent on training it's only right it should go to Lionel. He's a man – he'll always have a living to earn. A woman will probably marry one day.'

'I don't want money from you,' Lionel rumbled from the depths of the easy chair.

'And I don't want to get married,' Amy cut in. 'I want to be able to earn my own living, be a free and independent person like you've always been, Mother. Since Father died you've managed to keep the family on your own.'

'It was your proud, free spirit which first attracted me to you, Violet. I was captivated by it – a wild and beautiful creature of freedom, an exotic bird of the skies.'

'Tamed now, Frederic, for I'll never leave you.'

Violet looked at her daughter in silence. Independent? Oh yes, my beloved child, but at what a price! I'd have given the world to be married to the man I loved . . .

Amy whipped the tablecloth off the table with an angry flick. 'I would hate to be dependent on a husband,' she asserted, 'beholden to him for the food in my mouth and the clothes on my back. I want to be able to provide all my needs for myself – and yours too, Mother,' she added swiftly, casting her mother a loving look.

Violet smiled. 'There's no harm in going to the interview at any rate – you can see what they offer. You don't have to take the post.'

'Fifty-five pounds a year when I'm qualified, don't forget,' Amy said impishly.

Violet gave her an affectionate pat on the bottom as she passed. 'There's more to life than money, my girl, as you'll find out one day.'

Lionel was watching them morosely. 'Happen there is, but it's a damned uncomfortable life without. That reminds me – that scholarship is for needy folk – they'll probably want to know just what we do have.'

Violet held her head up. 'Then we'll tell them – what you and Amy earn, and about my little annuity.' But not about the money Frederic still bethinks himself to send now and again – far less often than he used to do. That's my private business, thought Violet.

Lionel was still sniffing. Violet looked at him sharply. 'You've got a cold again, Lionel Mallinson. It's lemon and hot water for you and up to bed right away. I don't want that cold going down on your chest like it did last winter and we couldn't shift it. Come on now, upstairs with you. I'll bring the lemon up in a minute.'

Grumbling and protesting, Lionel allowed himself to be persuaded.

When he had gone, Violet turned to her daughter. 'You know, Amy, there's nothing I'd like more than

33

to get Lionel out of the gasworks. It's not good for his chest at all. He should have a pretty fair chance of that scholarship if we get Mr Beardsley to speak for him.'

'That's right,' said Amy. 'Mr Beardsley did say he'd be glad to give Lionel an excellent reference any time he wanted it. There can't have been a brighter lad in New Street Board School than our Lionel, ever.'

Oh, he inherited a shrewd brain right enough, thought Violet, and a retentive memory and the gift of application too. If there were examinations to be passed, Lionel should have a pretty fair chance indeed. She took the flat-irons from the cupboard and set them on the hob.

'I don't like to hear you talk that way about marriage, Amy,' she murmured. 'At your age I was already wed.'

Amy looked up at her sideways, one eyebrow lifted. 'I've been thinking about that, Mother. I was born in the January and you said you were married the previous spring, but I've never found out just when . . .'

Violet slapped the brass trivet down on the hearth. 'Never you mind about my business – just you see to your own. Make a good job of ironing your blouse for the morning.'

She could swear that as she turned away to walk into the back scullery there was a mischievous twinkle in Amy's dark eyes.

Dinner had just ended in Langdenholme. The Reverend Percy had been called away before dessert to visit a parishioner who was gravely ill and not expected to survive the night. Charlotte Holroyd patted the seat beside her on the chaise longue and smiled at her son.

'Come, Charles, sit and talk for a while. You're not dashing out again tonight, are you? I'd like to talk to you about your future.'

Berenice yawned. 'That means you want Charles to yourself, I take it. Never mind, I have a new novel I can read in my room.'

'If you wouldn't mind, dear.'

Charlotte watched as her daughter swept up her skirts and left, then she turned to her son. He was still standing in the hearth, his back to the fire and his long legs astride. Why did men always assume this stance, she wondered irritably.

'Do sit, Charles. I get a crick in my neck looking up at you.'

His good-looking young face remained impassive. 'I prefer to stand, Mother. I imagine you wish to discuss again just how much of Grandfather's estate I am to acquire on my twenty-first birthday. We've been over all that before.'

His mother sighed. 'Yes, I know, but you never quite seem to see my point of view on the matter. You know Grandfather left it to my discretion just how much of the estate was handed over to you on your majority – my instructions were to maintain the estate for you, keep it intact and endeavour to augment the assets.'

'Which I am sure you have done, Mother.'

'Now don't be sarcastic, Charles. I'm only obliged to increase your allowance when you're twenty-one, you know – nothing more.'

'And you can continue to administer the estate until such time as you cast off this mortal coil, I know. Well, I have no objection to that, Mother, none at all.' He flicked an imaginary speck of dust from his jacquard waistcoat. Charlotte felt uneasy, not certain whether he was still mocking her, then the feeling was replaced with irritation.

'Oh, you're just like your father, never being sensible when you ought to be,' she grumbled. 'Just like a man, not taking a woman seriously – well, you ought to, since I devote so much time and energy to caring for your interests. I'm no fool, you know. Your estate would not be of half so much value if it weren't for me.'

He took a deep breath but it barely disguised his impatience. 'I know, and I am truly grateful, Mother, really I am.'

'Then why don't you sit and talk about it?'

'Because I recognise that this is a prelude to another lecture about mending my ways, spending more time at home, giving up playing cards and going to the races, and so on and so on . . .'

'And looking for a decent girl you can marry instead of just chasing actresses and the like. Yes, you're right. Can't you see, I can't hand over Langdenholme and all the estate while you persist in behaving in this reckless manner? You'll have to show more sense of responsibility, Charles, before I can entrust to you everything your grandfather worked so hard to achieve. Yes, I would like to see you settle down, marry and live a regular way of life. Then I could feel content.'

He gave a flicker of a smile. 'I expect I will, one day, but not yet – I'm too young. But don't worry, it will come. Just promise me one thing, though – don't go choosing a wife for me, will you?'

Charlotte looked up, startled. 'Well, as a matter of fact . . .'

'No,' said Charles firmly, 'not Edith Drake. I saw the way you were sizing her up at dinner the other night. No, definitely not Edith Drake.'

His mother sighed. 'Very well, Charles. But you do promise me you'll think about it, won't you?' She was toying with the cushion beside her, but Charles knew that despite her diffident manner she was in great earnest.

'When I find a suitable lady, I assure you you will be the first to be told, Mother,' he said drily.

His mother smiled. 'There, I knew you'd see my point of view in the end. What do you think of these cushions, Charles? I embroidered them years ago, when you were a baby, but I think they're looking a bit drab now. What do you think?'

'Very pretty, Mother,' he said.

The grandfather clock in the vestibule began to chime. Charlotte's hand flew to her mouth. 'Heavens, it that the time? I have to be at a meeting of the governors of the Technical College in half an hour. Be a dear and ring for the carriage to be brought round for me while I get ready, will you?'

In the high-ceilinged room upstairs in the Technical College several men seated around the long mahogany table – governors, aldermen, the Clerk to the Governors and the Principal – stared in silence at the one woman present. They were uneasy. Left to themselves they would have argued the matter out candidly, man-to-man, so to speak, but the presence of a plump, tight-lipped lady who left them in no doubt that her views were as forcible as their own, and that she was daughter to the man whose scholarship they were debating, rendered the position so nebulous that not one of them dared to try to force a decision.

The Chairman cleared his throat and tried again. 'Well, to sum up so far, it would seem we have disposed of all the bursaries with the exception of the Cedric Moorhouse scholarship. Over this one we seem to have reached something of an impasse – unless Mrs Holroyd is willing to reconsider?'

She made no reply. The Principal tried to come to the chairman's aid. 'Perhaps if Mrs Holroyd were able to give us some reasons for her objection to the candidate Mr Fletcher recommends so strongly . . . ?'

Charlotte darted him a furious look. 'I hardly feel that is necessary, in the circumstances.'

The Clerk to the Governors spread his bony hands. 'But you did request us to short-list the most outstanding pupils, Mrs Holroyd, and there was no doubt that this young fellow,' glancing at his notes, 'er

37

– Mallinson – stood out head and shoulders above the rest.'

'His report from Mr Beardsley is the most enthusiastic and approving one I have read in a very long time,' agreed the Principal.

Charlotte Holroyd's face was growing a richer red in colour. Aware of the pressure, silent but intense all around her, she folded her arms across her plump bosom. 'There are others on the short-list, I recall,' she said grimly. 'Who are they?'

The Clerk consulted his notes again with a sigh. 'The next is a lad named Booth, unemployed but with a very good recommendation from his headmaster. Eldest of seven children. Father is an unemployed bricklayer, a widower.'

'Then he's the one,' pronounced Charlotte. 'He deserves the Moorhouse scholarship much more than the Mallinson boy.'

The men looked at each other, bewildered. The Chairman, busy cleaning his spectacles, put them back on his nose and regarded her in surprise. 'You think so, Mrs Holroyd?'

Charlotte glared at him. 'I just said so, didn't I? One of seven children – Mallinson is only one of two – and his father unemployed. You said that Mallinson's mother, though a widow, does have an annuity and a daughter working. So I see no problem – my father clearly meant the money to go to a needy lad, and this young Booth sounds just the lad. I propose Booth.'

Her icy stare challenged the men to disagree with her. They glanced uneasily at one another; the Principal blew his nose; the Chairman gathered his papers and took a deep breath.

'Well, gentlemen, we now have a fresh proposal before the meeting. Booth has been proposed for the Cedric Moorhouse scholarship. Do I have a seconder? All in favour?'

Slowly, one by one each hand around the table rose

in assent. Charlotte Holroyd leaned back in her chair, the tightness about her lips slackening now into a shadow of a smile.

'Agreed unanimously,' murmured the Chairman, clearly relieved, 'and now let's move on to item number seven on your agenda, the matter of the provision of further funds for the purpose of adding more books to the library.'

It was after the meeting had ended and Mrs Holroyd had swept majestically from the room that the Chairman was free at last to voice his private opinion to the Principal.

'By heck, Dr Garside, but I'm glad that meeting's over. That woman fair puts the wind up me, she does that. Always has to have her say, but I've never heard her talk so daft as she did tonight. There's no rhyme nor reason in what she were saying – I mean, fancy saying three-and-six a year is nowt for a lad to find for fees! She wouldn't be told it meant much more than that, what with books to buy and all, not to mention the wages he'd lose as a day student.'

Dr Garside rubbed his chin, nodding. He'd have liked to add his own views, that Mrs Holroyd's only argument against the Mallinson boy, that he 'came of bad blood', was a ridiculously feeble one. Whatever his parentage, the boy evidently had ability and could have done well, but without a scholarship to fund him through the six-year textile course he'd probably never have the chance to prove it. Mrs Holroyd and all her narrow-minded, prejudiced like had a lot to answer for.

'Well anyway, what's done's done,' said the Chairman. 'Now I must have a word with you about calling a meeting with the town councillors. If the Hawksmoor Corporation is to take over the running of the College – finances being what they are – then I reckon it would be as well to have some further consultation on the matter.'

As the Principal moved away his place was taken by a rotund little man. The Chairman raised a plump finger. 'Ah, Roebuck – just the man I wanted to see. Now, what was this you mentioned the other day about the Corporation trying to put in a bid to buy the estate from the Hardcastles? Seems a very presumptuous move to me, even if we had the money; the Hardcastles have owned all the land hereabouts since the Lord knows when.'

'Happen they have, them always having had most money, but there's no call for them to go on owning it for ever.'

'But it'd cost a fortune to buy them out. The Corporation hasn't got that kind of money.'

'They could have, if they took advantage of a loan.'

The Chairman's sandy eyebrows rose. 'A loan? Who from?'

The little man laid a finger to his red-veined nose. 'Ah, I know a source. But it would mean discretion on our part.'

'You can always count on my discretion, you know that.'

'Well, let me tell you that when I was in Austria recently – you know, that Trade Commission I went on – I met a very influential personage. He knew a lot about Hawksmoor affairs, specially considering he were a foreigner, and he said he would be prepared to put up the money.'

'Would he, by heck?' said the Chairman, his eyes round in surprise. 'Then I think we ought to talk to one or two members of the Estates Committee about it.'

'I'll see to that,' said the little man firmly, 'especially since I'm Chairman of it.'

Both men edged around the table, making for the door. In the doorway the Chairman could resist his curiosity no longer. 'By the way, Roebuck, who is this foreign gentleman? Is he very rich then? Might I have heard of him?'

The little man was waddling off down the corridor but his voice came back over his shoulder. 'Oh aye, you've heard of him, right enough. His name is Baron Rothschild.'

That night, as the Chairman followed his wife up to bed, he couldn't help reflecting that it had been quite an eventful day, one way or another – coping with the redoubtable Mrs Holroyd, managing to keep the peace at the meeting and talking of buying the town and freeing it from the Hardcastles. Really, being an alderman of Hawksmoor brought more hazards in its wake than his wife ever dreamt of. He'd tell her a bit of it in bed; after all, it wasn't every day one could drop a name like Rothschild.

At breakfast next morning Percy Holroyd sat reading the *Hawksmoor Chronicle*. As Charlotte entered and took her seat he put the paper aside, anxious to avoid her usual complaint. For once she sat in silence, waiting for the maid to serve her tea and porridge. Her silences could sometimes betoken a worse atmosphere than her complaints, and Percy wondered how best to ward off a day of tension. He picked up the newspaper again.

'There's a piece in today's paper that might interest you, my dear,' he said tentatively. Charlotte made no sign of having heard. 'You know,' he went on amiably, 'all the discussion about how the town should celebrate the dear Queen's Diamond Jubilee.'

'What of it?' said Charlotte, ladling sugar generously over her porridge.

'Well, instead of a new public library there's a chap writing saying we ought to build a tower. He says:

"I think the fault of our town has been that too little attention has been paid to its ornamentation . . . Hawksmoor, with its widely extended municipal

41

boundary, has a feature within its borders which I believe to be unique. I know of no city or borough in the kingdom with an elevation of nine hundred feet above sea-level such as we have on Castle Hill and I therefore propose that a tower should be built on the summit, at least a hundred feet high, making a total of one thousand feet." '

Percy looked over the top of the newspaper at his wife expectantly. A proposal such as this ought to have provoked her instant reaction by now, but she was scraping the bottom of the porridge bowl unconcernedly. Percy laid the paper aside.

Charlotte signalled to the maid to bring some kedgeree from the sideboard. As the girl spooned it on to the plate, Percy ventured once more to ease the ominous silence. 'What is it, Charlotte, my dear? Aren't you feeling well today? One of your nervous headaches perhaps?'

She scowled at him and motioned to the maid with a quick flick of the wrist that she had quite enough fish on her plate. The maid drew back to the sideboard and waited for the next summons. 'Don't be silly, Percy,' Charlotte said smoothly. 'I had a very trying time last night at the meeting but I am happy to say all is well and I do not feel in the least disturbed this morning.'

Whatever the disagreement had been, Charlotte had clearly got her way in the end, Percy surmised, or she would not be speaking of the incident so calmly. It was safe to enquire.

'I'm sorry to hear you had a trying time, my dear, but I'm sure you resolved the matter satisfactorily.'

She laid down her knife and fork and leaned across the table. 'You can be sure I did,' she said with that sibilant firmness which told him someone had suffered last night. Food forgotten, she launched into the tale. At the end Percy could only murmur a string of 'My, my's,' and 'Oh dear's.' For a few seconds there was silence while she let him digest the information.

Charles swept breezily into the room and took his seat at table. His mother smiled at him benignly. 'I was just telling your father how I made certain that the Mallinson boy did not profit from your grandfather's bursary,' she remarked. Charles, occupied in murmuring his wants to the maid, was paying no attention. Percy felt obliged to make some protest in the interests of humanity. 'I really can't see what you can have against the boy, my dear. After all, he can't be held responsible for what happened before he was even born.'

'Nonsense!' Charlotte snapped. 'He inherits the same bad blood – he's a Mallinson, isn't he? Son of the man who tried so hard to ruin Father? He's tainted blood, he and that sister of his, and I've no intention of helping them, no, not in any way.'

'Are you talking about my cousins?' asked Charles.

Charlotte's complexion reddened under the rouge she had applied so lightly to her cheeks. 'Don't say that word,' she hissed.

'What word?'

'Don't ever recognise those creatures as relations of ours! Father disowned Violet, and so her children are disowned too. I won't have you saying they are cousins to people like us.'

'But they are, Mother. Blood cousins.'

Charlotte's voice rose an octave and Percy recognised the danger signals. He rose from the table, making a muttered excuse about visiting an old lady. Charlotte wasn't listening. Percy left quietly.

'How can you say that, Charles? You, with all the advantages money could buy for you – excellent schooling, splendid contacts – why, all our friends are a nice class of people. How could you compare those poor Mallinsons with us?'

'I didn't. I only said they're related. Closely. You

43

can't deny that, Mother, much as you'd like to. Maggie, bring me some bacon and egg, will you?'

'Now listen to me,' said Charlotte, and there was venom in her tone. 'I don't ever want to hear you say that again, do you hear me? I don't ever want you to come into contact with those people, related or not, neither you nor Berenice. I haven't gone to so much trouble over the years to turn you into gentry – yes, I think I can safely say that – only to have you thinking of people like that, as if they had anything in common with you. They haven't – they've nothing in common. Leave them to their way of life and you make the best of yours, do you hear me? Which reminds me . . .'

Charles laughed good-humouredly. 'Not now, Mother, please, not at breakfast. Let me eat my fill of this splendid bacon first. Don't clear away yet, Maggie, I'll want more bacon and egg, in a minute.'

His mother snorted and rose, pushing back her chair abruptly. As she swept from the room he could not help noting once again how she always seemed to leave a scent of lavender in her wake, mingled with a hint of disinfectant. It must be all that hospital visiting she did.

Violet kept one eye on the clock as she laid the table for the evening meal. They should be home any minute, those two, and even though she dared not allow herself to hope too much, knowing from long experience how often that could lead to disappointment, she nevertheless, was eager to hear how Amy had fared.

She'd looked very smart when she set off to the interview, her blouse crisply starched under the neat dark jacket, and not a speck of dust on her best woollen skirt. Neat as a new pin, but then she always had been proud of her appearance. Chin high, she'd worn a confident smile as she left home, but Violet knew her daughter well – she'd never allow apprehension to show. Please God, she thought, let her not be too bitterly disappointed if she doesn't get the post; she might then, with typical impulsiveness, do something silly. So full of love, that girl, she'd do anything for you, but so hot-headed with it. Unlike Lionel – he might brood over a disappointment, for days even, but he'd snap out of it soon and get on with life. Much more philosophical than his sister. Shades of Frederic again – she could still remember the words, faithfully captured in her diary.

'*C'est la vie, ma petite. We cannot always have what we want, but life must go on.*'

Violet lit a taper from the range and took it to the gas lamp, touching it to the mantle and watching the flame turn to a mellow glow. These new gas mantles were far pleasanter than the old fish-tail burners, she reflected, but on no account would she give in to the children's persuasions to go in for one of the new-fangled gas cookers. She didn't trust them; far safer to stick to cooking with the range as she'd always done. Anyway, the range had two ovens, and it was cheap to run with Lionel able to get coke from the gasworks at sixpence the hundredweight, and there wasn't the risk of contamination from that evil-smelling gas. It was all very well for the children to say a gas cooker could be hired from the Gas Company for only a few pence a week, but they didn't take into account things like health.

Lionel, for instance, would go out in all weathers in only his thin old jacket, despite having a good overcoat he could wear. The lines about Violet's mouth softened as she thought of him. If only he could get away from the gasworks – even if he did work in the office there, trying hard to work his way up from ledger clerk; he hated it and that foul, pervasive gas still got to him.

She heard the click of the outer door and straightened to listen. Heavy footsteps in the lobby told her it was Lionel.

'Hello, love. Amy not with you?'

45

Looking past him for the smaller figure of her daughter, she did not see at once that all was not well. He dropped his snap tin on the corner of the table so carelessly that it fell to the floor. Instead of stooping to retrieve it, he flung himself into a chair. She looked from the fallen tin to him, and saw with a stab of apprehension the pallor of his face, the burning hollows of his eyes.

'Aren't you well, love? Here, let me give you a hot cup of tea while we wait for Amy.' To reach the kettle on the hob she had to pass him. As she did so, she laid a hand on his forehead and found it clammily hot.

He brushed her hand aside with an irritable moan. 'Let me be.'

She was staring at him, startled, when the living room door suddenly opened again and Amy burst in, whooping with delight. She seized hold of her mother and began whirling her around. 'I've got it, Mother, I've got it! I'm going to work in the office!'

'Let me go, love, you're squeezing the breath out of me.'

'Don't you hear me? I've got the position. Oh, Lionel, isn't it marvellous?' Amy ruffled his hair, ignoring his protests, and danced around the table, pirouetting and holding out her skirts. The glow on her young face filled Violet with happiness.

'It's wonderful, love, and I'm proud of you.'

'It's so important to be able to do something you really want to do, isn't it?' breathed Amy as she subsided into a chair. 'Now if Lionel gets his scholarship then we'll all be happy. Oh, isn't life exciting? I'll get straight down to learning more of my Pitman after tea. And I'll give my notice to Mr Sidgwick tomorrow. Just think, in two weeks I'll be an office clerk!'

Her mother smiled, but the smile faded as she caught sight of Lionel's face. Far from reflecting his sister's joy, his pale features were contorted. Violet's elation fled.

46

'Lionel? Are you in pain?'

He shook his head, his face twisting even more, then suddenly he buried his face in his hands. The women looked at each other, aghast.

'He's weeping,' murmured Amy in disbelief.

Violet knelt beside him, touching his knee, unable to bring herself to put her arms around him lest he shake her off. 'What is it, son?' she murmured, trying to sound calmer than she felt. Inside, her heart was fluttering in fear.

Amy was more direct. She seized her brother by the shoulders, then put her hand under his chin, forcing him to look up.

'What's up, lad? Come on, out with it, tell us what's wrong.'

Reddened eyes staring from his white face, he spoke in a flat voice. 'I'm not weeping. It's the scholarship.' There was a catch in his voice. 'I haven't got it.'

'How can you know? The letter hasn't come yet,' said Violet.

'It doesn't need to – I've been told.'

Amy frowned. 'Who by?'

He got up abruptly and went to stand moodily by the dresser. 'Does it matter who? I haven't got it, and I can't go to the Technical. Ironic, isn't it, just when you've got what you wanted.'

Violet spoke sharply. 'Now that's enough, Lionel. You should be pleased for Amy, whatever your own disappointment. But how do you know – are you sure it's right?'

'Oh aye, it's right enough. I heard it from Maggie.'

Violet was bewildered. 'Maggie? Maggie who?'

Instead of answering he began fingering one of the plates on the dresser. Amy filled in for him. 'Maggie Braithwaite. Lionel's been sweet on her for weeks.'

Violet spread her hands, at a loss to understand. 'But how should this Maggie know before you do? Who is she?'

47

'A girl who goes to our Bible class, Mother – that's how he came to know her. She's in service.'

Lionel turned to face them. 'Aye, she is. In service at Langdenholme.'

'Langdenholme?' echoed Violet.

'Aunt Charlotte's place? I didn't know that,' said Amy

The boy's lip curled. 'There's a lot you don't know, Amy, a lot the likes of us never get to know.'

Violet, hearing the savage tone in his voice, felt afraid. 'What are you getting at, Lionel?' His eyes burned like red-hot coals. He ought to be in bed, she thought. His strange way of talking could indicate that he was feverish.

But his answer came coldly enough, each word sounding as though it had been hewn from crystal icicles. 'Your sister, Mother, the eminent Mrs Holroyd – she made certain that I would not go to college. She refused my scholarship, that's what I'm getting at. What price now brothers and sisters rejoicing at each other's success, eh?'

For a second Violet stared at him, then turned away, trying hard to keep her voice even. 'I'll dish up the tea – pass me the ovencloth, Amy.'

The girl did so, then began unbuttoning her jacket. She too was staying calm, and inwardly Violet blessed the child for taking her cue. Lionel was standing by the fireplace, staring moodily into the fire. Amy nudged him gently aside to reach for the kettle.

'Can you be sure Maggie's got the tale right, though, Lionel?' she said quietly. 'She can get excited and get things a bit mixed up, I know – not that she isn't a nice girl, because she is, but she can get a bit carried away.'

He jerked a chair out from under the table and sat down. 'She hasn't got this wrong. She heard every word at breakfast and told me tonight. All about not lifting a finger to help any of us, Mother being a disgrace to the family, you and me being bad blood. So she's proud she talked the other governors into refusing me – though it seems I were the best. She was having nothing to do with a Mallinson.'

He jabbed his fork into the dish of potatoes Violet set before him. She and her daughter exchanged looks.

'We can manage without Charlotte's bounty,' Violet murmured at last. 'We can find the college fees.'

Lionel shook his head. 'No – we can't manage without my wages. It's out of the question. God, but that woman's got a lot to answer for. I tell you what, Mother, if ever there's a Holroyd in need of our help, he'll wait a bloody long time before I'll lift a finger, by God he will.'

'Lionel! I won't have you speaking like that!'

Amy looked up, fork half-way to her mouth. 'Bad language or not, Mother, he's right. What has your sister ever done for you in all these years? She's no right deliberately to block Lionel now too, especially if he was the best student!'

Lionel flung his fork down. 'I can't eat. I feel sick.'

Violet laid a hand on his. 'Perhaps bed would be . . .'

'Oh, for Christ's sake!' Snatching his hand away he pushed back his chair so hard it fell backwards on the floor. Without stopping to pick it up he rushed from the room. Violet half-rose to follow him, but Amy took hold of her sleeve.

'Let him go, Mother. He needs to get over it alone.'

Reluctantly she sat down again but try as she might she could not eat. Amy appeared to carry on eating unconcernedly but as she finished the last mouthful and put down her knife and fork she turned to her mother.

'He's right, you know. Whatever you might have been brought up to think, your family loyalty is misplaced where your sister is concerned.'

Violet was wringing her hands in her lap. 'I'm so confused, I don't know what to believe any more. To think my own sister would deprive my son of what is rightfully his – oh, it's so cruel . . .'

'Condemning him to go on working in the gasworks where his chest could get worse – I know what you fear, Mother, and not without reason. Your sister is a bitch – no, don't try and stop me – she is, and her husband must be a weak fool to let her be . . .'

'Percy's not a bad man, Amy.'

'I said weak. And her children must be too, to let her be such a law unto herself, it seems to me. I'm glad I don't know my cousins – I don't think I ever want to know them.'

Violet gave a wry laugh. 'You don't know Charlotte. No one can change my sister. Don't blame Percy or your cousins.'

Amy piled the three plates and rose. 'I won't. I just don't want ever to know them, that's all. And I agree with Lionel – there'll be no love lost between me and a Holroyd, never. We don't need them – we can make our own way without them. But if ever they want a favour from us, well, I'll remember what they did for Lionel.'

Amy moved away to the sink, and as she dropped the plates into the bowl with a clatter, Violet thought unladylike words came from her daughter's lips. She couldn't be certain, but it sounded for all the world like 'Bloody upstarts, who do they think they are?'

THREE

By morning Lionel had such a high fever that there was no question of his getting up to go to work. Violet wasted no time in sending for the doctor.

'Acute bronchitis,' the doctor pronounced when he came downstairs again. 'Same as last year. I did warn you it would be wiser to find that young man another job if possible. Anyway, it's bed and warmth and rest he needs now, and some medicine. Here's a prescription.'

Recalling last winter Violet regarded him apprehensively. 'Will it be like last time, doctor? He was delirious, seeing things that weren't there.'

'Not necessarily. Get him through this fever first – keep bathing his forehead with cool water but keep him warm. He'll be in bed for some time, even when the fever's gone, probably even longer than last time. His chest gets weaker with each attack, you know.'

Violet hung her head, feeling personally responsible for her son's illness. The doctor touched her arm. 'Don't worry, Mrs Mallinson. You've brought him through before.'

She forced a smile. 'Yes. Thank you, doctor.'

'And I'll call again on Monday. Good morning, Mrs Mallinson.'

By the time Amy came home from the shop on Saturday night he was desperately ill, hallucinating and frightening his mother with the ferocity of his words. Sweat poured from him as he tossed and turned, writhing continuously so that she found it difficult to bathe his head.

Amy took one look at him. 'Here, Mother,' she said, taking the bowl of water from her, 'let me take over for a bit. You go and have a rest.'

Violet rose wearily. 'I'll go and get the tea ready. I haven't had a chance . . .'

'You're worn out – no sleep all night and then this all day. You get some rest.'

Her mother cast her a grateful look. 'There's some nice soup left over from the oxtail. It'd do him a world of good if you can get him to take it.'

'I'll see to it. You lie down. Now go.'

51

Sunday was easier, since there were two of them to share the load, and by Monday his fever was beginning to recede. By Thursday he was sitting up, pale and weak, and starting to take food again, much to Violet's relief.

'The worst is over,' the doctor confirmed, 'but he needs rest and nourishment for some time. Is it possible you could send him away, to the country perhaps, to relatives or friends for a week or two? He would benefit from getting away from the smoke of Hawksmoor for a time.'

Violet hesitated. 'I have no friends in the country, I'm afraid, doctor.'

'Nor relatives?'

She shook her head firmly. 'No.'

'Pity. Well, a good long rest at home then, and after that see about another job for him, that's my advice.'

Amy came home full of excitement about her new post, but sobered on hearing the doctor's words. She thought for some moments.

'He could go to London, couldn't he? You have friends there.'

Violet looked at her sharply. 'What friends?'

Amy shrugged. 'You have letters from London from time to time.'

Violet looked away quickly. 'Ah, yes. Legal matters those, that's all.'

She was aware of Amy's curious gaze. 'I thought Linthwaite and Dobson were your solicitors.'

'So they are – well, young Mr Dobson is, I suppose, since Mr Linthwaite died – they see to the annuity business. Now, I expect you'll want your tea quickly if you're off to Bible study class tonight.'

She turned to escape to the scullery, but Amy was not to be deflected.

'And some shares, wasn't it? It's the interest or dividend from London, is it?'

'Something like that,' Violet muttered as she left the

52

room. By the time she came back Amy's attention had turned to her brother's affairs again.

'Maggie Braithwaite's always asking after our Lionel. I expect she'll ask again tonight.'

'Kind of her. Tell her he's mending nicely.'

'Do you think he could ask to be changed to another job when he goes back, Mother?'

Violet sighed. 'There's none, seemingly, out of reach of the fumes unless it's watering the meters. That's no good for him, out in all weathers. Just about every house in Hawksmoor has a gas meter.'

After tea, as Amy stood before the fire, combing her hair and surveying her reflection in the oak-framed mirror above, Violet was watching her thoughtfully. 'Did you say our Lionel was sweet on this Maggie Braithwaite?' she asked.

'Seemed like it, when he was last at the class. They sat together at the back and he walked her to the corner of her lane after.'

'Then why don't you ask her if she'd like to call and see him? Might cheer him up a bit.'

It was a mistake, Violet realised later with hindsight, to tell Lionel. For the first time in days his pale face showed a flicker of interest in life. But when Amy brought back the news that Maggie had declined the invitation, he relapsed into total disinterest in everything around him. Even when he was strong enough at last to come downstairs he only sat about moodily, refusing to eat or read or even talk. Violet was distressed. There was nothing she could think of to restore his optimism, for all the life seemed to have gone out of him.

He'd be better when the last of the wintry weather fled and spring's warm sunshine came, she reassured herself, but the weeks passed and although Amy seemed happy enough, Lionel only coughed and stayed silent. Until the day Maggie Braithwaite presented herself on the doorstep.

She smiled shyly. 'I didn't come before,' she confessed as Violet led her into the living room. 'It seemed too cheeky, like, me not really knowing Lionel all that well.'

If she hadn't known him well before, she certainly must have done by the time she left that afternoon, Violet mused; an hour alone together had left Lionel with a distinct flush to his cheeks and a light in his eye which had not been there before she came. Violet was grateful for the girl's timely arrival, and hoped she would call again soon. She did, three days later, carrying a dish of blackcurrant jelly. On the doorstep she handed it to Violet with a grave smile.

'Me mam says there's nowt like it for a bad chest,' she murmured shyly. 'Like a lot of clever folk, Lionel needs a lot of looking after, doesn't he?' Her fingers flew to her mouth. 'Oh, I say, I'm sorry. I didn't mean that to sound like tha does not look after him. Oh, I am clumsy – I'm sorry.'

Violet patted her arm and led her indoors. She could warm to a girl like Maggie, she decided, especially when she saw how revitalised Lionel was once again by her visit. That girl could call here as often as she liked.

Amy evidently found her agreeable too. 'You can't help liking Maggie. Everyone down at Bible class does. She's pretty quiet, but she always has a smile for everybody. And she's smitten with our Lionel, that's for sure. He could do a lot worse, I reckon.'

Inwardly Violet agreed. The child was pretty but not enough to make her vain and she was neat and well turned out. If she could cook and sew . . . She pulled herself up sharply – what way was that to be thinking, and him only seventeen years old? Time enough for all that when he'd found out what he wanted to do with his life – that was the first priority.

It was Amy who reminded her that Maggie worked

at Langdenholme, when the girl came to Sunday tea. For once Lionel was also at table.

'I dare say you could tell us quite a lot about the Holroyds,' Amy remarked drily.

Violet saw Maggie's cheeks colour. 'Now then, Amy, don't go prying,' she said quickly. 'What they do is of no concern to us, relatives or not. Their life and ours have nothing at all in common, so don't go embarrassing poor Maggie like that.'

'I'm not,' Amy protested. 'I'm just curious, that's all.'

'Nay, it's not that, Mrs Mallinson,' the younger girl said shyly, 'it's just that I can't stand them Holroyds. Me mam says I can try for a post elsewhere.' She looked up with a frown. 'Thy relatives, didst tha say? I didn't know as they were related to thee – oh dear, I've done it again, haven't I, saying I couldn't stand them. I'm that sorry, Mrs Mallinson. Oh heck, I'm always putting me foot in it.' She turned to Lionel, her eyes pleading forgiveness.

Violet saw Lionel's hand reach across the table as if to touch the girl's and then hesitate. 'Nay, you're not, lass. But what'll you do if you leave there?'

She drew her hand away to fold it across the other in her lap. 'I'll be all right. Mrs Baker up Gledholt said she'd like me to come to her – lovely place she's got, but not as big as Langdenholme. I fancy I'll like it there.'

'I'm sure you will,' murmured Violet. Her sympathies were all with this child who had brought such a glow back to Lionel's thin face. He still looked peaky, though; a bit of fresh air wouldn't do him any harm now the warmer weather was on its way. It did him no good at all to mope about in the house all day, refusing to go out. Soon he'd be well enough to think of going back to work, the doctor had said.

Violet pushed a freshly baked pie across to Maggie. 'Here, have a bit of apple pie, love.'

Lionel passed her the cheese plate. 'And a bit of cheese with it. You know what they say: apple pie without the cheese, is like a kiss without the squeeze.'

Violet saw the girl's blush, but she accepted the cheese.

It was gratifying to see how eagerly Lionel responded when his mother suggested he should walk Maggie to the tram. 'I know it's not dark yet, but it's not wise for a young lady to be out alone at this time.'

'I'd be glad to,' he said, rising to help the girl on with her coat. Violet watched the two young people as they left, each looking a little gawky. Amy wrinkled her nose as the door closed behind them.

'Well, I knew she'd taken a fancy to him, but I didn't think she'd make it that obvious. She must have soaked herself in lavender water – did you smell it? Love's young dream. What a soppy pair they are.'

Her mother laughed. 'You won't think so when it comes to your turn, just you see. You'll be just as daft when the right young man comes along.'

'Not me! Young men are all a pain in the neck.'

'You don't know any yet. Wait and see.'

'Don't I then? The office is full of them, some with pimply faces, some as thin as drainpipes, not one you could call presentable, yet every one of them seems to think he's the bee's knees. You can have 'em all for me. I wouldn't touch 'em with a barge pole.'

Violet was humming as she cleared the table. She stopped and looked at her daughter. 'Maybe not now, but one day, you'll see. You'll change your tune, sure as eggs is eggs, just you see if you don't.'

For a moment Amy chewed her lip thoughtfully. 'I doubt it, and if I did care for someone, I'd run a mile sooner than let him see. Anyway, I think I'd best sew that button on my blouse now ready for morning.'

Violet, standing by the stone sink, put a hand to her side. 'Why not let me sew it for you, love, while you see to the pots? And I'd be glad of a hand turning out the cupboards if you wouldn't mind – your young legs are better suited to climbing up there than mine.'

'Of course I will. Is it spring-cleaning time already then?'

'There's cupboards and drawers that haven't been turned out in years. I'd be glad of some help.' She turned away from the sink and reached for the sewing basket, trying not to let the girl see the strain which must show on her face. That pain in the side was getting to be a nuisance.

At the tram stop Lionel stood shivering next to Maggie. It was not so much the chilly evening air that made him tremble as the knowledge that she stood so close, hardly a breath away. He turned up his jacket collar, making an inadvertent hissing sound as he drew in a breath between clenched teeth.

'Oh, thou art cold!' she murmured in concern. 'Go on back home – the tram can't be long.'

'Nay, I'd rather wait and see thee safe.'

He saw her look up and smile, and felt the blood rush to his cheeks. Had he betrayed his feelings too clearly? He hardly knew himself what they were, so confused and bewildering had they been of late. That letter from the manager hadn't helped either. He groped in his pocket, pulling out a white square, and saw her curious gaze as she looked down at it.

'It's a letter to my gaffer,' he explained gruffly. 'He wrote and said as I'd get the sack if I weren't back at work by Monday. I've written to say as I'll be there.'

She smiled impishly. 'And judging by the state of it tha hast forgot all about it. Want me to post it for thee on the tram? It'll be delivered in the morning then.'

'Aye, if thou would.' He could not bring himself to meet her gaze as their hands touched. A tremor ran through him, and the joy he felt surprised and elated him. A distant rumble diverted his attention and he looked away down Westgate, over her head. 'It's coming now, is the tram.'

She looked up quickly and he saw wistful blue eyes regarding him. 'Shall I see thee soon? What I mean is,' she added hastily, 'wilt tha be well enough to be at Bible class next time?'

'Aye, I reckon.'

As the tram clanged to a halt before them and the driver nodded a greeting, he could not bring himself to cup her elbow to help her mount the step, much as he ached to touch her, however fleetingly. He saw her place one slim foot on the lowest step and then turn to look at him. Under the gaslight her hair gleamed like a halo, and he swallowed hard. He gave an abrupt wave and turned as if to walk away, but his eyes could not leave her. She looked so slim, so fragile and vulnerable – more than anything he wanted to snatch her up and whisk her away.

She was gone and the tram was labouring up the hill out of sight. The momentary touch of her hand on his still burned. He raised the hand to his face, trying for a moment to see if he could smell the scent of her flesh on his, then brushed his lips lightly across where her touch had been. Dear little Maggie! He would count the days until he could see her lovely, haunting little face again. As he retraced his steps towards home his heart felt lighter than it had done for weeks, even if it did seem to flutter and behave strangely in a way it had never done before.

Later that night Amy lay curled up in bed, feeling the darkness folding about her like an embrace. But she did not feel at ease. She had been restless already, dissatisfied about the office and reluctant to admit it, but now she felt even more disturbed. It was those old papers in the box.

'Get down all that stuff up in the top cupboards,' Mother had ordered. 'It's stuff we never touch from one year end to the next. It's high time we sorted it out and threw a lot of it away. Get it all down and I'll go through it when I've time.'

Amy had still been stacking the boxes carefully in the corner when Mother finished sewing the button back on her blouse and slipped out for an hour. 'Just to see Mrs Brierley about those hassocks that need re-covering for the church. I said I'd give her a hand if she needed any help.'

So Amy had carried on taking down the dusty boxes and tins alone. It was the very last one that had proved tricky, piled too high with old programmes from church concerts and tracts and some dog-eared exercise books, curling at the corners from age. One of them had slith-ered off the top of the pile. On picking it up the yellowed pages had fallen open, and the words, faded and spidery, had caught Amy's eye.

'Such wild and frenzied passion I have never known till now. I thank God that he brought my beloved Frederic into my life, just when I believed I could never love again.'

The words had hit Amy as forcibly as if it had been a blow to the face – Mother, known all her life for gentle-ness and a sweet, imperturbable nature, to have known passion? The thought seemed sacrilegious, somehow. Mother was old, near enough forty, there were lines of tiredness around her eyes and she complained often of rheumatism these days – she'd always been old, hadn't she? Always a mother, and one could not believe such things of one's mother. It just didn't fit. And who was Frederic? The exercise book had carried a date on it – 1879. That was the year Amy had been born, and presumably her father was still alive then, so how could Mother have written such words at that time?

She had not meant to pry, but these searing words

59

begged for further enquiry. She might have overcome her guilty feelings and read on, had the back door not opened suddenly. She had only just shoved the book hastily out of sight before Lionel came in, coughing and rubbing his thin hands together, clearly chilled and anxious to stand close to the fire.

It would be no use asking Mother to explain. She always remained politely uncommunicative whenever Amy asked about those early years.

'Everyone needs to keep one little part of themselves to themselves,' she used to say. 'Everyone has a need for a little privacy.'

The only way to find out more would be to have another surreptitious look at the exercise book – and that she determined to do, just as soon as the opportunity presented itself.

Mother, at about the age she was herself, consumed with passion for a man not her husband? The very idea seemed strange and unnatural. But was it? It could account for why she spoke so softly of Amy's future change of heart where men were concerned. Amy snuggled down into the depths of the feather mattress, turning over in her mind the picture of Mother those words in the book had conjured up, but when she heard her mother return, singing softly to herself in the kitchen as she made her preparations for bed, she tried hard to banish the picture. It seemed somehow disloyal to think such thoughts of the loving woman who tiptoed into the bedroom, undressing quietly in the dark before lying down beside her.

'Mother?' It was no use. She could not rest.

The figure beside her moved slightly. 'Are you still awake, love?'

'I just wanted to ask. Did you ever love any other man apart from my father?'

It might have been imagination but there seemed to be just a fraction of a pause, a tiny catch of breath before the answer came. 'What a time of night to be asking about ancient history. Go to sleep, lovey, if you're to catch the early tram in the morning. Good-night, sweetheart. God bless.'

In the next room, Lionel began to cough. Without a word Mother got out of bed and, putting on her robe, went to dose him with honey and lemon.

FOUR

The wind was blowing dust and litter all around the statue of Sir Robert Peel in St George's Square as the tram clattered to a halt at the stop. Amy climbed down from the tram, brushing the grit from her skirt, and smiled as she caught sight of Cissie Barlow. She was clutching her hat to her head, trying not to let it blow away in the stiff breeze.

'Wish I'd put another hat-pin in, like me mam said,' she said with a grin.

'You're late,' Amy remarked. 'You should have opened up shop by now, shouldn't you? Mr Sidgwick'll be after you.'

'Shop's shut. Haven't you read the paper?' said a round-eyed Cissie. 'Mr Sidgwick dropped dead on Tuesday, just as we were locking up. Apoplexy, the paper said. Being buried at St Thomas's at two tomorrow, he is. New manager at the shop next week. Hope he's nicer than Mr Sidgwick, though. I ought not to say that; I hope he keeps me on.'

Amy was stunned. Mr Sidgwick dead? It didn't seem possible. Death had not come so close to her life before, and it was not easy to believe. Even if Mr

Sidgwick had not been a likeable man, it was not easy to think of him dead. Poor Mrs Sidgwick, the faded lady who had sometimes come into the emporium to ask his advice – she would be all at sixes and sevens without him. It would be a fitting mark of respect to attend his funeral, Amy thought.

'I'll see if I can come tomorrow, Cissie, if I can get time off. Must fly, or I'll be late.'

'Happen I'll see you then,' said Cissie. 'Oh, me hat!'

With a quick wave Amy hurried away up Railway Street, leaving Cissie to chase after her hat.

Mr Pogson, the office manager, kept running his podgy fingers through the end of his moustache, lifting it to bristle even more than usual. 'So you expect me to give you the afternoon off?' he demanded. 'Are you prepared to make the time up afterwards?'

'Only an hour off, sir. I'll come back after the service.'

'And work the hour after the others have gone?'

Amy sighed. 'Very well.'

Nodding, he bumbled away into the main office.

Mistake after mistake. That seemed to be the pattern of her life, Amy reflected ruefully as she set off from the office that afternoon. A stiff breeze still chased along the streets, swirling her skirts tightly about her legs as she made her way out of the town centre and headed along the Manchester road towards the church. It had been a mistake to believe that life as an office-clerk would be far pleasanter than as a shop-girl, and a greater mistake still to play into Mr Pogson's hands. He would squeeze every drop he could from his advantage tonight if she was left in the office alone with him. He could not lock up until she left.

If she'd been naive once, she certainly was not so any more, not since starting work at Wadsworth and Firth's. The partners themselves, Mr Firth and Mr Wadsworth, were the essence of propriety, gentlemen of the old school – whenever they chose to appear on the premises, which was not often. But all the other men there, from Mr Pogson down to young Albert the most junior clerk, they were birds of prey the lot of them, vultures waiting to pounce on an unwary girl.

They were a sickening lot, but they had some excuse in that they all took their cue from their plump and oily manager. The other girls all seemed to take it in their stride.

'They're not so bad as the fellows up at Hepworths when I was a junior there,' the senior woman clerk, Miss Wigfall, once remarked in a brief moment of familiarity. 'Not a day passed but you could be sure to have your bottom pinched, or worse. Just take care not to go into the stockroom on your own, that's all.'

Well, she had little trouble probably because she was the senior, called formally by her name and not just Eliza, and she was walking out steadily with a burly young man who was often to be seen waiting outside on the pavement for her at six of a Friday evening. No wonder Miss Wigfall held a rosier view than the other girls about conditions in the office.

Ahead of her, Amy could see figures entering the door of St Thomas's church, several well-dressed men and ladies, clearly people who did not have to go out to work for a living, or who at least held high enough positions to be able to take time off. She seated herself unobtrusively in a pew near the back. Down near the front she could see Cissie's head, bent to whisper to the young man next to her. On the front pew sat the diminutive figure of Mrs Sidgwick, veiled, and her head bent in prayer.

'Abide with me,
Fast falls the eventide.'

Voices sang in a hushed, reverent tone and there was a faint sound of sobbing mingled in the words – Mrs Sidgwick, no doubt. The vicar spoke eloquent words about the deceased, about his piety, devotion and conscientiousness, the sad loss to his family and to the town. At last the mourners rose to leave. Amy, unwilling to follow the cortege to the graveside, remained seated in the pew as the silent figures passed her by. She remained, head bent, her eyes on the prayerbook in her hand.

The church was empty now but for the organist in the loft. The last notes of music faded away into the rafters. Amy got up to leave.

A man stood outside the door, his hat in his hand and his gaze resting on the group of mourners at the graveside. Amy felt a stab of half-recognition. His regular features, golden beard and fair head gleaming in the pale sun – where had she seen them before? He wore an overcoat of expensive cloth and was elegantly turned out; he could be no one she had ever met, and yet . . .

He turned, catching sight of her, and she saw him start. For a second he looked as if he were about to speak. Searching blue eyes probed hers, and she felt as if her heart stood still. At the same moment she felt a sudden stab of pain in her thumb.

For several seconds she stood as if paralysed, overcome by the strength and beauty of his face. An electrifying current seemed to pass between his eyes and her own, and she shivered, held in their thrall.

Then he opened his lips as if to speak, but no words came.

From out of nowhere Cissie appeared, and she took hold of Amy's arm.

'Eh, I'm glad you've not gone, Amy. Now we can walk back to town together.'

Regaining her self-control, Amy turned and began to walk away. At the corner she looked back over her shoulder. He was still standing there, tall and beautiful like a Greek god, then he was gone.

'He's lovely, isn't he?' Cissie chuckled.

'Who?'

'That gentleman you were looking at. I saw you were watching him in the church too. Know him?'

'No. Do you?'

Cissie shrugged. 'He were in the shop not long back. Mr Sidgwick served him, not me. Only saw him the once. Once seen, never forgotten, eh? He's not for the likes of us, any road. Them sort always mix with their own.' She giggled, and prattled about her new beau from the shop next door. Amy was barely listening. Her thumb was still pricking. Strange, she thought, it reminds me of that line – is it from *Macbeth?*

> *'By the pricking of my thumbs,*
> *Something wicked this way comes.'*

But there could be nothing wicked about that young gentleman – he was so fair, so beautiful, and there was nothing but directness in those clear blue eyes. She might never see him again, but she knew she would forever remember him as representing all that was perfection in a man.

In the town centre she parted from Cissie and made her way back towards the office, still seeing in her mind's eye the vision which made her senses ache, turning the murky air of Hawksmoor into a rosy glow.

It was Mr Pogson who dissipated the glow. She was aware of his quick glance from her to the clock as she came in and took off her hat.

'Fifty-five minutes to be made up,' he remarked, pointing his pen at her as the clock reached six and the others covered their typewriters, locked their drawers and prepared to go. He went back into his office and Amy continued to type as the others left and the door closed behind them. The last letter completed, Amy laid the sheet of paper aside and stared at her machine, the name Barlock printed on it burning itself into her sight, but seeing in her mind's eye only the blond Adonis outside the church door.

The doorknob gave a sudden rattle and Mr Pogson emerged from his office, pencil in hand.

'I heard your machine stop. Finished?'

Startled out of her reverie, Amy nodded and held out the letter. He waddled forward, taking it and perusing it closely. She watched as he ran the pencil tip along each line. Finally he nodded.

'No mistakes today. Good.'

Encouraged, Amy half-rose. 'Can I go now?'

He frowned. 'Nay, there's half an hour yet to be made up. Can't have short measure, you know – that's bad as stealing.'

She coloured. 'But I've done all I was set to do – there's nothing else.'

He glared. 'It's for me to say if there's owt else, miss, not you. You can go get more paper and ribbons out from the storeroom ready for morning. And fill the inkwells. You're not due out of here while seven.'

The storeroom smelt musty and dusty as Amy moved boxes and cartons to reach the typewriter ribbons. Mr Pogson remained out of sight while she moved to and from the office, but reappeared while she was pouring ink into the lading-can ready to fill the inkwells.

'You've splashed some,' he pointed out, nodding towards her. Amy looked down. A small dark stain stood out on the whiteness of her blouse. He came closer, pencil clenched between podgy fingers and his gaze still resting on her breast. Amy turned away and busied herself.

'I've been thinking.' His voice came over her shoulder, and she noticed the unaccustomed softness of his tone. 'You're not a bad lass, not bad at all. You could do nicely here.'

'I'm glad you think so, Mr Pogson.'

'Aye, very well indeed. You've a bearing about you, much more so than the other lasses. Miss Wigfall tells me she's to be engaged shortly, and hopes to marry by the end of the year. I'll be needing to promote someone in her place. Soon, very likely.'

Amy turned eagerly. 'You mean, it could be me? Already? I've not been here very long, you know.'

'I'm not promising owt – yet. But there'll be some changes made and, like as not, you could better yourself – if you play your cards right.'

He touched the tip of his pencil lightly on the stain as he spoke. He stood so close, his face level to her own, that she could see the gleam in his eyes and smell the unpleasantness of his breath. She was turning away again when she felt his hand seize her arm.

'Not so fast, miss. I said, if you play your cards right. That means pleasing your boss, don't you know?'

She could feel the blood rising to her cheeks. 'But I do, don't I? You said my typewriting was good today, my shorthand's getting faster all the time and I don't slack.'

The stubby fingers dug deeper in her upper arm. 'Nay, don't play the innocent with me, Amy. I know you're not daft – far from it. You're a bright lass, you are, and you could profit by that, if you'd a mind.'

She watched the wet mouth shaping the words, exhaling foul breath and equally foul suggestion, and felt her throat constrict in nausea. Her first impulse was to hit out at the leering face, but caution prevented her.

Mother had always proclaimed one maxim for troublesome men: '*Treat them politely but remain cool, my lovey. Keep them at arm's length and don't allow familiarity.*'

Easier said than done, but then, Amy realised, she could not risk losing her position yet. She must placate and evade the creature. Picking up the ink can with her free hand she turned, ignoring his grip. Involuntarily he released her.

'There, it's striking seven,' she said. 'Mrs Pogson'll be keeping your tea hot. It's very kind of you to think of me, being a likely person to promote, I mean.' She poured ink, avoiding meeting his gaze. 'I'll certainly do my best to please, that I will, and I'll not mention what you've said to the others.'

It was a veiled threat, and he recognised it. He cleared his throat. 'Ah, yes, that would be best, I reckon, at the moment. But I'll make more use of your services for my own needs. I'll send for you to take dictation in the morning.' He paddled back into his office, closing the door behind him.

Alone with him in his office, that would mean. Amy sighed inwardly as she put on her coat. Escape would not always be so easy.

So preoccupied did Amy remain that evening with dreams of the beautiful young man that she forgot completely about Mr Pogson, and it was not until her mother went out that she recalled her earlier intention. That glimpse of Mother's diary several days ago had awakened a curiosity she could not repress. Underhand or not, she was determined to sneak another glance.

The church hassocks which still needed repair, coinciding with Lionel's visit to the Bible study class, gave the perfect opportunity.

'And there's the church sale of work coming up soon,' Mother remarked. 'I'd best help Mrs Brierley get some of the stuff cut out ready for the other ladies to sew. I'll not be very late.'

Neither Mother nor Lionel would return for an hour or two – Lionel possibly much later if Maggie was at the class too. When they had both gone out, Amy began to look for the diary.

The boxes had been moved; Mother had evidently found a place for them. It took some time to find them. They were not in the living room or the bedroom, but in the attic, where Mother usually put away things she would be unlikely to use for some time. The boxes, covered by a cloth, lay in a far corner. It took only a few moments to find the one which had excited her interest, and Amy re-covered the boxes with care. It was too chilly to linger up there so Amy carried the exercise book downstairs, put more coal on the fire and settled down to read.

Her fingers trembled as she opened the book. Guilty, yet consumed by curiosity about those passionate words she had glimpsed, she had to pry; she could not help herself. Maybe she had misread it, maybe she had misunderstood. One way or another, she knew she must find out the truth.

Begin at the beginning and skip through, she decided. No sound disturbed the silence save the slow tick of the clock and the crackle of the fire – she would be sure to hear the click of the latch soon enough to hide the book away.

But still she could feel her heart race as she read the opening words.

'My Tom is gone forever. My Amy is safe at Father's house. I must make a new life for myself, and so I go to London, to see whether Mr Newman may help me. He seemed a kindly man.'

For an hour Amy sat mesmerised by the gently sloping copperplate hand. Such neat, controlled writing, so much at odds with the sentiments she read. Mr Newman, it seemed, had been surprised but warmly welcoming, and Mother had been overwhelmed by the beauty of his gracious home in Poynton Square. Amy skipped quickly over the description, noting instead how Mr Newman's hospitality had grown into amazing generosity.

'Today Frederic insisted I should have a new gown and coat, befitting a lady who was daughter to the Mayor of Hawksmoor, he said. I could not expect him to present me to his elegant friends in my outworn

clothes, but so graciously he makes the gesture that he makes me feel it is I who do him a favour. Such is the considerate mark of a gentleman, and I account myself indeed fortunate.'

Amy chewed her lip thoughtfully. Either this man was too good to be true, or Mother was unaccountably naive. Why on earth should an obviously prosperous London gentleman take in a provincial woman, mayor's daughter or not, unless he had some motive? Philanthropy only? Amy's experience of men so far led her to doubt that.

'Frederic is so thoughtful. When I ventured to suggest my presence in his home might be misconstrued he hastened to reassure me. No eyebrows would be raised, he said; it would be made clear to all that I was to be accorded the respect due to a lady.'

Amy snorted. From the passionate phrases she had read the other day, he had not continued to treat her as a lady. She read on.

A word caught her eye – her own name.

'Charlotte asked me what did I know of love, to be able to abandon my precious Amy and go away alone. How little she knows. I adored my child even before I bore her. Today my wonderful Frederic asked me the same question – "What do you know of love, my little bird?" he asked me as he sat beside me on the chaise-longue in his beautiful drawing room. "So briefly wed, so soon widowed – what can you know of love?" I did not answer him, but I can see still the sunlight gleaming on the polished parquet floor as he murmured to me, "I could teach you arts such as you have never dreamt of." I did not know what he meant.'

70

Amy turned the pages, tongue flicking along dry lips as she read the passionate phrases. It was clear from Mother's own opinions that, disarmed by grief, she had been readily susceptible to this Frederic Newman's persuasive tongue. Poor Mother, vulnerable and desperate for love and safety – no wonder she had succumbed. Amy felt a stab of disillusion – her own Mother, who had always advised her to keep persistent men at arm's length.

The man sounded beautiful, according to Mother's loving description – the waving black hair, long nose and keen eyes, the tapering beard and sensitive hands. He had done his work well and Mother was clearly deeply in love with him. But was he with her? Or was he simply using a pretty but gullible woman in need?

Passages in the diary throbbed with exclamation.

'How tenderly he touches me! How gentle he is to me!' And there was exultation where Mother's hand had written, *'Today he spoke of his love for me, and bade me stay with him forever, mistress of his home and of his heart.'*

The joyful words left no doubt that she adored this Frederic Newman. She wrote proudly of all they did together – entertaining, dining out at his friends' houses, walking in the park, riding in his carriage. *'The only place where I may not accompany him is to the Temple on Saturday.'*

Amy frowned, puzzled, but at that second the sound of the door latch made her start in alarm. Footsteps sounded in the lobby, then voices. She leapt from the chair and darted into the scullery.

The diary! She could not let it be seen. Hide it, and quickly, she thought. Drawing it from under her apron, she looked around feverishly for a hiding-place before the door from the living room should open. Under the rag rug – that would have to suffice for now. She would

71

retrieve it later, for Mother would be sure to lift the rug for cleaning in the morning.

The diary secreted, she stood on the rug, conscious of the slight bulge, and waited. No one entered the scullery, and after a few moments she tiptoed to the door and laid her ear against the panel. It was Lionel who was speaking.

'Nay, I only wanted to see thee alone for a few minutes where we wouldn't be disturbed, that's all.'

Thee? He never said thee – unless it was to someone else who spoke that way. It could not be Mother, for she had always frowned on the word.

'I know, love, but I promised I'd not be late home.' The voice was timid, indistinct, but Amy recognised it as Maggie's. She hesitated, reluctant to intrude upon the couple. If only they would leave quickly so that she could return the diary to the attic.

'Nay, tha musn't! There was alarm in Maggie's tone and Amy was filled with embarrassment. A furtive reader of her Mother's private thoughts, she was now also an inadvertent witness to her brother's advances. There was only one thing to do.

She clattered the pile of pans stacked on top of the wash-boiler, anxious to warn the couple they were not alone. Lionel's sheepish face appeared at the door.

'I didn't know you were still up, Amy. I brought Maggie in for a cup of tea, it being such a cold night and all.'

'Nay, I can't stop,' Amy heard the girl protest. 'I must go before I get scolded again, thanks all the same.'

'I'll walk thee down.' Amy watched her brother's thin, gawky frame as he left, then, remembering the diary, she took it quickly back upstairs. When she had replaced it under the cover in the attic she made ready for bed, feeling a mixture of disgust with herself for prying and – though she was loth to admit it – with her Mother.

Mother, always respected and admired as a lady of breeding, even if of reduced circumstances, had once behaved as a girl no better than she ought to be. She, the model of propriety who always exhorted her daughter to behave with decorum, she had known illicit passion. It was almost too gross, too far-fetched to believe. And yet, it gave Amy a strange sense of warmth and compassion to know her mother had once been as carried away as she herself could be in fantasy. That beautiful young man at Mr Sidgwick's funeral today, for example; he would fill Amy's dreams, she knew it. She could write words about him every bit as rapturous as those Mother had penned about Frederic Newman.

She pulled on her flannelette nightdress and climbed into bed, revelling in the warmth of the stone hot-water bottle wrapped in a piece of blanket at her feet. Words from the diary flashed into her mind.

'You have taught me how to love, Frederic, in a way I never thought possible. Today you called me beautiful, a true child of nature. I love you with all my heart, my precious man.'

As Amy settled down to sleep she felt only love and understanding for her mother. It was somehow very reassuring to know that beneath her calm, poised exterior had once lain a woman of spirit who could let her heart rule her head.

As Violet trudged homeward from the church ladies' sewing meeting many thoughts flitted through her tired mind. Her pinpricked fingers were stiff and aching from pushing the needle through the tough tapestry of the hassocks but she refused to believe the relentless rheumatism in her legs was beginning to attack her hands. A night's sleep and her hands would be flexible and pain-free again, she was sure they would. She turned her mind to her children.

Lionel was a cause for worry. That cough still hadn't really left him, but he'd insisted on going back to work. If only he could go to the Technical . . . Her mind battled with the problem. Perhaps if she took in washing again as she used to do in the bad days – but then, she was forced to admit, her hands could never endure all the washboard-rubbing and wringing.

But at least the lad seemed less troubled and restless these days. That young Maggie had a lot to do with it, and she felt grateful to the girl. Amy now, she was deeply restless and so far Violet had not been able to discover the cause. The office job didn't seem to be all the child had hoped for, but there was no clear reason why. If only she would take up with a presentable young man, but she never seemed to show any interest. Quite the contrary, she seemed positively scornful about men. If only the child could learn the pleasure of loving, and of being loved.

'You have taught me how to love, Frederic.'

One day, perhaps, Amy would write words such as that, and with the same fervour. God grant the child would be as lucky as she had been, but with a happier ending to her story.

She undressed in the dark so as not to disturb Amy, blew out the candle and climbed into bed. Though her back was turned, it was clear to Violet that the girl was awake, for there was tension in the slim body.

'Awake, love?'

A faint murmur came in reply.

'Something bothering you? Work, perhaps? Has that Mr Pogson been at you again?'

The figure turned. 'It's not work, Mother. Nor Mr Pogson, though he would be at me in another way given half a chance.'

'Oh, Amy!' Violet couldn't help her shocked tone of disgust. To her surprise Amy laughed.

'Come off it, Mother – you know what men are like. You've gone through it all yourself.'

'What do you mean? Men are usually courteous if a lady makes it clear—'

'Stop it, Mother! You've always told me that, but I know different.'

'Just because Mr Pogson—'

'Not him – you! I know what you did with Frederic Newman. I know you've been used too, and called it love. Exploited, Mother – that's what you were. How can you, of all people, try and teach me how to—'

'What do you mean, Amy? How do you know about Frederic?' Violet could hear the coldness, the disbelief, in her own voice.

Amy grunted. 'I read your diary, that's how.'

'You-did-what?' She felt sick, sick at the thought of her hidden past coming to the girl's knowledge, sicker still at the thought that her precious child had spied, behind her back, into the dark corners of her life.

'I'm glad I did.' There was no repentance in Amy's voice, muffled under the bedclothes. 'I know now how a woman can be used. I know why you never talked much about Lionel's birth – because he's not really my brother.'

'He is, oh, he is!' Violet protested. 'You are both my children.'

'But with different fathers. Lionel's father was a wealthy Jew, it seems, not a poor workman like mine.'

'Your father was a skilled man, a pharmacist, a father to be proud of. And Lionel is your brother, well, half-brother at least.' She reached out to place a comforting arm around Amy, but the girl brushed her away, swinging her legs out of bed and sitting, her back to her mother, on the edge of the bed.

'Much use it did Lionel,' she muttered. 'A wealthy

father who disowned him – what kind of man is that to love?'

'He didn't disown him. He just wasn't able to marry me, that's all.'

'I read it – because you were only a Gentile. My God! You were good enough to be his mistress, but not his wife! And you fell for it, Mother!'

Violet breathed a deep sigh. 'You're right, I did. I believed he planned to marry me. I cannot tell you the pain—'

Amy turned quickly, laying a hand on her shoulder. 'I know. I read what you wrote, that he always seemed to side-step when marriage was mentioned. And when you told him you were pregnant—'

'Liaisons are one thing, he said, but marrying someone not of his own faith was out of the question. Poor, dear Frederic, I loved him so much, but he was what he was . . .'

'Weak,' commented Amy.

'No, a product of many generations of marrying only one's own kind. Inherited tradition. He could not break away.'

'But *you* had broken away from your home and upbringing.'

'Circumstances were different. I was desperately poor, a widow with a child—'

'And came home poor and with two children. How did you explain that?'

Her mother shrugged. 'I never needed to explain anything. I suppose people thought I was already pregnant before your poor father died. I don't know – it didn't matter.'

'You could have stayed in London.'

Violet sought her daughter's gaze but in the gloom she could see only the pale shape of the night-gowned figure. She reached out and pulled the girl back into bed.

'You read about Lord Denaby then?'

'That he would have taken you over from your Frederic – yes, I did. I also read what you overheard them saying about you.'

'Don't speak of that. I pushed it from my mind years ago.'

It was a lie, and she felt sure Amy knew it. How could a woman ever forget these words?

'What's she really like then, Newman, this little Yorkshire pudding of yours? Lively filly, would you say?'

'Pyrotechnics, my dear fellow. Light the blue touch-paper then stand well back. You'll never know what hit you. Explosive, a woman of fire, you might say.'

She could still recall the sound of laughter and clink of glasses from the drawing room as she stood in the shadow of the stairs and her scarlet-faced retreat. Amy was right. Who was she, with her ignorance of the ways of men, to counsel a daughter? She laid a finger on the girl's cheek in the dark.

'Do you still love him, Mother? You did then.'

'The young are blind and foolish, love. Don't be too upset at what you read. I should be angry with you for prying, but remember this – when we are young we write down what we believe to be the truth, but with the hindsight of years—'

Amy clung fiercely to her mother. 'Let's talk no more of it, Mother. Goodnight, and God bless you.'

Feeling the intensity of the girl's hug, Violet fell silent. She was content that her secret was out. As Amy turned over, she curled herself around the girl's back. Like two silver spoons, she thought. There was comfort in the warm, firm young body, and it eased the ache in her side.

'You think no different of your brother now you know, do you?' she murmured.

Amy lay silent for a moment. 'He's still the brother I've always loved.'

'I'm glad of that, love. And I think I've no need to

77

ask it, but you'll not mention what you know to him, will you?'

There was a deep sigh. 'Not I. He's troubles enough of his own. Goodnight, Mother.'

'Pass the salt please, Charles.'

Absently Charles passed the silver pot across to his sister. She stared at his hands in horror.

'Good Lord! Just look at the filth under your nails! Have you been in the stables again or helping the gardener? Charles! Are you listening to me? I refuse to sit and eat with you with your hands in such a state.'

Charles smiled amiably. 'Hold your tongue, Berenice. You're getting to sound just like Mother. We could have a rest from nagging just for once while she's not here. Where are they, by the way?'

'Dining at the Lumbs'.' Berenice draped the damask napkin across her knees and tucked the corner into the waistband of her skirt. Charles took the salt-cellar and poured copious amounts into his soup.

'Charles! You'll never be able to eat that! What's the matter with you? You're miles away.'

He smiled again good-humouredly, tasted his soup and pulled a face. 'Ugh! Yes, you're right, I was day-dreaming.'

His sister cocked her head. 'What about, this time? Billiards, cards, horses? Or that little actress you've been taking out to supper lately?'

'Little Ismelda, you mean – no, she's gone now. The company was only in Hawksmoor while the play lasted. They've gone on to somewhere in Lancashire now. That little *affaire* is at an end, I fear.'

'Good job Mother didn't hear about it, but she will one day – you have so many little romances.'

'What's this, little sister? Jealousy, because romance hasn't entered your young life yet? It will, I assure you, it will.'

'I hope so, and soon. Life is so boring with little to do but read and sew and play the piano.' She eyed her brother speculatively. 'There's still that far-away look in your eyes, Charles. Have you begun a new romance or something?'

He sighed and pushed the soup away. 'Not yet. But I did see the most delectable little creature at the funeral today. A ravishing dark-haired girl with the most devastating eyes I've ever seen.'

'You see – and you grumbled when Mother said you had to go to represent the family. You have all the luck. Who was she?'

'I don't know; she was with Sidgwick's girl assistant.'

'So she's probably only a shop-girl too. Oh, Charles! How could you! She's not your sort.'

' "Not one of us," as Mother would say? Perhaps not, but she was a real beauty, I can tell you.'

'Well, you don't know who she is, so you can't start a romance there,' Berenice remarked with a wry smile.

Charles chuckled. 'I could if I wanted to. I could always go into Sidgwick's shop and find out about her. God, but she was a real eyeful, that one.'

Berenice laid aside her spoon. 'I give up. You really are incorrigible. What are you going to do tonight? Will you stay in for once and keep me company?'

'I doubt it. Edgar invited me to his place to play billiards. I said I might come. Did I tell you I did the most incredible in-off last night?'

'No. I don't want to hear.' She signalled to the maid to remove the soup dishes then sighed deeply. 'So that means I'm condemned to spending the evening alone with my book again. You men have all the fun.'

'Fun!' exclaimed Charles. 'How much fun do you think it is to have to attend funerals because Mother is too busy to go? There's no fun in that, I can tell you.'

Berenice shrugged. 'Well, at least you get out and about. I have to stay indoors and read.'

'What are you reading? Another of your slushy yellowbacks?'

'It's a lovely story about a girl forced to marry a much older man, believing her lover to have been killed out in India. It's so sad. It's called *Love's Cruel Flame*. Mother would die if she knew I'd borrowed it from Sophia.'

Charles pushed back his chair and stood up. 'I don't think I'll eat any more – I can always have supper with Edgar later.' He laid a hand on his sister's shoulder as he passed her. 'Poor Berenice,' he said, and there was a hint of a chuckle in his voice. 'I'm so sorry for you, only being able to read about love. Never mind, one day . . .'

Berenice seized his hand. 'Listen, Charles, I persuaded Mother to let me choose my own maid this time instead of her. Why don't we go to the fair at Cope Bank on Monday. Will you take me? It would be such fun – there's a hiring-fair there, you know. It's not far.'

Charles considered for a moment.

'The fair? Why not – it would make a change. A fellow finds it hard to find much of interest on a Monday. If the weather stays fine – yes, I'll take you.'

Berenice beamed. 'That's wonderful – a new maid of my own and your company for the day. It'll be like old times, before you took up with all your cards and horses and billiards. Oh, I do look forward to Monday.'

Charles smiled and, as he took his hand away, Berenice caught sight of his fingernails and shuddered. How on earth could any woman let him touch her with hands like that, even if she was only an actress or a shopgirl?

FIVE

Lionel and Maggie walked arm-in-arm down Cloth Hall Street, passing outside the London and Midland Bank with its fluted columns and huge copper dome. Lionel drew Maggie under the shadows of the portico.

'Nay, Lionel, the manager lives upstairs – he'll see us!' she protested.

'He'll neither see nor hear us, lass – Oliver told me he's deaf as a doorpost. They've had gunpowder-proof locks put on the strongroom in the cellar, he says, but Mr Barraclough'd never hear if someone did try to blast them. Come here, give us a kiss.'

Still protesting, she let herself be drawn into the shadows. For long, close moments they clung to each other until at last she drew away.

'Nay, listen, I want to hear what tha thinks about me leaving – going to Mrs Baker's up Gledholt. Should I go while I've still chance?'

He sighed. 'After what tha told me about thy mistress today, I'd not hesitate if it were me. She'd no right. She's a cow, that woman.'

Maggie grew reflective, but kept close to the lean warmth of him. 'Nay, Miss Berenice said I could have them chemises – they only needed the lace tacking on again, but Mrs Holroyd took 'em off me before I could even take 'em downstairs. She were that mad with me . . .'

'I'd leave, especially if yon Mrs Baker still wants thee.'

'She is thy aunt, Lionel – I thought tha might not agree with me.'

'She's no aunt of mine!' he exploded. 'Think on what she did about that scholarship. It should have been mine; thou heard her – it was thou as told me she put a stop to it. Don't ever call that creature my aunt again, dost hear me? She's nowt to me – nowt!'

'I'm sorry, love.' Maggie's voice came faintly in the darkness and Lionel, repenting of the sharpness of his tone, drew her close again.

'Nay, don't hesitate, lass. Give thy notice and leave as fast as they'll let thee – and I tell thee what, I'll give me notice in too. If I don't make shift to better myself I'll be stuck in them blasted gasworks for the rest of me life. Let's both take a leap together, Maggie lass – I'll go looking for a new place first thing Monday.'

'We're on holiday on Monday, Lionel – it's Easter Bank Holiday, think on.'

'Oh aye, so it is! Shall we go to Pringle's Pictures again? Tha liked the films – remember me taking thee to the bioscope?'

'Nay, there'll be the travelling circus down at the Beast Market. Wilt take me? Go on, say tha wilt – I love them clowns and tightrope-walkers.'

Her eager little face glowed in the shadows and he touched her gently under the chin. 'Aye, I'll take thee, love. I'd do owt to please thee.'

She giggled. 'Then get me home before I get shouted at – come on.' Pulling him by the hand she led him out into the light of the gaslamps, and together they walked away up the street, his arm about her shoulders. 'And I'll do as tha suggests love – I'll brave Mrs Holroyd's tongue and tell her tomorrow as I'm off. She'll have a word or two to say about that, I reckon, or me name's not Maggie Braithwaite.'

'Not for long, it isn't,' muttered Lionel. 'Soon as ever I can manage it, it'll be Maggie Mallinson. How dost like the sound of that?'

'Oh, Lionel!' She buried her nose in the sleeve of his jacket. 'Oh, love, I'll be that proud,' she murmured.

Amy stared at Mr Pogson's podgy red face in dismay. The hands of the office clock showed six and the others were all preparing to leave.

'Work late again tonight? Oh no, not again! Can't you ask one of the others if it's that urgent?'

His face spread into the oily smile she had come to loathe. 'No, I can't. None of the others is as good at figures as you are, and the stocktaking has to be done before weekend – it's Easter, you know.'

'But it was me who stayed late last time—'

'And will do again, if I've so a mind. What's the matter – is there a young man waiting for you?'

'No, there's not. But my mother—'

'She'll keep your tea hot. Now get going – count up what's in the stockroom, what's out in the office, and see if the totals tally with mine. Shouldn't take long if you shift yourself – look lively.'

But when the heavy oak door had banged shut behind the last clerk and the only sound in the office was the slow tick of the wall clock, Amy knew the stillness was only a prelude. Tonight, she felt sure, the manager had only contrived this excuse to keep her behind, alone, for his own purposes.

But half an hour later when her columns of figures were half-completed and Mr Pogson had made no move to come out of the inner office she began to give him the benefit of the doubt. Perhaps, after all, Mr Wadsworth and Mr Firth had given him explicit orders to produce the figures before the Easter break. She was busying herself in the stockroom, re-counting the pen nibs to be certain, when she became aware of heavy breathing behind her, accompanied by a faint smell of violets. It was Pogson, and he was eating those parma violet cachous he often chewed in an effort to sweeten his breath.

83

He did not speak as she turned, nor did he move his cumbersome body out of her way as she made to pass him. In the narrow space left between the boxes of stock and the doorway she would have to touch him if she wanted to pass.

'Excuse me, Mr Pogson.'

Still he did not move. Amy hesitated, then, turning her back towards him, tried to pass him. He spread his thick body so that there was no room to squeeze past. At the same moment she felt his clumsy hands on her waist.

'Mr Pogson!'

There was a throaty chuckle and the thick fingers slid up over her breast. Amy gasped. 'Come now, lass, don't make out as you didn't expect it,' he muttered. 'You been leading me on for weeks, and don't think as I didn't know what you were up to.'

'You're wrong! I mean, you're mistaken, Mr Pogson. I'd never lead anyone on. Please let me pass.'

Her heart was thumping and anger choked in her throat, but she tried to keep cool.

'Oh aye! Always the lady, you – always your nose in the air, making out as you're a cut above all the other lasses. But I know better. I've seen you look up under your lashes at me, I've seen you swinging your hips – you know what you're about, that you do.'

'No! Truly! You've got it all wrong!'

'Have I, then? Well, put me right – weren't you trying to make sure as I noticed you for promotion? Isn't that it?'

His red face pushed itself close to hers and Amy turned her head away in distaste, the scent of violets choking her nostrils.

'It was you who talked of promotion, not me,' she muttered, glad at least that his hands had fallen from her, although she was still wedged in the doorway with him.

'Aye, it was me, but haven't you tried to be nice as

84

pie ever since – amiable to a degree, you might say? Haven't you come down often into the stockroom while I could see, maybe hoping I'd follow? I'm not daft, you know.'

Amy glared. 'I only come when I need more paper or a rubber – I wouldn't stoop to that!'

'Then you're not so sharp as I gave you credit for. Now Jenny and the others – they've more sense.'

His stubby fingers were climbing again, struggling clumsily with her buttons. Amy let her list and pencil fall, slapping his hands sharply and breaking free. Then she turned to glare at him.

'You must be mad, to think I'd willingly let you paw me, promotion or not. You can do what you like with the other girls, but you'll not have your way with me, you evil creature! Be damned to your promotion – you can do what the devil you like with it! I'm leaving!'

'And don't come back, Miss High-and-Mighty!' he called after her. 'Not only no promotion for you in my office. Don't come back here tomorrow, or ever.'

'I won't,' she called back as she snatched up her jacket.

'And don't ask for a reference neither – you'll get none from me!'

'And you won't get one from me either!'

Hurling her defiance, Amy slammed out of the door. The thought of his grasping fingers and foetid breath filled her with such repugnance that she felt joyful at the prospect of never setting eyes on him again. Men! They were predatory, lustful creatures, the lot of them!

Cissie was hovering at the tram stop in the square. 'Oh, Amy! I was wondering if you'd gone – I wanted to see you. I've lost me job, the new manager doesn't want me.'

Her face looked stricken. Amy took her arm. 'Never mind love – so have I. We'll look for posts together. We'll get on a sight better, just you see.'

'But where will we look, Amy? I've not much of a reference to go on.'

'And I've none at all, but who cares?' She squeezed the girl's thin arm. 'The world's our oyster, Cissie. We'll go exploring, you and I, and the day will come when we can look back and be glad. Fate is making us move on, don't you see?'

Cissie looked doubtful. 'I hope you're right.'

'I'm sure I am! Look – here comes your tram. Go out with me on Monday – we'll go down to Cope Bank and have a bit of fun. Ride on a donkey and go out in a boat on the lake. We'll make plans then.'

Cissie's face brightened. 'Right, then. Call for me? Midday? Oh, I hope me mam's not mad with me.'

Amy watched her small face framed in the window as the tram trundled away, then bent her steps towards home.

Violet regarded her daughter's angry face with concern. Though she felt filled with dismay she could not help secretly agreeing with her actions.

'I just want you to think carefully, love, before finally making up your mind. You know how hard good positions are to come by.'

'It's too late, Mother. He dismissed me.'

'But he might well reconsider if you went back in a calmer state of mind. I'm not urging you to do it, mind, only to think. It's so easy to be impulsive when you're distraught and so easy to regret it later.'

'Like you, Mother?' There was gentleness in the girl's tone. Violet smiled and ran a hand over her aching side.

'Ah yes, I was impulsive once, but I wouldn't want you to make the same mistakes I did – throwing the baby out with the bath water, as you might say. Don't throw away the old, the familiar, to rush off for what seems new and exciting. There's safety, at least, in the old, even if it does seem boring at times. Just because you're disappointed. . . .'

Amy clicked her tongue. 'Not disappointed – angry, Mother, angry at the way men try to exploit us. They do, you know – you were exploited, though you may not choose to recognise it.' She came close to her mother, eyeing her speculatively. 'You still love him, don't you? You still cherish a passion for the man who used you.'

Violet's lips firmed into a thin line. 'Now that's enough, Amy. You know nothing about it – and you had no business prying into matters that don't concern you. It's past, it's dead and gone, and anyway it was my private life.'

Amy lowered her head. 'I'm sorry. You're right. But I still believe men use women to their own ends and lots of women put up with it, either out of love or of necessity. Well, not me – I won't put up with it. I'll look for a new post, and be damned to Mr Pogson and all like him!'

'Amy! That's not a ladylike way to talk!'

'And was he gentlemanly, the way he behaved? Can't you see, Mother, you're supporting their way of thinking – that there's one law for them and another for us. Well, I'm blessed if I'll subscribe to it. From now on it's me that'll use men, and not them me.'

'Bad grammar, Amy.' Violet wagged a finger but her daughter brushed it away.

'But good policy, Mother. I'll take care of myself from now on and trust no man.'

Violet sighed. 'One day, God willing, you'll find the man to prove you wrong, a man who loves you sincerely. Then all doubt and distrust will be banished. I'll pray for that for you.'

Amy laid a hand on her mother's sleeve. 'Though you never found it for yourself. Oh, Mother! You deserved better.'

Violet smiled, a bright, unnatural smile. 'I had you

and Lionel – what more could a woman want? Now come on, help me side the dishes from the table.'

Late that night Violet sat alone by the dying fire thinking over the girl's words. Pray heaven the child didn't do something rash and impulsive, for it was in her blood. At her age – ah yes, at much the same age Violet herself had thrown caution to the winds to chance a life in London, and what had it gained her? A man whose face would haunt her all her days, and shame; being offered by Frederic to another man because he could not marry her, and the only way left to save face was to free him and return to Hawksmoor. How could she have gone to Lord Denaby's arms, carrying Frederic's child? Even if her condition had been known, he could not marry a Gentile. Hiding in a cheap London boarding house until the baby was born was the only solution. Coming home with a new baby raised no eyebrows, and once Frederic knew he had been only too anxious to help.

'I'll see you both provided for, Violet, but he can never bear my name.'

Lionel Mallinson would have been Lionel Newman, had life been fair. Violet sighed, easing herself in the chair to ease the ache, then picked up the volume of verse Lionel had brought from the library.

> *'Remember me when I am gone away,*
> *Gone far away into the silent land;*
> *When you can no more hold me by the hand . . .'*

She closed the book sharply, refusing to let her mind wonder whether Frederic ever gave thought to her these days.

A dismal mist hung over the chimney-pots of Hawksmoor early on Monday morning, but by the time Amy arrived at Cissie's the sun had responded to the holiday mood of the day and was pouring its mellow glow over the smoke-grimed cottages of Brook Fold. As Amy lifted the sneck on the back gate to go into the yard, she saw Cissie outside the shed and her small, wiry father's backside protruding out of the shed door.

'Me dad's feeding the pigeons,' Cissie explained as her father straightened, a bird in his hand, and nodded to the visitor. 'It's coming up time for a big race. Me dad's good at pigeon-racing.'

Amy looked at the sleek pigeon in his work-worn hands. 'It looks a fine, plump bird,' she commented.

'Plump's no good,' the little man said shortly. 'Thin and with hard muscle – that's what they need. And pink flesh, and feet that's dry and warm to touch. This one'll be in full bloom by the time he's to race.'

Cissie laughed. 'You always talk like they were flowers, Dad,' she teased.

'So they are, lass, come to bloom and fade again, just as fast as roses do. Now get out from under me feet and let me get on.'

The girls left the yard, walking off down the lane arm-in-arm. Cissie sighed. 'Like us, isn't it?' she murmured.

'What is?'

'Come to bloom and then fade fast. I hope as we find the right young men before that.'

Amy squeezed her arm. 'I swear you think of nothing else, Cissie Barlow – young men, that's all you talk about. What about that fellow in the shop next door?'

'Albert? Oh, he's off up the country to see his uncle. I'm on me own this week – so, Amy Mallinson, if I can find another beau to fill the time, I will, I promise you. Hurry up, love, let's get down to the station. He might be on the train, or happen he's waiting up there at Cope Bank, who knows?'

She bubbled happily all the way on the train up to Brockhurst, and as she chattered Amy visualised her own picture of the perfect man – the Adonis of the golden hair and beard outside the church that day. The special excursion train was packed with people who, like themselves, were freed from work for the day and in high festive mood. At Brockhurst the little station was thronged with excited holidaymakers, all heading for the pleasure-gardens, and as they spilled out on to the street they met and mingled with many more arriving by field paths and pouring down the hillside. Even the greyness of the windswept moors seemed to have taken on an Easter freshness under the glow of the sun.

Arriving at Cope Bank, Amy felt breathless with excitement; there was so much to see and do, from donkey-riding to eating from stalls selling fruit and nuts, brandy snap, hot pie and peas or beef and pickled cabbage.

Cissie was ravenous. 'I've had no breakfast, saved me appetite for this,' she said, tucking into currant pudding and cold roast veal. Stomach satisfied, she turned her attention to the people around her, the young men in particular. Everyone was laughing and jostling, wearing their Sunday best and eager to make the most of the day.

'There's waxworks in that tent, and a menagerie over there,' exclaimed Amy. 'What would you like to see? We could go for a boat ride – I'd like that.'

Cissie wrinkled her nose. 'I'd rather stay here, on land,' she murmured. 'Tell you what – you go for a ride and I'll meet you later at the fortune-teller's, eh?'

Amy shrugged. It was all the same to her. To tell the truth, Cissie's incessant chatter about young men was becoming a little wearisome. Alone, she could see and savour the sights for a while. She strolled around the grounds, watching with amusement the high spirits of the children released from school, the pleasure of grandparents with their children and the exasperation of young mothers. It was a lively, busy throng, and after a time Amy felt the need for space. She made her way to the lakeside.

A pleasure-boat, moored at the water's edge, was filling up with laughing passengers being helped aboard by a thickset young man in a cloth cap. He turned and, looking up and catching sight of Amy on the bank above him, surveyed her from under black eyebrows. His eyes glittered like coals.

'Room for one more,' he said tersely. Without a second's hesitation Amy slithered down the bank, putting out her hand for him to assist her. He gripped her upper arm and Amy lifted her skirts as he helped her on board. A buxom young woman pulled her youngster closer to her to make room for Amy on the crowded seat. Amy nodded her thanks and paid her sixpence, then watched the young man take the oars.

From where she sat she could see his broad shoulders bend and straighten, the muscle tightening under the coarse cloth of his shirt. There was something fascinating about his back, the long hollow that ran the length of his spine, and she had to jerk her gaze away sharply as he glanced back over his shoulder. Instead, she gazed at the eddy of receding figures on the bank and the sunlight splintering on the water.

It was chilly out in the middle of the lake. Amy turned up her collar. The young mother fussed over her child.

'I tell thee tha'll have thy muffler on whether tha likes it or not,' she chided. 'And for goodness sake sit up straight or tha'll get a charlie on thy back, slouching like that.'

The boy made no answer, but simply broke into pieces the remains of a sandwich in his grubby hand and tossed it to the gaggle of ducks hungrily pursuing the boat. Amy shifted her attention back to the straining shoulders of the oarsman. All around him voices chattered, teasing and happy, but he seemed absorbed in a world of his own as his arms moved in strong, rhythmic strokes. It was only when he brought the boat round to moor again at the jetty and sat motionless while the holidaymakers began to disembark that she became aware those thoughtful, deep-set eyes were focussed on her. She clambered out, not waiting for his arm.

As she was moving away along the bank there was a sudden cry and a splash behind her. Looking back she saw the buxom young woman bending over the water's edge, crying out and pointing.

'My lad! He's fell in! Somebody get him out!'

Amy saw a blue-shirted figure dive headlong into the lake and strike out towards the child. People gathered to watch as swift, clean strokes brought him to the child; and moments later the man from the boat was climbing, dripping, out of the lake and handing a sobbing little boy over to his mother.

'The wicked lad!' she shrieked, kneeling to slap and hug him close. 'We'll have to get thee home and dried out afore tha catch they death – and thee in thy new sailor-suit too!'

She dragged him away and Amy saw the man wringing out water from his sleeves and trouser legs. She approached him with a shy smile.

'She didn't think to thank you, she was that relieved,' Amy said. 'You deserve thanks.'

'It were nowt,' the man replied.

'You should get into some dry clothes – someone is sure to have something you can change into in one of the stalls. What's your name?'

'Clegg. Tobias Clegg.' His tone was surly, as though he resented her questioning, and as he turned his back on her, Amy went to move away. But something held her.

'I just wanted to thank you, at least,' she murmured.

He half-turned, looking at her over a hunched, dripping shoulder, and his slanting deep-set eyes glowed.

'No call for that. I did nowt but pull a lad out. Tha'd a done the same thyself if there were nobbut thee here.'

She felt confused, and felt the blush rise to her cheeks. 'Ah, well, maybe. But you should change out of those clothes – '

'Don't fuss me like a babby,' he said quickly. Then, catching sight of her expression, 'I'm sorry – I'm a rough sort – didn't mean to offend.'

A girl, a tiny dark-skinned figure with hair black as a gypsy's, appeared at his side carrying a blanket, and she reached up to drape it over his shoulders.

'Here, lad – it's the blanket from the wagon. It'll do till we get thee home.' She turned an enquiring gaze on Amy, who suddenly felt ill at ease and unwanted. She nodded to them both and walked away towards the collection of stalls and booths, aware of two pairs of black eyes staring at her back.

'Oh, Lord! Berenice, can't we go home now? I'm so bored!'

Charles yawned, spreading his kid-gloved fingers across his mouth. His sister picked her way carefully across the muddy grass, anxious not to spoil her pretty new shoes, tightening her grip on his arm.

'Not yet, Charles. We came purposely to hire my maid, remember? And the hiring hasn't begun yet. There's time for us to have our fortunes told first.'

'Not me! You can leave me out of all that female superstitious stuff! My fortune is what I make it, not what some grubby, greedy tinker-woman chooses to predict for me!'

'Then you can wait patiently for ten minutes while I hear mine – and after that we'll go to the hiring booth.'

He groaned. 'I'll wait, but not patiently, mind. I'm already thinking ahead to the game of bridge tonight. I don't want to be late.'

'You won't. We'll be home in good time for dinner, I promise.'

Charles was no longer listening. In front of them, already standing outside the fortune-teller's tent was a young woman, and his heart quickened as he caught sight of her. Dark curls peeping from beneath the bonnet, slender figure and that dainty, erect bearing – he recognised at once the captivating girl outside the church that day at Sidgwick's funeral. As they approached her, Berenice let go of his arm.

'Oh, there's someone else waiting,' she said in that petulant tone which often irritated him.

The girl turned, obviously overhearing. 'It's all right, I'm only waiting for my friend,' she said awkwardly. 'Ah, here she is.'

Another girl emerged from the tent, seized her arm and led her away. Charles saw the enticing creature glance back over her shoulder at him before she was lost to view in the crowd. Berenice was tapping him on the arm.

'Do you hear? I won't be long – don't move away or I'll never find you in this crowd.' And she disappeared inside the tent. Charles hesitated, then made up his mind. His heart was thumping with delight, just as it had that day at the church – God, but she was a magical creature, well worth braving Berenice's anger for. Such an opportunity might never arise again; he must follow and find the girl while Berenice was occupied.

'Ooh! It was so exciting, what she said to me,' Cissie was enthusing, clutching Amy's arm tightly. 'She said I'd marry by the time I were twenty, have five children, four of 'em sons, and my husband would be in a good way of work. I'd never want for nowt, she said; though we'd never be well-off, still we'd never lack owt that mattered.'

'That's good,' said Amy, but she was still trying over the multitude of bobbing heads to catch a sight of the glorious golden-haired Adonis outside the fortune-teller's tent. It was no use. He was nowhere in sight. Disappointment swelled in her. He was beautiful and her every fibre had thrilled at the sight of him, so much

94

so that she had babbled in confusion to the young woman he escorted.

'Nay, and that weren't all,' Cissie was saying, her face pink with excitement. 'She told me I'd make a decision that would change my life – for the better! And dost know when, Amy?'

'No, love. When?'

'Today! She said I'd make a choice today that'd influence my life! What dost think of that?'

'Very good.'

'Very good? I tell thee of summat so important it'll change my life – art listening to me, Amy Mallinson?'

'Yes – yes, of course, Cissie. What kind of decision? Are you thinking of making one today?'

'I didn't know as I was, but tha never can tell. Oh look! What's going on here?' She pointed to a booth where a stocky, weatherbeaten man was talking to a row of young women and girls assembled on a rough wooden stage. Below them several onlookers were gazing up, pointing and commenting among themselves.

'It's the hiring!' exclaimed Cissie. 'I've never seen one afore, but I've heard tell of 'em from me cousin. Girls as wants posts go up, and people choose if they want a maid or summat.'

Amy frowned. 'It's like the cattle market,' she said crisply.

Cissie nudged her and chuckled. 'Nay, the girls can eye the employers over too, can't they? That's more than cows can do. And they can barter for their wages. Hey – that's it, Amy!'

'That's what?'

'That's what I can do – offer meself, happen get a post out of Hawksmoor, a job as'll change me life. I'm going up.'

'No – wait! Think first, Cissie!' She clutched at the girl's arm, but Cissie snatched it away.

'Nothing venture, nothing gain, Amy lass. I can always turn it down if I don't like sound on it!'

She bounced up the steps and sauntered almost saucily towards the stocky little man. Amy saw them exchange a few words, and then the man indicated a place at the end of the line. Cissie went to stand next to a pock-marked girl with a squint. Amy saw the plump woman in front of her nudge her husband.

'Here, Alf, that one looks sturdy enough. She'd do us, I reckon.'

The man grunted. 'Do for thee round the house right enough, but not a lot of use to me – look at that pasty face, and them arms don't look brawny.'

'It's help in the house we're wanting, Alf, not a farmhand to help thee deliver lambs – tha can get another lad for that.' She paused a moment, looking up at Cissie, who stood confidently, head held high. 'Nay, on second thoughts, happen tha's right, Alf. She looks a bit brazen, that one. What about that little dark one?'

'Or that one,' prompted Alf.

'Who? Which one?'

'That one – with the rosy cheeks.'

His wife followed the direction of his finger, then shook her head firmly. Amy smiled. The girl was buxom and pretty, a threat to any careful housewife with an errant husband. 'Nay, not her, and that's a fact,' she said.

A woman with a pinched face and sober but well-cut clothes motioned to Cissie, and Amy saw her come down the steps and then listen to the woman's words, nodding every now and again. With luck Cissie was about to find what she was looking for. Suddenly Amy's attention was diverted by the strange sensation in her spine, like the slow touch of a cold finger starting at the nape of her neck. She turned, and her gaze met the clearest blue eyes boring into her own, and the cold finger gave way to an electrifying shudder. It was

Adonis, standing there as real and tangible as if her repeated fantasies about him had somehow finally succeeded in materialising him. Alarm rippled through her, as she saw his lips part to speak.

'Forgive me, it is unforgivably rude of me to address you – '

It was too much. The deep, sonorous timbre of his voice was a caress, as presumptuous as if he had physically reached out and touched her. Overcome, heart pounding and all reason fled, she broke away from his mesmeric gaze and turned, taking flight in the only visible escape – up the steps. The little man in charge raised thin eyebrows, then came across to her.

'Service, is it? Or shop, or office work?'

'Ah, yes, anything – service,' Amy stuttered.

'Join the line. Cost thee a week's wage. Agreed?'

'Oh, yes.' She was not listening to, nor registering what he said, aware only of those piercing blue eyes still holding her in view, but resolutely she refused to meet that gaze. Instead she looked over the heads of the crowd below, looking away into the distance where sunlight still rippled on the lake.

'Snooty, aren't thee?' The girl with the squint was speaking to her. 'Twice I've asked thee thy name. I sharen't ask again.'

'I'm sorry – it's Amy.'

'Here, you,' said the little man, tapping her on the shoulder. 'That young lady wants a word with thee. Go on down, and let me know what's settled.'

As Amy moved carefully down the wooden steps she glanced around her. There was no sight of the blond-haired gentleman. A pretty young woman with a pink bonnet, which Amy recognised as being from the most expensive range in Sidgwick's Emporium, was smiling at her.

'I'm looking for a personal maid – on trial for a month. Have you experience in service?'

'No, but I'm quick to learn. I've worked in a shop and an office.'

'I see.' The young woman looked a trifle crestfallen. 'But I see your own things are well-pressed, your lace collar beautifully goffered. Can you curl hair?'

'I do my own, with rag curlers.'

The girl cast a glance over Amy's head. 'My hair is very fine – could you do it like yours?'

'I'm sure I could; mine is fine too.' She was beginning to warm to the idea. It had been an impetuous thing to do, going up those steps, putting herself on offer like that, but there'd been no time to think with those eyes and that incredibly beautiful voice destroying her wits . . . Besides, pandering to a well-off young lady's vanity seemed, on the face of it, to offer a far easier way of life than submitting to the vagaries of temper and distasteful approaches of a man like Mr Pogson.

'Yes, I think I like the look of you,' the girl was saying, eyeing her up and down speculatively. 'It's only a trial period, remember, for a month. We'll see, then. Where do you live?'

Amy jerked her attention back. 'Oh, in Hawksmoor.'

'That's good; so do we. But I think I'd prefer you to live in, so you'll be there to see to my wants last thing at night, and see to my hair and so on first thing in the morning. I've arranged that you can have a small attic room. Are you prepared to live in?'

Amy did not hesitate. If she had taken hasty action which was going to alter her way of life, then she might as well go the whole hog. 'Yes, I am.'

'Splendid. Uniform will be provided and laundered. When can you start? Tomorrow?'

'Ah, well — '

'The next day, then. My name is Berenice Holroyd. What's yours?'

'It's Amy, Amy — ' Her voice died in her throat as Adonis suddenly reappeared from nowhere, standing by the side of the young woman and cupping her elbow. A slow, gentle smile curved his lips and Amy could not breathe. The girl looked up at him.

'Oh, there you are, Charles! I wondered where you'd got to. This is my new maid – I do hope Mother will approve.'

'I'm sure she will.' His voice held a deep, magical quality which set Amy's pulse throbbing, and his eyes moved up and down, appraising her. 'And what is her name?'

'Amy.' Amy suddenly found voice to say, and for some inexplicable reason she suddenly felt the need to keep back some vestige of privacy. 'Amy Robinson.'

'Then we'll look forward to seeing you at the house on Wednesday,' said Miss Holroyd. 'You can't miss it. Langdenholme is the big house at the top of Greenhead Lane.'

She took his arm, nodding goodbye. He looked down at Amy.

'Goodbye, Miss Robinson. I look forward to seeing you again.' And the couple mingled with the crowd and vanished from her sight.

Black eyes in a weatherbeaten face were watching her closely, and vaguely she was aware that it was the boatman, Tobias.

'Didn't know tha were looking for work,' he said.

She shrugged, but made no answer. Her wits were not yet functioning properly, still bedazzled by the beauty and electrifying presence of Adonis.

'If ever tha wants work again, think on I can use thee,' Tobias was muttering. 'Jericho Farm. Just up yonder.' He waved a muscular arm uphill towards the moor. She was gazing into space, unaware of him. 'Dost hear me, Miss Robinson?' he said more loudly.

'I'm sorry – what?' She looked at him, his dark, sober eyes and earnest expression, and felt contrite. 'You're still damp!' she exclaimed.

'No matter. I said if ever tha needs it, there's a place

99

for thee up Jericho Farm, up yonder. Nowt as fine as tha'rt used to, but warm and comfortable. Think on.' And he strode away. Watching his broad back as he plunged into the crowd she suddenly felt sick.

Langdenholme, Holroyd! What a slow-witted fool she had been! She had just accepted work in the house of her own aunt! Berenice was her cousin – and so was the magnificent Adonis. He must be Charles.

'Week's wages, I said,' said the little man with the notebook.

'Yes, yes, of course.'

Cissie caught her arm, eyes aglow. 'I start tomorrow, Amy! The gypsy were right, weren't she? A decision today, she said. Oh Amy! There's a whole new life beginning for me, and there's no looking back.'

She squeezed Amy's arm tightly in her excitement, a little disappointed that her friend showed little reaction to her good fortune. Then suddenly she caught sight of a young man.

'Oh, look, Amy! Isn't he lovely, that man down at the boat look – what fine muscles he has in his shoulders! Ooh, I could fancy him!'

Down beyond the lake Berenice Holroyd leaned on her brother's arm, still thinking over her choice and wondering about her mother's reaction.

'Mother said to pick someone clean and well-turned-out, preferably someone with an air of refinement. That girl Amy fills the bill, don't you think?'

'Definitely, my dear,' he answered absently.

'Oh, and someone willing to please. Do you think Amy is anxious to please, Charles? She looks agreeable enough; I'm sure she wants to please.'

'It is devoutly to be hoped,' murmured Charles, 'devoutly.'

SIX

Lionel's news the next day startled Violet. He, always so biddable in the past, had somehow got a mad fire in his soul which even her patient words could not extinguish.

'I've got it, and I'm going, and that's that,' he'd flung at her in the end. 'I'm old enough to make up me own mind.'

'But in a dyehouse, Lionel. That's no place for you! A dyehouse is full of steam.'

'You wanted me out of the gasworks – well, now I am. And I'll get better wages. Aren't you satisfied?'

'Out of one lot of fumes into another – how can I be?'

'There's nowhere in Hawksmoor where the air's clean, Mother – it's smoke and soot and dirt wherever I go, except up on the moors. Would you have me go away to work in the country?'

'I would if we could – '

'But there's no work, no money – I have to work in town. Anyway, I've told 'em I'll start tomorrow.'

'Where?'

'Halliday's.'

He turned away from her, surly defiance in his eyes. Disbelief and anger flooded her. She had no choice but to tell him about that day, all those years ago.

'So Halliday sacked your father,' she concluded, trying to keep the anger out of her tone. 'He'd have ruined us – we could have starved. I'd not want a son

101

of mine beholden to Halliday's after what they did to your father.'

Amy, who was sitting silent in the corner, glanced up at her mother, and Violet read the meaning in her look. All right, Tom had not been Lionel's father, but it was near enough the truth.

Lionel slumped in a chair, his thin face pouted into that sullen look which always twisted Violet's heart. 'Oh, Mother! You're talking of ancient history, near enough twenty years ago. Why, old Halliday is dead and gone now. Anyway, we need the money. I'm going tomorrow, and that's that.'

'We don't need it that badly. We can wait a while and see what else turns up and I've a bit put by.' Desperation showed in her voice.

'No. Amy's not earning now. And I need money for meself, too.'

'What for?'

He looked up, and she saw the fire in his eyes. 'To get married, that's what for. Me and Maggie. We want to get married.'

She had no answer to counter that, recalling how determined she herself had been at his age to marry Tom. She held her tongue then – and so, surprisingly, did Amy.

On Wednesday morning Violet awoke to a ragged sky and a chill in the air, and felt distinctly at odds with the world. Not only had that dull ache in her side made her sleep only fitfully, but the patches of sleep had been riddled with strange dreams she could now only half-remember.

From outside came the usual morning sounds, clogs clattering along the street and a dog howling mournfully, sounds which had fed her dreams, she realised, and tried to push away the superstitious thought that the far-off sound of a dog's howl was said to presage death. She had enough troubling her mind already.

She looked down at Amy, still sleeping, and her dark hair spread all over the pillow. She had gone to bed early, but all day she had been unusually withdrawn and quiet. Unused to being at home, perhaps, instead of at work, depressed or guilty at having lost her post? And she'd made no comment about Lionel, either. Violet felt uneasy. Amy had always had a private side to her, but this was an unnatural quiet, as if something was troubling her, something she did not want to disclose, and Violet knew better than to pry. Amy would come to it in her own time.

But if Violet had been prepared to accept Amy's reticence for the time being, she was certainly not prepared for the utter blank wall she was to face later when Amy came downstairs. Violet could hear her washing herself in the scullery while she was preparing sandwiches for Lionel's snap tin. Whether she approved of his new job or not, she was not going to let him go hungry till nightfall. He took the tin from her and left for work.

'Good luck, lad,' she murmured, and he gave her a faint smile before closing the door behind him. Amy came into the living room, her face shining and pink and her hair smoothly brushed and coiled. Violet poured tea for them both.

'You're all dressed up like you were going to the office,' she murmured. Amy sipped the tea in silence, avoiding her mother's eyes. Violet felt a tremor of apprehension. 'Are you going out? Looking for a new post, perhaps?'

Amy set the cup down on the saucer with deliberation. 'I'm going to work.'

'Work? Where?'

Amy shook her head, glanced at the mantel clock and reached for a slice of bread.

Violet began to feel irritated. 'Amy, did you hear me? Where are you going?'

She watched slim fingers gripping the knife as it

103

spread butter over the bread. Still the girl did not look up. Irritation burst forth. 'Now look here, I've had enough of this, Amy. Where are you going, and what are you going to do? Are you going to tell me?'

'No, Mother.' Small teeth bit firmly into the bread and began chewing.

Violet felt she could burst into tears with vexation. 'Why ever not, may I ask? A mother ought to know where her daughter's going, especially if it's to start a new job. But why didn't you tell us last night? You heard Lionel say you weren't working – why couldn't you tell us?'

Amy swallowed the bread and met her mother's eyes at last. 'Because you won't approve, so if I don't tell you, you can't say anything. That's why.'

Violet trembled, alarmed. 'I wouldn't approve? Oh, love, what is it? What have you done that I wouldn't like?'

'Now don't take on, Mother – it's nothing disgraceful.'

'Then what? What wouldn't I like? Oh, Amy, tell me *something*, at least!'

The girl looked again at the clock and got up from the table. She took her jacket from the peg. 'I'll tell you this much, Mother. It's a living-in post, so I won't be back tonight. It's in service.'

'Not back? In service?' Violet stumbled as she rose from the table, and made to take her daughter's arm.

Amy moved away out of reach. 'Don't fret, Mother. It's a good post, on a month's trial. I'll be able to give you same as I always did.'

'It's not the money – '

At the door Amy picked up a bag. Violet had not seen her bring it downstairs. Then she turned.

'I'll be back Sunday. I'll tell you more then. Now don't worry.'

As Violet moved towards her, arms outstretched, Amy leaned briefly towards her, gave her a quick kiss on the cheek, and was gone. For several seconds Violet stood, stunned, feeling that somehow her brain had got left behind in the tangle of events. Lionel and Amy, both gone on the same day to start new jobs, and neither asking her advice before taking the plunge. Numbed, and feeling strangely bereft, she slumped down on the chair again and buried her face in her hands.

It hurt, she realised, hurt her unbearably that her children had clearly outgrown her. They needed no help now in making their decisions, but it hurt that they did not consider how hurtful it was to make her feel so unnecessary, so unexpectedly. Until now they had always turned to her, expecting neither rebuff nor impatience, but taking it as their due that they would always have her instant attention and affection. And it was right that they should.

But now suddenly the fledglings had found their wings, both at the same time, and they did not understand that she had lost the reason for her being – her function as parent. Without them, her life was somehow out of focus, meaningless . . .

Violet shook herself, dried her eyes and rose stiffly. Silly, self-pitying creature, she reproached herself. They still need you. They'll come back, Lionel at dusk hungry for a good hot stew, and Amy on Sunday, full of news and eager to tell what she had done. They had not left her life entirely, only shown that they no longer needed her guidance on every aspect of their lives. It was natural that they should learn to be independent. Hurt was sinful and selfish; regret was the most she could allow herself.

Later that morning she was pegging Lionel's shirts out on the line strung across the yard, deep in thought. As she took the last peg from her mouth to fasten the last shirt, the backyard gate opened. A tall figure, well-dressed and carrying a cane, came towards her with a slight smile.

'Violet, my dear— '

'Edwin!' She could hardly believe it. Ever since that day – what was it, eight, no, nine years ago – he had paled at learning of Lionel's illegitimate birth, she had not set eyes on Edwin Glover.

'No one answered the front door, so I came round the back,' he murmured. He stood awkwardly, clearly ill at ease. It must have taken a great effort for him to return after all this time. Her heart lifted.

'Edwin, I'm glad to see you,' she said softly.

His face brightened. 'You are? Oh, I'm so glad! All this time – I couldn't forget – I wanted to see you.'

'Come inside, and I'll put the kettle on. Oh, Edwin, I am glad to see you.'

Amy approached the tall stone gates at the top of Greenhead Lane which marked the entrance to Langdenholme. As her footsteps crunched up the gravel drive she felt her heart thudding in excitement, apprehensive at the prospect of coming face to face once again with Adonis, and still overcome at her audacity in taking up the offer of a post here. Not just because she had no experience at all to qualify her to be a lady's maid, but to work for her own aunt and cousins, and incognito at that! It was almost like the adventures of one of the heroines of a popular yellowback.

At the head of the drive Amy hesitated. The servants' entrance was usually round the back of big houses, she knew – but this was Aunt Charlotte's house. Aunt Charlotte was a beast, treating Lionel the way she had. Amy walked steadfastly up to the front door and rang the bell.

'I'm Amy Robinson, the new maid,' she announced, and saw the maid's eyes widen, as she stepped back to let Amy in. The girl's hands fluttered.

'I'd best take thee down to Mrs Cartwright,' she said.

Mrs Cartwright turned out to be the sturdy, keen-eyed cook-housekeeper, busy supervising breakfast in the kitchen. She gave Amy a quick, critical look up and down.

'Esther, fetch the clean apron and cap for Miss Berenice's maid – what's thy name?'

'Amy.'

'Take Amy's coat, then show her Miss Berenice's room. Tha can take her her morning tea since Maggie's gone,' Mrs Cartwright added, taking up the huge earthenware teapot and pouring tea into the small teapot on the ready-laid tray. Amy tied the apron string, put on the neat cap in front of a mirror over the dresser and picked up the tray to follow Esther. As they emerged from the baize-covered door of the servants' quarters, she caught a glimpse of a man's back, a man in a dressing gown, as he crossed the vestibule and went into a room, closing the door. Amy felt a lurch of recognition.

'That's Mr Charles,' said Esther, starting up the stairs. 'He's down early for breakfast for once. Mustn't have gone out last night.'

Amy followed the girl's slim figure up the wide, balustraded staircase. Langdenholme was certainly a fine house, beautifully furnished and everything gleaming, testimony to the diligence of the servants or the exacting nature of the mistress. Turkey carpet and handsomely panelled walls gave an impressive background to the portraits and landscape paintings ranged up the staircase and all along the corridor to the bedroom door where Esther paused and tapped lightly.

No answer came. 'Go on in,' urged Esther. 'Wake her gently – she's not in the best of moods first thing.'

She opened the door, waited until Amy carried in the tray, then closed the door. In the half-light of the curtained room Amy could make out the bed, the head buried in the pillows and the dressing table. She put down the tray and drew back the curtains.

'Go away,' said a sleepy voice. 'It's too early.'

'It's almost eight,' said Amy.

A groan from the bed. 'Give me my tea.'

Amy poured tea from the little china teapot into a cup. The figure stirred, groaned again, and sat up slowly. 'Sugar?' Amy asked.

'Two. Oh, it's you. Just a dash of milk.'

Amy carried the cup and saucer carefully to the bed, waiting there till a slim hand reached out uncertainly. Miss Berenice was evidently not finding it easy to come to terms with a new day. Amy watched her, shapely and pretty with her tousled hair, and could feel only a sense of wonder that this young woman was her blood cousin, child of her mother's sister. And though she was reluctant to admit it, even to herself, she felt glad that the girl was her cousin, sister to Charles and not his wife or fiancée as she might have been, from the way she clung to his arm at Cope Bank. Amy remembered the leap of alarm when the thought first came to her.

Berenice was watching her curiously. 'Are my family down yet?'

'I don't know. Mr Charles is, I believe.'

The girl stretched and sighed. 'Good. Mother's not about then – you haven't met her yet?'

'No. Only Mrs Cartwright, and the maid Esther.'

'You must say "Miss Berenice" when you address me, Amy. Go down and fetch hot water for me to wash, and then you can lay out my clothes for the day. I'll tell you where everything is kept.'

It was as Amy was returning with the huge jug of hot water from the kitchen that she encountered the mistress of the house. A vast, black-embroidered bosom barred her way at the head of the staircase, and sharp eyes fixed on hers.

'Who are you, girl?'

On the instant Amy took a deep dislike of her aunt, the voice sharply aggressive, the bearing intimidating. 'I'm Miss Berenice's new maid,' she answered.

'Are you indeed?' The eyes travelled up and down, then the bulky figure stepped aside. 'Well, see you do your work well. We tolerate no slackers in Langdenholme.'

Amy had a wicked impulse to want to tip the contents of the jug over that menacing, embroidered bosom, but she managed to quell it and walk on by.

'What's your name, girl?' the voice demanded from behind her. Amy did not turn.

'Amy.'

'Amy what? And say "madam" when you speak to me. Where on earth were you trained, child!'

Amy looked back. It was a severe temptation to speak the truth, to cry out 'Mallinson' in defiance, but she held her tongue. The time would come when she would tell this woman, this aunt of hers, what she really thought.

'Amy Robinson – madam.'

There was a tinge of mockery in her tone on the last word, but the woman did not seem to notice.

'Well, see you serve us well, Amy, and you will be well treated. See to Miss Berenice now, and then you can give a hand in the dining room. That silly, wilful Maggie has left with no thought to the inconvenience she's caused us.'

Berenice was sitting on the edge of the bed. She laid her cup aside and watched as Amy poured water into the basin. While she washed, Amy laid out on the bed the undergarments the girl directed her to find.

'And I think I'll wear the violet gown today – you'll find it in the wardrobe. I want to look nice. I've got a new piano tutor coming; it'll be nice to have company for once.'

'Don't you often have company?' asked Amy, taking down the dress and inspecting it for creases.

'Only when Mother entertains, and they're usually old fuddy-duddies, aldermen and that. Nobody really interesting. Now this Mr Benson who's coming today is young – and he comes from London.' She glanced over her shoulder mischievously. Amy reflected how pretty she looked, vivacious and attractive in a way that almost denied she could be her mother's daughter. Perhaps she inherited her father's agreeable nature – Mother had often said he was a very pleasant man.

'Don't you have family – relations, I mean – who come to visit?' Amy could not resist the urge to see how her cousin would react to the question. The girl shrugged and reached for a towel.

'Not really. Father's brother lives in Dorset so we hardly ever see him and his family. My mother has a sister and she has children, but we never see them.'

'Too far away, like the others?'

'No, no. In Hawksmoor, actually, but we don't meet.'

It would be too venturesome to ask yet another question, ask a reason why. Not yet. 'Pity,' Amy remarked. 'Especially as they're so close.'

'Ah well, there it is,' said Berenice. 'Mother just won't have it. Now, do you think those shoes will go with my violet dress?'

Questions of colour-matching settled, hair brushed and coiled to her satisfaction, Berenice made one final reference to her relatives before going down to breakfast.

'It's not us, you know, not my brother and I. It's Mother who's so dead set on this business of not recognising our cousins. Some ancient family feud, I gather, something dreadful my aunt did years ago. Family skeleton – she'd be furious if she knew I talked to a servant about it. But I think I rather like you, Amy Robinson. We'll get on well, you and I.'

She smiled as she rose from the dressing stool, and Amy warmed to the girl. There was no malice in her, that was certain, but the mother was a horrid creature. She had spited Lionel, and for that she would never be forgiven. Odd that such a creature could have a daughter so pleasant – and a son who, cousin or not, could make a girl tremble from head to foot.

While the family was at breakfast Amy took the opportunity to slip out of the back door and walk along the balustraded terrace. Out in the cool spring morning there was no sound but the song of the birds in the trees down beyond the rose beds, and the rustle of leaves. She walked along to the end where the leaves of the laurel bushes shivered, sighed and fell silent. There was a stillness in the air, a shimmer that promised sunshine, and the atmosphere seemed charged with an air of expectancy.

Something was going to happen – and soon, she could feel it. Taking the plunge of invading the enemy's territory, coming face to face again with the man who excited her beyond all reason – something was bound to happen. And cousin or not, she looked forward to the encounter with eagerness mingled with apprehension.

SEVEN

Violet Mallinson's unease was beginning to fade. It was so easy after all to talk to Edwin, to unburden her concern. They sat by the fireside, sipping tea from her best cups and he listened intently, nodding every now and again.

'I know how you must be feeling, Violet lass, for I've been through all that meself.'

So he had; she'd almost forgotten. His own children grown and gone and his wife dying so young – of course he knew the pain of bereavement better than she. His calm voice, charged with concern, softened her anguish, soothing and protective as it always was in the old days, before gossip had somehow wrested him from her. She longed to ask what had happened. He evidently read her mind.

'I want to take thee out, Violet, down the town on me arm. I'd be that proud. But I must tell thee first – I'd never have left off seeing thee before, but I were told tha'd no time for me.'

'Oh, that's not true, Edwin! Not true at all!'

'Well any road, that's what Charlotte would have me believe. She said tha loved the father of thy lad. So I took me hook.'

Violet could not resist laying a hand on his sleeve. 'Oh, Edwin! If only I'd known – I thought it was because . . . because . . .'

The cup rattled as he set it down and laid his hand over hers. 'Nay, not for that, love, not for that. I thought tha'd wed him.'

He deserved no less than the truth. Violet raised her chin, meeting his gaze directly. 'I would have done, Edwin, but it could not be. It was over long before I met you.'

He smiled gently, patting her hand. 'Come on then, lass, put thy coat on. We're going out. I promised I'd go to a meeting this afternoon, and it'll be that grand to have thee on my arm.'

Ten minutes later Violet was aware of lace curtains twitching as she walked down the street on Edwin's arm. It filled her with a strange mixture of shyness and excitement, to be escorted by a gentleman again after all these years, and she realised with a start that for a whole hour now she had not given a thought to either Lionel or Amy.

'What's this meeting we're going to, Edwin?'

He smiled down at her. 'Co-op, love. About the new education department they've begun for ordinary folk, using one per cent of the society's profits. We've already set up a public reading room in Albion Street and now we're buying more books.'

'But I can't go to that – I'm not a member.'

'We'll soon fix that. There'll be folk there you'll enjoy meeting, and they'll like you, Violet. Don't disappoint me.'

She squeezed his arm, ever so slightly. 'Of course not. I'll be proud to come. Education for ordinary folk, eh? I approve of that, indeed I do.'

Perhaps that could help Lionel, she thought privately. It was time she moved in the outside world again, to learn what could benefit her and her children.

'Aye, the wording is to further the promotion of instruction, culture and recreation. And one per cent is no mean figure, Violet – do you know, we had over six hundred pounds this year? We've a clever fellow from Oxford giving lectures, a fine choir building up in the singing class, and now we've begun shorthand classes. There's no limit to what we can do, lass. We'll be setting up scholarships before long.'

Violet could feel her excitement growing, and a distinct sensation that life was about to alter course once again and this time, she hoped, it would be for the better.

By the time the Holroyd family were due to gather for dinner, Amy still had not set eyes on cousin Charles since that breakfast-time glimpse of his back. It was very disappointing, and she was almost grateful that her aunt had insisted that she should help in the dining room. It was almost seven now. Amy resolved to thank Maggie for leaving, so presenting her with the opportunity.

All day she had been kept occupied, pressing blouses and camisoles for Berenice, mending her stockings and tidying her disordered room.

Of the occupants of the house she had seen and

113

heard nothing, save the distant sound of piano chords from the music room during the afternoon. When she had taken afternoon tea to Berenice in the drawing room, there had been a smile playing about the girl's lips, but she had not ventured any conversation.

The dinner gong sounded. Mrs Cartwright's blue eyes widened in surprise when Amy took the soup tureen from her with evident eagerness.

'Now take good care not to spill it when you ladle it out,' she admonished, wagging a stubby forefinger. 'That's far too good and nourishing to waste – and it's taken me the best part of the afternoon.'

As Amy entered the dining room Mrs Holroyd paused for a second in mid-flow of her monologue. She stared, then evidently recalled who Amy was and carried on.

'So I told Mr Bamforth that I thought it essential for one of the Technical governors to be represented on the Co-operative committee. I knew he wouldn't like it – him being chairman – and he obviously wants to keep me out, but I wasn't going to be put off like that. I think we should be represented, don't you? What are you waiting for, girl? Bring the soup to table and serve it.'

Amy was standing by the sideboard, soup tureen forgotten in the chill of disappointment. He was not at table – only the mistress, mouth opening and closing incessantly, a balding, portly man who must be Uncle Percy, and a clearly bored Berenice. As she began to ladle soup for Aunt Charlotte, Berenice spoke, and Amy's ears pricked up.

'Where's Charles, Mother? I thought he was to be back for dinner?'

The mistress's lips tightened. 'So he was. I swear we've spoilt him dreadfully, Percy. Do you know where he is?'

'Er, no, I'm afraid not, dear.' Amy could see the poor fellow's timid, apologetic attempt at a smile, and she felt sorry for him. She could not resist a faint smile as he looked up to thank her, and she served him an extra spoonful. Berenice waved a hand, declining the soup.

'Well, now, about this committee,' Aunt Charlotte went on, draping a napkin across her broad lap, 'what I say is, if they're to provide education then they need people who know about education. I could be invaluable, and I told Mr Bamforth so. I'm willing to give of my time – '

'He could be at the Drakes',' said Berenice.

Charlotte stared. 'What?'

'Charles. He could be down at the Drakes. He quite likes Edith.'

'I hope you're right. As a matter of fact I have the Drakes coming to dinner tomorrow night, with young Edith, so I hope Charles doesn't do this to us again tomorrow. He really is most thoughtless. Now what was I saying? Ah, yes . . .'

Throughout the meal Amy stood dispiritedly by the sideboard, coming forward to serve, remove dishes and serve again, and not once did the mistress let up. Her voice ranged over the table, the diners, the furniture, seeping into the carpet and curtains until the room seemed utterly pervaded and dominated by her. She was like some cheap, unpleasant perfume, thought Amy, assailing and abusing one's senses. Aunt Charlotte was a thoroughly obnoxious woman.

Her husband and daughter seemed to retract into their own private worlds, their only defence to seek oblivion from her verbal assault. Amy would have disliked her intensely if she had been a stranger, but knowing her aunt's malice her dislike had no choice but to mount into contempt and hate. Poor Berenice and Charles, to have that creature for a mother.

The door opened, and he was there, tall and smiling genially as he crossed to the table, pulling out a chair. His mother glared at him.

'Sorry, Mother,' he smiled, and turned to beckon to Amy. 'Soup, please, if it's still hot enough.'

She moved like an automaton to the table, willing a look of recognition in his eyes, but none came.

'Well, really, Charles!' his mother expostulated. 'Do you call that an apology? Where have you been?'

Without looking up he raised a hand, signalling to Amy that he had enough soup. 'Oh nowhere special, you know. I called in the Adega for a game of billiards and got talking. Lost track of the time. Sorry, Mother, I really am.'

Father and daughter occupied themselves with the meal, silent for a moment while the mother drew in a long, sibilant breath in acceptance of his apology. Charles smiled broadly.

'Frank Shaw told me his wife had taken on young Hetty at their place. They're finding her quite satisfactory. I thought you might like to know, Mother.'

'Who? Oh, Henrietta, you mean. Well, the Shaws are easily pleased. She wasn't up to my standards.' Charlotte's heavily lidded eyes closed in disdain.

Berenice ventured to demur. 'I thought Hetty was quite a good maid, Mother. Very neat, never obtrusive. Well-mannered too.'

'I know about these things. She was – passable, I suppose, but not what I would require for long. Henrietta could be quite unmannerly at times – you can't keep a maid who answers back.'

At last the reverend Percy Holroyd drew breath to speak. 'As I recall, my dear, she only told you her name was Hetty, and she wanted to be called that and not Henrietta.'

His wife darted him a furious look. 'Everyone knows Hetty is short for Henrietta. I wanted her called Henrietta, and surely that was enough – with Miss Hardcastle coming to dinner too? The girl was wilful, stubborn to a degree. She had to go.'

'Even if she was christened Hetty, dear? She was,

you know – I officiated at the baptism, sixteen years ago.' Almost at once Percy Holroyd regretted his words.

'Percy! You're being obtuse! Allow me to run my own household, if you please – I am the best judge of servants, and I'll make certain they come up to my standards, or else—'

'Yes, my dear. You're quite right.'

Before long, Charlotte and Berenice left, and it was only as Amy was serving dessert that she caught his eye and saw the sudden gleam.

'Ah – it's Amy, isn't it?' he said. 'Father – remember Berenice and I went to the hiring fair? I told you about it.'

For the first time Amy saw a glow of animation in the older man's eyes. But the interest was in his son, not in her, she realised, for Uncle Percy leaned across to Charles. 'Indeed, I recall it. That was the Monday night we sat and played chess together, and sampled some of that old port Miss Hardcastle made a gift of to me. Ah, a pleasant evening that was.'

'Because Mother was out,' his son rejoined, and Amy saw the twinkle of laughter in his eyes. He was looking at her, his spoon to his lips, and once again she felt the electric charge shivering through her body.

The meal over, the two men rose and left and she cleared away the dishes, stacking the tray to carry down to the kitchen. On the third trip back to collect the last of the glasses, she became aware of a figure in the shadows of the vestibule.

'Amy.'

His voice, deep and resonant, made her shudder with excitement. 'Yes, sir?'

He came forward, an easy, graceful movement that made her think of a cat. He looked down at her, a smile in his eyes if not on his lips. 'I can only say that I regret the sad circumstances of our first meeting,

117

Amy. It is a pity we had to meet like that.' The voice was purring, a caress in the way he spoke her name.

'Sad, sir?'

'You don't remember? I first saw you at Sidgwick's funeral. You evidently didn't see me.'

'Oh, I did! Yes, I did, sir!'

The smile reached his lips now, and she felt she could melt under the radiance of his expression. 'I'm so glad, Amy. I would hate to think I was alone in that experience. We must talk more – later. Will you bring me my bedtime chocolate – to my room?'

The fair head cocked to one side in question. Amy felt flustered. 'Well, I don't know – I have to see to Miss Berenice – I don't know if it's my duty – '

'Oh, it will be, with Maggie gone. She always brought it before. Tell you what, once you've seen my sister settled, tell Mrs Cartwright I want my hot chocolate sent up at once.'

'Very well, sir.' She lowered her gaze, fearful at the tumult his teasing eyes raised in her.

'Don't be alarmed, little Amy. We'll talk, that's all.' He turned to saunter away towards the drawing room, and as he laid his hand on the doorknob he cast her one more quick smile. Amy almost dropped the tray as she made for the dining room, her heart beating in exultation. Alone, with Charles, in his room – the danger of discovery, the malicious delight of deceiving that revolting aunt of hers, the whole prospect of the intrigue was so daring that she felt she could burst with excitement.

Edwin Glover pressed Violet's hands between his own as they stood in the little gaslit lobby.

He looked at her soberly. 'I've enjoyed the day with thee, Violet lass. I can call again soon, can I?'

'To be sure, Edwin. I'll look forward to it.' There was no mistaking the warmth in her tone.

His expression brightened. 'Then I will. Tell thee

what – I'd like to take thee over to Ramsbottom with me to see my brother. He wrote that he's not well at all, and I'd like to visit him. Tha'd like Ramsbottom, Violet. Its name means a valley of wild garlic.'

She smiled squeezing his hand. 'I'd like that, Edwin. I'd like it very much.'

He spoke gruffly. 'I'm glad. I'm that glad I came.'

'Oh, so am I! I did so enjoy my day – and meeting your friends. I'd never have come across James again, I'm sure, but for you.'

'James Stott Pearson, dost mean? Oh aye, he's a sound fellow is Pearson. Works hard, him and his wife, for the society. Magistrate he is too. Solid, reliable sort.'

'He always was as a lad. I knew his mother well, you know.'

After Edwin had gone, Violet sat by the fire. Considering how saddened she had been only this morning, she felt strangely content. Content at having Edwin back in her life, if only as a good and trusted friend, and content to know from young James – though hardly young now; he must be nearing forty, like herself – that Jessica had prospered. Jessica Pearson. What a warm and caring friend she had been, all those years ago in Hunter's Yard. Consoling Violet after Tom's death could not have been easy for her when her own daughter had run away.

They had lost touch when Violet went to London. Jessica had left Hawksmoor when she returned. It was gratifying to learn from James that she had remarried, very contentedly, and that Rose had got in touch again to say she was well and happy and lived in America, now.

She could still visualise Rose, the slender, elf-like creature who used to assist Tom in the dispensary. Pretty, she was, and bright too, but lacking the restrained strength of her mother. Insignificant really, in comparison. Now James was his mother all over again – quiet, reserved, mannered and full of human kindness. It would be pleasant to accompany Edwin to more of these meetings.

Edwin was a man much of the same mould, patient and honourable. It was vexing to think that, but for Charlotte, their friendship could have flourished and blossomed years ago. Some day Providence would repay that spiteful sister of hers for all her malicious doings, she felt sure of it. If ever anyone deserved Nemesis it was she. Living in comfort the way she did, with husband and children still by her side, she ought to be humane enough to allow others their few pleasures.

And it had been a pleasure to see Edwin today, of all days. They had walked home in the late afternoon sunlight, arm-in-arm in companionable silence. For once she had found herself taking note of her surroundings, feeling a glow of pleasure even at the sight of the long shadows cast across the cobbled streets by black mill chimneys.

Witch's fingers, she remembered. That's what she had always called them in her childhood mind, when they had brought a sense of menace, black, silent and ominous. Strange how things once disliked could become even pleasurable when in the company of someone who cast an air of serenity over a fretful mind.

Mrs Cartwright handed Amy a steaming cup and saucer to place alongside the biscuits on the tray.

'There's Mr Charles' cocoa, then, or chocolate if that's what he wants to call it, but it's cocoa to us.' She sniffed, as if in deprecation of the pretensions of better-off folk. Amy took the tray upstairs. The vestibule was still lit by the oil lamp on the hall table, the mistress having had all the gas lights put out before she sailed up to bed. Berenice was already abed, sleepily reading her yellowback and, if her bedtime conversation was anything to go by, weaving fantasies about handsome young Mr Benson, the piano tutor.

Amy could feel her palms sweating as she tapped at Charles' door. There was a pause, and then a low 'come in'.

He was seated in a chair by the fire, a book lying open on his lap. Amy tried to ignore the fact that he was wearing a plum brocade dressing gown which gleamed in the firelight, but not so glossily as his waving hair and that beautiful golden beard. He smiled and tapped the night table at his side. Amy approached him, her heart thumping, and laid down the tray beside him. Then she stood back, awaiting an order or dismissal.

'Stir it for me, Amy.' The slow caress of that voice made her heart lunge. She came close again, conscious of his nearness and of his eyes appraising her. Plunging the spoon into the creamy liquid she stirred, then stiffened as his hand rose to touch her. A wild frenzy leapt in her blood.

The next few moments were nothing she had ever known or even dreamt of, the tall figure uncurling from the chair, standing before her and reaching his arms about her. His lips were moving, murmuring words of passion, words that sang in her ears and thundered through her brain, making her incapable of reason. And then the words ceased, and his mouth took hers. The wild frenzy intoxicated her, and she felt his touch move and tighten, relax and move again.

At last a glimmer of reason dawned in a befuddled brain and she pulled at his hands, breaking away from him.

'You mustn't! You really mustn't!'

Involuntarily hands smoothed hair and apron, and she looked around, confused and uncertain. He stood relaxed, a smile hovering about his lips.

'Amy, Amy, don't take on so! You know we both felt that same feeling, the moment we laid eyes upon each other. Now don't deny it – you did, didn't you?'

She snatched up the tray and made for the door,

alarm and delight fighting for supremacy. 'It's wrong –
we shouldn't – I'm the maid . . .'

'And a very delectable one too, Amy. You knew
how I felt about you – I saw how your eyes avoided
mine, at the fair and at dinner tonight. Confess it, Amy
– you are not unmoved by my adoration, are you?
Confess you feel something for me too!'

He was moving close again, the magnetism electrifying her once more. 'No, it's not right—'

'But you did, didn't you?' The voice was still purring,
caressing, but insistent.

'Yes. That is, I mean—'

He chuckled. 'I knew it. But I was too sudden for
you. That was very remiss of me. But if I promise to
woo you more gently, will you come to me again,
Amy? Tell me you will.'

She was still fluttering in agitation when he took her
hand, lifting it to his mouth and kissing her fingertips
with all the gentleness of handling a frightened little
bird. 'Promise me, Amy,' he murmured.

'Very well, if you wish. I must go now.'

He made no further move to delay her. Amy felt
gauche as she hurried out of the room and closed the
door behind her. He was still chuckling to himself.

At the end of the corridor she leaned against the
wall for a moment to regain her breath and composure
before facing Mrs Cartwright. God, he was a magnificent creature, she thought, beautiful as a god, but
with such insolent arrogance to fling himself upon her
like that! A fascinating devil, was cousin Charles, but
she would fall no easy victim to his urbane charm.

Exploiters, that's what men were. Charles Holroyd
would be no Frederic Newman for her, to woo with
smooth words, only to deceive.

'Oh no, cousin Charles; I shall be wary of you –
though it won't be easy when you are the most
beautiful, the most magnetic and devastating man I
ever set eyes upon. But I shall profit by Mother's

mistakes – and I shall remember that you are son to the woman who ruined both her life and Lionel's.'

EIGHT

Spring was giving way to early summer, the sun's rays making valiant attempts to penetrate the thick layer of sooty smoke that overhung Hawksmoor. Lionel Mallinson, engrossed in his love for Maggie, hardly noticed as he laboured in the dyehouse that his cough was troubling him far less than it used to; he was only aware of feeling happy, absorbed in working for his one goal in life – to be married to Maggie.

His mother, too, seemed content. Frequent excursions with Edwin Glover made her far less prone to questioning her son, and he was glad for her. It was far better that she should be living her own life, not just experiencing it at second-hand through her children. She welcomed Amy's visits home, but no longer probed every corner of her life.

'You're happy in this post then, love?' she asked.

Amy gave a reassuring smile. 'It'll pass – for the time being. I don't expect to be there for ever, but it'll do.'

'Good family, is it?'

'Very respectable, Mother. Couldn't be more so.'

'Then why don't you tell me who they are?'

'I have my reasons, Mother. Just rest content that I have a good job, in a fine house, and I'm happy.'

And to the surprise of both her children, Violet seemed content with that. It afforded Amy a great sense of relief; it gave her a feeling of power to think she was the only person to know that she was in her own aunt's home. She hugged the secret to herself. One day she could put it to good use.

Cousin Charles. Amy's heart melted at the thought of him. Shrewd and cunning with his wily wooing as he was, she still intended to keep the upper hand, but his ways were so winning.

'Let me kiss you, Amy. You know you like it.'

'It is not fitting, master and servant.'

'Come now, Amy, I felt your response. I need to taste your sweetness, and I know you want it too. Only a kiss, I promise.'

So far, it had been only kisses, and she was enjoying the game, yielding only so far and then backing off, enjoying teasing and seeing the disappointment in his blue eyes. But she did not enjoy the visit of the Drake family when they came to dinner; he seemed to be lending far too attentive an ear to Miss Drake's amiable chat.

Not that she was envious, Amy told herself, for how could anyone envy a girl who simpered, looked up from under her lashes and laughed approximately every half-minute whether any amusing words had been spoken or not. And that cornflower-blue gown she wore was cut just a little too *décolleté* to be ladylike.

'Mother says the colour of my dress matches my eyes exactly,' Amy heard the girl say as she was busying herself at the sideboard. 'Do you agree?'

Amy turned, just as Charles, leaning back in his chair, was surveying the young woman reflectively, his gaze travelling from her bodice to her eyes and down again. Amy felt decidedly put out as he nodded.

'I think she's right. You are to be complimented, Miss Drake.'

The mother smiled in the same satisfied manner as her daughter. Mr Drake just stared, the bewildered expression on his ruddy face accentuated by the short, wiry cut of his hair which protruded from his scalp like a scrubbing brush. He gave up attempting to follow the sartorial conversation and addressed himself to Percy Holroyd.

'I reckon as you've probably had a word with this new fellow who's joined our congregation, vicar,' he said with deliberate care.

Percy nodded. 'Indeed, and a very pleasant gentleman he is too. Come up the hard way, he has, and a very good living he's making for himself now. A model of enterprise and industry.'

'A self-made man, you might say,' agreed Drake.

Charles looked up from his plate. 'Who worships his creator,' he said drily. At the sideboard Amy could not resist a smile, but his jibe seemed lost on the company.

'I should like to play Gossamer after dinner. Would you like to play, Edith?' Berenice smiled invitingly.

'It's called ping-pong now, not Gossamer,' corrected Aunt Charlotte. 'Perhaps you would like a game with Charles, Edith?'

'I should prefer to see the Japanese ivories you spoke of earlier, Charles,' said Edith Drake, and as Amy brought the sorbet to table she longed to let it fall on the gently heaving cornflower-blue bosom. And at the end of the meal she bit her lip in bitter vexation as she was left to clear the dishes while Charles escorted Edith from the room.

'Let's go down to the music room now,' he was saying, 'and we can look at the ivories there in quiet.' He caught Amy's eye as he passed the sideboard, but there was no recognition in his look. She might just as well have been part of the William Morris wallpaper.

For the first time in weeks Charles did not ask for his hot chocolate to be sent up to his room that night after the Drakes had gone. Amy saw Miss Berenice safely tucked up in bed, her thick hair twined with curling rags and a new romance she had sent Amy to fetch from the lending library in her hand, and then hovered expectantly in the kitchen, but the summons did not come.

Mrs Cartwright, her chores for the day completed, sat knitting by the fireside, and as the clock chimed eleven she laid the knitting aside and took off her spectacles.

'There, he's not going to ring for his cocoa now, Amy. Might as well get off to bed, lass.'

Amy bit her lip. 'Perhaps I should knock at his door and ask. He might be reading and have forgotten the time.'

The housekeeper snorted. 'Him – read? Not him. More likely he's got a bottle of brandy up there and he's fallen asleep. I'd get to bed if I were thee.'

But at the top of the servants' staircase Amy hesitated, then turned and went to his door. No sound came from the room. Perhaps Mrs Cartwright was right and he was already asleep. Disappointment filled her. After all those nights of persuasion, she could not bear to think he had lost interest – or worse still, diverted his attention to that simpering Drake girl.

Tomorrow she would have the afternoon off and perhaps not see him at all. She tapped softly, and waited.

A faint murmur. Heart quickening, she went in. He was reading in the armchair, still fully dressed, and with a dreamy expression on his handsome face. He did not look at her. Amy shifted from one foot to the other.

'I was wondering – would you be wanting cocoa tonight, sir? You didn't ring.'

'What?' He still didn't look directly at her, just leaned his length back further in the chair. 'Cocoa? Oh, no, thank you. Not tonight.'

Disappointed, she moved reluctantly towards the door. The low voice pursued her. 'Amy – I wonder what you think . . .' The voice died away.

She turned. 'About what, sir?'

126

'About a man choosing a woman. Do you think he should, dally, shall we say – or settle down seriously with a wife?'

She coloured, feeling the hot sensation that rose in her. He must be thinking of Edith Drake.

'That depends.'

'On what?' The blue eyes challenged hers now, and she could swear there was amusement in their depths.

'On whether he's old enough, and responsible and secure enough, to settle. Dallying I don't approve of at all.'

'I was not asking your approval, Amy. And if he had the choice between a woman and a new horse – what then?'

'A horse?' She was baffled by his strange line of questioning.

'Yes – they both cost money. I can only afford one or the other.'

The cheek, the insolence of him! Weighing a woman against an animal indeed! There was no pause for thought. 'Then I should choose the horse if I were you. If you cared enough about the woman the choice would never enter your mind. Goodnight, sir.'

'Amy.' The voice was silkily insistent as she opened the door to leave.

'Sir?'

'When do you next have time off?'

'Tomorrow. But why do you ask?'

'Afternoon? Then be in the park, by the bandstand, at three. Goodnight, Amy.'

He stood up, unbuttoning his shirt and turning his back on her. Confused and in silence, Amy left.

Next afternoon Charles Holroyd gave a final glance in the cheval mirror, adjusted his mother-of-pearl tiepin, and went out into the bright sunlight. The few hundred yards' stroll up to Greenhead Park afforded him time

127

to reflect how successful his strategy had been – or rather, Cecil Roebuck's advice.

'Whoever she is, Charlie boy, make a reluctant woman jealous and she'll fall like a ripe apple into your hands. Believe me – it never fails.'

It seemed he was right. Just by failing to make advances to that delicious little Amy for once, he'd got her attention. Positively begging him to order his hot chocolate last night, she was, no doubt anxious for another little flirtatious encounter with him, and his cool disinterest had evidently got her excited. She'd be there, at the bandstand, and far more tractable next time, he was sure of it. She'd probably be there already, nervously rearranging her collar or bonnet-strings, flattered to fever point by a gentleman's attention.

He entered the park by the main gate and sauntered along the tree-shaded path which ran along the inside of the heavy iron railings until he could see the circular bandstand, half-way across the sweep of lawn. In the distance the parish church clock struck three, but she was not amongst the half-dozen or so figures strolling in the sun near the bandstand. He seated himself on an iron bench, reluctant to arrive at the meeting-place before she did. He wanted to watch her, unobserved, and savour her movements.

Moments later he spotted her, hurrying with swift, small steps to the bandstand. He did not move, but watched her pause, look around uncertainly, then walk with slow deliberate steps around the building. Twice he watched her reappear, revelling in her erect bearing and the slight sway of her hips. Then he rose from the bench and crossed the lawns towards her.

The slight frown on her forehead vanished when she caught sight of him, and she stopped and waited with a half-smile as he approached. Cecil Roebuck was right – jealousy was succeeding in bringing this little beauty into easy reach, he thought. It would not take long now.

Lionel and Maggie strolled, arms about each other's waist, down the rough track leading past the ruined farm building out on to the moor beyond. Lionel felt at peace with the world. Here, where the bracken-covered slopes of the valley lay between them and habitation, the mind and soul could feel free of the choking smoke and dirt of town. Here one could feel a serenity impossible down there.

A stiff breeze billowed out Maggie's skirts as she left his side and ran to chase the birds, and he revelled in the clean, sweet smell of the air, so unlike the wind down in town, where it could only moan in the tele-graph poles and chase scraps of garbage along cobbled streets.

Small brown birds darted everywhere, swooping now and again on the heather, then flying on in quest of food. Maggie's eyes gleamed.

'Look, Lionel, titlarks! They're looking for daddy-long-legs! Aren't they pretty?'

'They can't sing like proper larks,' he grunted, but as always he was impressed by her knowledge. Coun-try-born and bred until recently, she knew so much of country lore and her delight at being here filled him also with delight. Since knowing her, his days seemed overflowing with peace and happiness.

Some day, they would have a little home of their own in town, and make weekend trips to the country, picking bluebells in the woods in springtime, gathering blackberries in the lanes in autumn – life with Maggie looked blissful indeed.

Yet, somehow, a cloud blew up to spoil the sunlit serenity of their day. It all seemed to start when Maggie glanced up at him, tucking an arm through his.

'I've got a lovely new bonnet for Whit, Lionel – me Aunt Clara gave me some lovely pink ribbon to go on it, too. I'll be able to put a bow of it on me basket to match – that basket I told thee I'd lined with silk to put me flowers in. Oh, I'll be that smart! Tha'll walk with me on the Whit walk, won't thee? I'll be right proud.'

'But I can't, love. I always walk with me mam and Amy on our own Chapel's walk. Me mam's busy embroidering the banner – I must go with her.'

Her lip drooped, and before long became a pout. By the time they turned back for home, she was barely speaking to him.

'Look, I'll see what I can do. I can't say fairer nor that, now can I!'

But there was an angry red sunset filtering through the smoke-haze over Hawksmoor as they got down from the tram, and she only turned a cold cheek for his goodnight kiss.

Charlotte heaved her bosom on to the dining table and folded her arms.

'Mrs Bingley told me today that Miss Hardcastle called on her and stayed for tea yesterday,' she told her husband.

Percy beamed. 'How very nice for her, my dear.' At once he learned his mistake.

'Called unexpectedly, Percy, not by invitation. Miss Hardcastle said she was driving by and simply presented herself on impulse – she's never done that to us. She's only come when we've invited her, and not always then.'

Pink of face, and looking like a ruffled pouter-pigeon to Percy's embarrassed gaze, she tightened her lips and spoke with evident envy. 'Mrs Bingley has only been in Hawksmoor for three months – three months, mark you – and already she's regarded as a close friend by the wealthiest people in town. It's not right, Percy, it's not – well – not good breeding in my opinion.'

It was clear now why she was so ruffled; she was

being overtaken in prestige by a newcomer, and that wouldn't do at all. Percy lowered his head.

'And it's unjust,' Charlotte went on. 'We're established as respectable, worthy people, me the daughter of the mayor as was, and heir to his money. I'm more the Hardcastles' level than she is.'

'Financially, I'm sure that's so, dear.'

'But somehow we've never quite acquired the degree of intimacy with Miss Hardcastle that she seems to have got already. Why is that, do you think?'

She glared at him, and he shrank as far as a portly figure could on a tall-backed dining chair. He felt distinctly shamefaced, Charlotte's tone implied that he personally was at fault for not having become intimate with Miss Dorothy.

'It's you who's the loser by it,' Charlotte went on, spotting a new line of attack. 'You could have got her to bring the Bishop to supper – why, you could have got preferment long before now if you'd played your cards right. Fancy letting a common woman from Wakefield push your nose out of joint. She's curried her right and proper – you see if she doesn't make something out of it, for that woman's an adventuress, Percy, or my name's not Charlotte Holroyd.'

Odd, thought Percy, how people could develop in Charlotte's estimation from being a respectable sort of person to being an adventuress in the space of five minutes. She could talk herself out of one opinion and into another as easily as she changed her dress – indeed, perhaps even more easily.

'Tell you what,' said Charlotte reflectively, 'there'll be all the celebrations for the Queen's Diamond Jubilee shortly – why don't you ask Miss Hardcastle to come to the tea for the Sunday school scholars? And perhaps you could get her to bring the Bishop to that.'

Percy shook his head. 'There'll be teas and sings and processions and the Lord knows what all over Hawksmoor – they'll both be busy at some event far more impressive than ours. Indeed, they might not be in Hawksmoor at all, but down in London on such an important day.'

Charlotte's face fell. She ruminated. 'Well, there's always the Harvest Festival – she could present the prizes to the scholars then.'

'Yes, that might very well be possible,' agreed Percy, 'but that's a long way off yet.'

'I know, I think I'll have a little musical soirée one evening soon,' went on Charlotte. 'And I'll invite Mrs Bingley.'

'You will?' Percy was lost. He could not follow his wife's train of thought at all – a moment ago she was dismissing Mrs Bingley as an adventuress.

'Yes,' said Charlotte with satisfaction. 'Everyone has to do a turn – play a piano piece or sing a song. I might get out my violin again.'

'And you'll invite Mrs Bingley?' repeated Percy, just to make sure.

'Yes – I know for a fact she can't play anything and can't sing a note. She told me so herself.'

Berenice sighed as Amy was brushing out her long, silky hair ready for bed. She surveyed her night-gowned reflection in the mirror thoughtfully.

'Are you content with your life, Amy?'

The girl's hand seemed to pause, just for a fraction of a second, before she continued her rhythmic movement. 'Yes, I think so.'

'I'm not.' Berenice sighed deeply again. Her maid did not voice the question she hoped for, so Berenice went on. 'I want to do something with my life, achieve something so that I'm remembered after I'm gone. A kind of immortality, I suppose.'

Did she detect a wry smile on the maid's face? Her voice was impassive. 'You're not thinking of going yet, are you?'

Berenice clicked her tongue. 'No, silly. But one has

to plan one's life, not just let it happen haphazardly. I don't want it just to drift by and then suddenly find I'm old and I've done nothing. I've got to plan something, otherwise Mother will plan it all for me.'

'You don't want her to?'

'Indeed, I don't. Marriage to some boring fellow she chooses, babies to make her a proud grandmother – oh no, I want more from life than that.'

The brush stopped moving. 'What do you want?'

Berenice shook her head sadly, admiring the swaying movement of her hair in the mirror. 'I wish I knew. Some way to leave my fingerprint on life – something that's individually me. I'd like to write a piece of music that gets published, like Elliot Benson did – something for posterity.'

'Then why don't you? I'm sure he'd be glad to help you.'

Berenice swung round on the dressing stool and caught her maid's hands. 'Do you think he would? Do you really think so?'

The girl smiled. She was really quite pretty when she smiled, Berenice noticed. 'If there's anything you set your heart on, the only way to achieve it is to get on and do it – and don't let anything stop you!'

'You're right, Amy! I will! I'll ask Elliot tomorrow! I've got a pretty tune running round in my head – I just can't think how to finish it off. But he will – oh, he's marvellous, Amy! A true artist if ever there was one.'

'I'm sure he is. If that's all now, Miss Berenice, I'll go and fetch Mr Charles' hot chocolate for him.'

'Do. Goodnight, Amy.'

Violet Mallinson eased her body into bed, lying on the side which did not hurt. It had been a wonderful day, with Edwin's congenial company and the excitement of an unaccustomed train excursion out of Hawksmoor. Ramsbottom had proved to be just as pleasant as he had promised, and there had indeed been wild garlic in the valley.

She had taken readily to his brother Robert and his diminutive wife Martha, who had welcomed her with gentle ease as if they had known her for years. And after tea she had insisted on helping Martha to wash up in the little scullery. As she dried the pretty china cups she had seen the insignia of crossed swords on the base and recognised Meissen, just like Father had all those years ago in Langdenholme. They had brought out their best for her and Edwin, treating her like an honoured member of the family. It was comforting to feel family warmth around her again, after so many years.

Less luxurious than the days in London with Frederic, perhaps, but genuine and sincere. All Frederic's lavishness had been part of a grand design to impress – not so these folk's.

Dear Frederic. It was impossible still to think of him without a tinge of nostalgia and love, whatever his faults. Did he now ever find a moment to think of her with affection, even regret?

*'Better by far you should forget and smile
Than that you should remember and be sad.'*

Pressing a hand to the ache in her side, Violet fell asleep.

In the flickering darkness of Charles' candle-lit bedroom two figures stood entwined, only a hand's reach from the bed. The taller figure manoeuvred the slighter one until the back of her thighs touched against the valence. She broke away.

'No, Charles, no!'

'You love me, don't you?' he murmured.

'It's not that – it's here, your mother's house – I couldn't! No, I must go!'

He caught her by the wrist as she turned to make for the door. 'Amy, my little precious, we can't go back – please!'

He saw the dark, troubled look in her eyes. 'I'm sorry, Charles. I told you – not here.'

'Then somewhere else?'

There was a pause before she answered. Small teeth chewed at her lip. 'Perhaps.'

'Then I'll arrange it, I promise. Tomorrow I'll tell you. But before you go . . .'

He drew her into his arms once more, murmuring in her ear. 'Trust me, little Amy, I'll never hurt you. I love you too much. Soon we shall be together – truly together – and you shall see how much I love you.'

Her lips tore away from his and she moved so swiftly he could not recapture her. At the doorway she stopped, looking like some frail wraith in the candle-light.

'If ever I give myself to you, Charles Holroyd, it will be on my terms, and as an equal. I will not wear cap and apron then.'

He laughed softly, amused by her feminine caprice – it was part of her charm. 'As an equal if you wish, little one, but neither cap nor apron would deter my ardour, I promise you.'

'As an equal,' she repeated firmly, 'or my name's not Amy Mallinson.' She closed the door firmly behind her.

Chuckling, Charles picked up the cup of cocoa, which had gone cold on the tray.

NINE

Violet did not want to believe what the gossipy neighbour told her, and could hardly wait until Amy came home on Sunday to question her.

'Mrs Garside tells me she saw you in Greenhead Park the other day.'

'Very likely, Mother. I work near there.'

'And you weren't alone. In fact she says you were with a young man – and she recognised him.'

'Oh Mother, really! You listen to too much gossip. Let's pour that tea out and have one of your delicious scones. Lionel, pass us the scone tin.'

But Violet was not to be deterred. 'I want to know, Amy. You've been keeping your doings a secret, not telling where you're working. There's a reason for it. I want to know why.'

She saw the slim tongue run along the girl's lip and recognised the sign. She was hiding something.

'Look, Mother, I work near the park. It's natural I should walk out on a sunny day there. It's so pretty now with all the flowers, children paddling in the pond and all.'

'You're at one of those houses in Greenhead Lane?'

'Yes, Mother.'

'So you've got to know the Holroyds – I know, I was told it was young Charles Holroyd in the park with you. Now why, Amy? What are you up to?'

Amy's gaze met hers levelly, and there was candour in her eyes. 'Yes, I was with Charles – my cousin. And

I was with him because I work at Langdenholme, and I've grown to like him.'

Violet felt a lurch of sickening disbelief. 'At Charlotte's house? Oh, Amy! How could you! After all she's done—'

'I know. I dislike her as much as you do. She's a dreadful woman. But Charles and Berenice are nice, Mother – you'd like them, really you would. And Uncle Percy—'

'Stop!' Violet could not prevent the cry of alarm. She refused to hear more. 'Whatever the reason, Amy, I don't want to know. Do you hear me? You lied to me—'

'No, I didn't!'

'As good as. You made sure I didn't know you were working at my sister's house. Oh, Amy, if you knew how she has betrayed me – and Lionel too. You can't have forgotten what she did to him. He'll never forget, will you, lad? Tell her she's wrong – she can't go back there.'

Lionel remained slumped, his eyes broody. 'It's all the same to me,' he muttered. 'I don't care.'

'Lionel! After her robbing you of your scholarship!'

'It means nowt now. I've more on me mind, what with that accident at work and now Maggie not speaking to me and all. I should never have gone on the Whit Walk with you. Losing Maggie'd cut me up more nor any scholarship.'

For a moment the two women stared at each other. Amy squared her shoulders.

'I haven't forgotten, Mother, truly I haven't. I thought I could make use of my position there, somehow—'

'To get revenge? Oh, child, there's no way the likes of us can score over them, no way at all! And what good would it do us? Now for Heaven's sake stop this nonsense and give your notice at once. It's such a humiliating position, you acting as servant to her!'

'I'm maid to Berenice, and she's nice, and Aunt Charlotte has no idea who I am.'

Violet was listening with a closed face. 'You will give notice and leave at once, Amy. Oh, if only I'd known—'

'You'd have stopped me. Well, I'm not leaving now, Mother. I don't want to. And there's no humiliation, when she doesn't know who I am.'

Violet stared. 'Not when she knows your name? And she brought you up – in that very house – for the first year of your life?'

'She doesn't recognise me now. And I told her my name was Robinson.'

Violet spread her hands. 'But why, Amy, why?'

'Because I wanted to get to know my cousins. And I like them – very much.'

Violet's eyes narrowed. 'You were in the park with Charles. Does that signify something?'

The girl pulled up her chin, and Violet read the meaning of the gesture before she answered. 'Yes, Mother. I love him. And I think he loves me.'

Violet reached for the chair and sank down. The pain in her side was so vicious now she felt sick. 'Amy, oh, Amy! It's unthinkable! Cousins can't fall in love!'

'But they do. We have.'

'No! Not Charlotte's son! I won't have it!'

'You have no choice, Mother.'

Violet looked up quickly. 'You don't think Charlotte would agree to this either, do you? It's too ridiculous, too humiliating! Oh, Amy – forget the whole stupid idea and come home at once.'

'No, Mother.'

She drew in a long slow breath. 'Amy, I know you're headstrong, but this time I will be obeyed. Give your notice and come home – with luck, she'll never know and no damage will be done. But I'll have you out of that house – I insist on it – or I swear I'll never call you daughter again.'

The two women's eyes met and locked in a long, challenging stare. At last Amy shook her head.

'I'm sorry, Mother. I must lead my own life.'

And before Violet could struggle to her feet the girl had picked up her jacket and left. Violet stood, trembling and holding a hand to the knifing pain in her side. She looked at Lionel, who was still moodily staring into the fire, and knew words were futile. He'd gone through too much today already, what with Maggie failing to turn up to meet him and that grisly business at the dyeworks yesterday. To watch one of his mates, the boiler-firer, climb down into the empty drum and then be scalded to death by a faulty valve suddenly exploding must have been terrible indeed. Poor Lionel. Suddenly she felt sick and too weak to think any longer. Life would have to go on in the outside world how it would, for all she wanted was her bed and sleep to bring oblivion.

The moor stretched away into the distance, desolate and wan in the rain-darkened air, rise upon grey rise. They climbed in silence, hand in hand, over the spurs of rock and wind-bent heather, leaving the broken track to skirt the green-grey area that marked the marsh. It was wild up here, not beautiful but magnificent, in an awe-inspiring way. Amy broke free from Charles' hand and sat down abruptly on a boulder to look back down the way they had climbed. She shivered.

'It's here you can almost feel the Gabriel hounds are close,' she murmured. Her voice was lost in the wind, but he smiled, amused by her wide-eyed look of apprehension.

'Not superstitious, are you, Amy?'

She shook her head, and her hair tangled around her head in the wild wind. He felt a surge of love for her; she looked so like a naiad – or was it dryad? – a wild spirit of the moor, primeval and of the earth. He longed to snatch hold of her there and then.

'Come on,' he said, holding out a hand. 'It's not far now.'

Obediently she rose and took his hand. As they neared the high point of the moor a gentle drizzle began to fall, but she made no complaint. She was an amiable, even captivating, little creature, he thought, and he was impatient to reach the privacy of the lodge.

'It's no more than a hut really,' he told her as they scrambled, breathless, over the boulders. 'But it's cosy, and no one will disturb us there.'

She let go of his hand, stopping suddenly. 'Smell, Charles! Just smell the rain!'

He laughed. 'You can't smell rain, you little goose.'

'Yes, you can! At least you can smell the earth and the heather – isn't it delicious? It smells so sweet and clean after the dirty smell down there.' She flung one arm behind her in the vague direction of Hawksmoor. 'Oh, isn't it wonderful – so clean and sweet and kind of pure, somehow.'

He looked down at her, moved by the radiance of her face. Hair now dampened by the rain and clinging about her shining face, she looked a picture of purity herself, clean and wholesome, far removed from the painted and powdered prettiness of that little Irish actress – what was her name now? The anticipation he'd been enjoying mounted to excitement. The lodge came in sight, nestling in a hollow alongside a pool.

Reaching it, he unlatched the door and ushered Amy inside. It smelt damp and dusty to him, but there was kindling by the open fireplace, thank heavens. Drawing the lucifers from his pocket he soon had a blaze going, while Amy took off her damp jacket and sat on one of the rickety wooden chairs to watch him. He could see by the way she nibbled her lower lip that she was agitated. She knew full well why he had brought her here – indeed, she had held out against him so long

140

because she'd insisted he must find a private place, where she could meet him as an equal, she'd said. He smiled. Her whimsical ways delighted him. In a moment or two he would make his move, but he wished to blazes he knew what was going on inside that pretty little head of hers.

He rose from his knees, and she smiled. 'It's so lovely walking on the moors, Charles, and with you. Thank you so much.'

He sat down beside her, taking her hands in his. 'I'm sorry it's raining. I would have had a perfect day for you, if I could have commanded it.'

She shook the long damp hair. 'I love rain, Charles, truly I do. I wouldn't have it otherwise.' She shivered.

He touched her arm. 'You're cold – take my jacket.' He took off his jacket and went to put it about her shoulders, but she leaned away.

'It's just as damp as mine is – put them both by the fire to dry.' She took his coat and then her own, and spread them both before the blaze. He knelt suddenly beside her.

'Hold on! There's a flask in the pocket – just what we need.' Withdrawing it from the pocket, he held it up triumphantly. 'Brandy – just the thing to warm us up.'

She leaned across him. 'And here's a pan. Fetch water from the pool, Charles, and we can make hot toddy.' She stood up, holding out the battered tin pan.

Charles laughed as he rose to his feet. What a quaint, imperious manner the child had! She was carrying out her game of equality to perfection – who would have dreamt a mere maidservant could afford such sport? He'd be the envy of Edgar and the others when they learnt about this little charade. Very well, he decided, he would humour her – for a time.

They sipped the toddy in turns from the flask cup, and he slid his arm about her waist as she squatted on the wooden floor. She felt slender, firm and tantalising, like all the others before her. He could smell her flesh, and buried his face in her neck. She did not move, but continued to study the blazing wood of the fire.

'It's strange, Amy, but I have this curious sensation that we have met before. Maybe in an earlier life,' he went on, murmuring into her neck in a manner never known to fail in the past. 'It's almost as though our meeting was predestined. It was meant to be, Amy.'

He slid one hand up gently to touch her breast, ever so lightly. She made no response, but took a deep breath. 'It's fate, Amy.' His hand cupped more tightly.

She nodded absently, and then hiccuped. 'I know – you're right.'

His hopes rose. 'You do? You recognise it too?'

'Yes. I do.'

Encouraged, he sat up, taking her face and turning it to his, but before he could kiss her she hiccuped and spoke again. 'I don't remember it, Charles, but I know we met. I lived in your house.'

There she was again, he thought, off on one of her flights of fancy. What a fey little thing she was!

'I'm serious, Charles,' she murmured. 'I spent the first year of my life in Langdenholme. My mother was away in London. She was your mother's sister.'

He stared at her, stunned and bewildered by her words, and his hands fell away from her. At last he began to make sense of it. 'Aunt Violet, you mean – then you must be my cousin! God, yes – I remember now! But why did you never tell me?'

She looked up at him, her eyes sober. 'I thought I did, once. But, anyway, why should I? Your mother would never recognise us.'

Memory was trickling back. 'Wait a moment – I remember now. Grandfather's funeral. You were there – you were burying your doll.'

He saw the startled look in her eyes. 'It was you,' she murmured. 'I never knew.'

'I gave you a rose,' he reminded her.

'And frightened me with talk of worms, I remember.'

'But why did you come back to Langdenholme – and as a servant, not telling us who you were? I don't understand that.'

'I didn't plan it – it happened when your sister offered me a post. I was curious to see what you were all like, my rich relatives who had all disowned us.'

'That was Mother, not us, Amy.' His tone was low, persuasive. Again he laid a hand on her arm, and she made no effort to remove it. He let the hand travel up to her cheek, and she hiccuped again. 'It would be best not to let her know, even now, or she'll send you away.'

'I wouldn't want that, Charles.'

That was all the confirmation he needed; she wanted to stay close to him. He cupped her chin in his hand. 'I know a certain cure for hiccups, Amy. Let me show you.'

She made no resistance as he bent her gently down on to the floor, but as he kissed her mouth and neck, exploring her body with eager hands, he felt her body respond to the urgency in his. The rough floorboards and the thudding of rain on the roof were forgotten, and all time and meaning were compressed into here, and now, and the needs of the flesh. She was beautiful, she was magnificent – and in a moment, she was his.

Later she fastened her dress in silence, but he could see the gentle smile about her lips. He lay on the floor still, hands behind his head, watching the graceful motion of her body as she moved towards the window and rubbed a patch of the dusty pane clean.

'Look, the sun is shining again.'

Slowly he got up and came to stand behind her, a hand on her shoulder. The hollow in the hills was suffused now with a warm glow of the evening sun, all trace of rainclouds vanished, and sunlight slanted gently on the rippling surface of the pool. Amy was tracing a pattern with her fingertip in the dirt on the windowpane.

'Happy, Amy?'

She considered. 'I wish it were still raining. I love the rain.'

'What a curious child you are.' His tone was filled with affectionate amusement, but she frowned.

'No, there's something pure and clean about rain – I told you. Water purifies, doesn't it? I feel so good when I feel it on my skin.'

He laughed outright. 'You are an odd one, Amy. Fey, that's what you are, a little dreamer.'

'No, I'm not.' Her voice had never sounded more serious. 'I'm earthy, Charles. I'm of the earth, a realist, not a dreamer at all.'

He frowned, puzzled by her sudden changes of mood. Actresses were easier to understand, even if half the time they were acting a part. But he'd have her again, of that he was certain – she was so different, so intriguing.

Suddenly she turned. 'Let's swim, Charles – in the pool! Come on, come swim with me.'

She was unbuttoning her bodice again, stepping out of her dress before he could protest. Seconds later she stood stark naked before him, eyes aglow with eagerness.

'Come on, I'll race you!'

She turned and sped out of the doorway while he was still unbuttoning his shirt, an eagerness rising in him to match hers. God, what a girl she was – so natural, so beautiful, he thought. He heard a splash. When he ran outside, feeling the wet springy heather under his bare feet, she was nowhere to be seen. For seconds he stood on the water's edge, transfixed with fear. Then she surfaced, long hair plastered about her head and shoulders. She smiled, then dived below the surface again, out of sight.

His heart swelled and contracted with a sensation he

had never before experienced. God, what a girl – a true child of nature! He dived, searching in the green-grey depths for her. Unseen, she swam up behind him, touched him, turned and vanished. He could swear she was laughing silently at him in that deep green silent world down there among the reeds.

From time to time he surfaced, gasping for air, and found her waiting, laughing. Once she seized his face, kissed him hungrily, then vanished below water again. Down he plunged after her, eager to continue the game, but again and again she eluded him, only to tease him when he surfaced again. At last she clambered out on to the bank and lay gasping, arms outspread. He flung himself down beside her on the prickling heather.

'Look, Charles – the sun is setting.'

Reluctantly he withdrew his gaze from her naked, wet body to look. Along the ridge on the western side of the hollow a fire of molten gold spread along the horizon.

'Just as if some alchemist had overturned his crucible,' murmured Amy. He rolled over, closer to her. She looked up at him.

'I've loved my day, Charles, rain and all. I've loved it all.' Her words held an air of frivolity, and he hastened to dismiss it.

'It's only just begun, my little Amy, I promise you. This is only the start.'

A slow, sad smile spread about her lips, and a sudden tiny fear clutched him. She seemed so far-away, so wordly-wise, as if she were in possession of some ancient wisdom far beyond his powers of comprehension. The word fey came to his mind again. He banished the unbidden sensation with a sudden move, covering her wet, cold body with his own. It was a strange and exciting sensation, his flesh slithering over hers. Then arms circled his neck.

'Love me again, Charles,' she murmured.

The slim, slippery body rose and fell under him, but for minutes she spoke no word, only moaned softly now and again. At last he felt her stiffen, hold her breath for a second, and then cry out as if in pain.

'Fill me!' she cried, then shuddered and fell still.

TEN

Mrs Cartwright was determined to stay cool, as befitted the one who presided over the kitchen, but it was not easy when the air was so hot and still the yard door had to be left open to allow the steam out and fresh air in. She wiped her brow with the back of a floury hand. It was even more difficult with a new kitchen-maid to train, and Amy apparently lost in a dream-world of her own.

'Now listen to me, Minnie Boswell,' she said, firmly but kindly, to the gawky, thin-faced girl who clearly felt ill at ease with her face scrubbed and a starched cap hiding her wispy hair. The girl stood awkwardly, weight on one leg, screwing up her face in an effort to follow and remember.

'Aye?' she said.

'Yes, Mrs Cartwright,' corrected the cook. 'Now, listen. Wash the cutlery first, dost hear, and then the plates and things. Pans last, think on. Oh Amy, give a hand with drying up, there's a good lass – we've that much on today, what with six coming to lunch. Eh, I don't know – they call it holiday for the Jubilee, but I'm flummoxed if I can see owt of a holiday for us in all that.'

Amy picked up a tea-towel and began drying knives and forks. 'Beautiful weather for it,' she remarked.

'Oh aye, Queen's weather they're calling it. Only hope as we've chance to see some of it, before the day's out. Here, where's the tureens? There must be one still in the dining room.'

'I'll fetch it,' said Amy.

There were voices in the dining room. Amy tapped before entering, but no one answered. She was about to enter when she heard the mistress's voice, and its tone did not indicate that her conversation was of the public kind that servants could overhear.

'I would never have believed it, Percy, never if I lived to be a hundred, if I hadn't witnessed it with my own eyes!'

'But you're mistaken, my dear, I do assure you.' The Reverend Percy Holroyd's murmur of protest was barely discernible. Amy hesitated. To return to the kitchen without the tureen would surely agitate an already flustered Mrs Cartwright, but it was clearly not the moment to interrupt her aunt.

Charlotte was rumbling on. 'There I was, doing my civic duty all day long, making certain the arrangements ran smoothly – as indeed they must for our dear Queen's celebration – there I was, slaving unstintingly on the town's behalf, and what were you doing while my back was turned?'

'I was working too, Charlotte, indeed I was. There was my sermon to prepare, and the scholars' treat, see all the commemoration medals were ready to present after the procession, make sure the ladies' committee had everything in hand for the meat tea—'

'And that, presumably, was what you were doing when I found you – conferring with the ladies' committee in the shape of Mrs Sugden, were you?'

'No, no, dear, not at all! She only called in the vestry to talk to me about subscriptions to the new public

147

library to mark the Jubilee – and there were other ladies nearby, seeing to the church flowers.'

'Nowhere in sight when I came in,' remarked Charlotte shortly. 'Just you and Mrs Sugden, far too close in that corridor, if you ask me, to be talking about subscriptions. Really, Percy! After all these years! Until now I would have pointed to you as a model of propriety and marital fidelity.'

'And you still can, my love, I assure you!'

'And to make matters worse, you had to do it while I had that obnoxious Mrs B with me – you know she'll go straight and tell Miss Hardcastle about it. What chance your preferment now, I ask you? You are remarkably stupid, Percy, to gamble your future – our future – for a furtive little – little – oh, I don't know what name to give such sordid behaviour.'

There was a long silence. The Reverend Holroyd had evidently abandoned all hope of redeeming his reputation. Amy knocked, and entered.

Charlotte stared icily at the ceiling above her husband's head while Amy retrieved the tureen and escaped. Poor Uncle Percy – Amy wondered what retribution was going to fall on his head once Aunt Charlotte had decided on a suitable punishment, but half an hour later Amy saw him leave the house to begin the day's rejoicings with his Sunday school scholars. With guests coming to lunch, and the Jubilee celebrations to continue for the next three days, maybe he could hope to be spared until all the fuss was over.

Charles would not be at lunch. He was with friends in London for the Jubilee, Berenice had said.

'Far more exciting than being in Hawksmoor, he says,' Berenice confided. 'I wish I could have gone with him, but then I wouldn't have had the chance to go to watch the fireworks with Elliot.' She regarded herself dreamily in the hand-mirror, then exclaimed in horror.

'Oh, God! A spot – look, I've got a spot on my

148

chin! Oh, now of all times! I shall look ugly for Elliot tomorrow!'

Creamed with Dearden's Antiseptic Balm, guaranteed to heal all spots and pimples overnight, and calmed by Amy's reassurance, she went off to play the piano. Amy made her way back to the kitchen. The house, for all its activity, seemed remarkably empty without Charles.

She stood in the pantry, her hands busy cleaning the silver cutlery ready for lunch, but her mind roaming, recalling the hut and the pool on the moors. From the kitchen she could hear Minnie's questions while she and Mrs Cartwright peeled vegetables for lunch.

'We're missing the procession through town,' she was grumbling. 'Mayor and everybody'll be there.'

'Procession is for gentry, not the likes of us,' said Mrs Cartwright.

'Like the Holroyds,' said the girl. 'Are they very rich? Me dad says they must be bow-legged with brass.'

'No business of thine, my lass. Nay, make sure there's no eyes left in them potatoes! No good only half-peeled.'

'There was folk in the town already when I came up, waiting for the procession to start. It fair made me feel excited too – I were in a hurry all over,' the girl chattered on.

'Put it out of thy mind, Minnie. Now fetch us the carrots from the cellar. And have a look if the jelly's set while tha's down – and don't stick thy finger in, mind. Folks don't want eating dirt off thy mucky fingers. Fine celebration that'd be.'

Later, as Amy was nearing the end of the pile of silver, she heard Minnie's high voice again.

'I wish I lived in, Mrs Cartwright. It's a heck of a long road up here.'

'Aye, well, if it'd been any shorter it wouldn't have reached,' remarked the cook. Then after a moment she added, 'Wouldst like to live in?'

'Oh, aye, I would!'

'Then I'll have a word with the mistress. There's room where Amy is.'

And somehow Mrs Cartwright contrived the arrangement, for the next night Amy found Minnie upstairs in the little attic bedroom when she came up to undress. The girl was already in her calico nightdress, on her knees by the bed. Amy felt resentful. Until now she had been able to hug and cherish memories of Charles and their secret encounter to herself, lying in bed and inspecting each snapshot memory in turn. Now there was an intruder.

'Now I lay me down to sleep,
I pray the Lord my soul to keep.
If I should die before I wake,
I pray the Lord my soul to take.'

Minnie finished her prayers and clambered into bed, turning back the covers on Amy's side.

'I'm that glad I don't have to go back to Samson's Yard,' she murmured sleepily as she snuggled down. 'There's a deal of sickness there now – it's got worse now the warm weather's come.'

That was not unusual, thought Amy. Typhoid and even cholera were frequent visitors to the poorest parts of the town, where overcrowding and uncleanliness reigned.

'Me mam's got quinsy – eats little else but boiled eggs,' confided Minnie. 'Little lad next door nearly died of whooping-cough, but he's getting over it. Now that Mrs Denny across from us has got smallpox, so they say. There's always summat, isn't there?'

Amy was gazing at her reflection in the cracked mirror, seeing only the water of the pool on the moors and Charles' smile.

'I love you,' he had muttered before his mouth had closed on hers. *And so you should, Charles Holroyd,*

150

for you possessed my soul long before you possessed my body. There is no reason why you should be spared the torment I have had to endure.

As she climbed into bed and settled down alongside Minnie's frail figure, the little body moved and curled up against hers. Amy lay immobile. The last time another human body had lain so close to her own was a night of tumultuous frenzy she would never forget, never, if she lived to be a hundred. Was she occupying Charles' thoughts now as wildly as he invaded hers?

In the deep leather armchair of his London club Charles reclined, sipping his brandy.

'You can say what you like, Rupert, but I can't summon up the slightest interest in your Pearl d'Arblay. Oh, she's pretty enough, I grant you, and coquettish in the extreme, but she seems shallow somehow. Like most actresses.'

Rupert's eyes twinkled. 'You wouldn't have said that a month ago. Oh, I can guess. You've found some little temptress of your own, some little charmer who has bewitched you out of your senses. Come on, tell us about it. You can't be selfish and hog her all to yourself.'

Charles did not smile as he stretched out an arm to replace the brandy glass on the table. 'Oh no, not this time, Rupert. This one means too much to me.'

'Aha! I detect the dangerous symptoms of love, Charles! Don't tell me the ubiquitous Charles Holroyd is forsaking all his other loves – I can't believe it! She must be the most exciting woman of all time to rob our Charles of his senses! Come on, you must tell.'

'No,' said Charles firmly, rising to leave. 'The minute this damn jamboree ends tomorrow, I'm off back to Yorkshire. And I shan't tell you a word about her.'

'Ah, so she's in Yorkshire, is she? Any chance I could come up and spend a few days at your place? Be a sport, Charles – I let you in on Pearl.'

Charles nodded his goodnights to other occupants of the club. 'Goodnight, Rupert,' he said drily. 'This one's for me – and me alone. There's never been one who stirred the blood as she does, and she's mine. Goodnight.'

Rupert picked up the newspaper with a sigh. 'Ah, well, I'll see if I can pick a winner at Newmarket tomorrow instead. Let's see now, if this fine weather continues the dry going is bound to favour Outcast. Think I'll have a sovereign each way on her.'

It was the last day of the Queen's Diamond Jubilee celebrations in Hawksmoor. Mrs Cartwright seemed glad it was at an end.

'All that junketing and comings-and-goings,' she muttered as she poured tea out of the huge earthenware pot and passed a cup to Amy. 'I'll be that glad to get back to normal, I can tell you. Where's that Minnie Boswell?'

'In the yard – she'll be in in a minute.'

'Boswell's a funny name,' remarked the housekeeper, lowering her voice. 'Not Irish, is she? They used to say as the Irish ate babies when I were a lass. Never seen it for meself, mind.'

'No, she's not Irish,' Amy assured her. 'Do you know when Mr Charles is coming home?'

The housekeeper shook her head, and her second chin wobbled. To Amy it seemed as though the woman's skin was a size too large for her body, for it fell in folds both at neck and waist, and probably elsewhere. 'There's never no telling, where Mr Charles is concerned. He comes and goes when he likes. Ah, there you are, Minnie, lass. Here, get us them strawberries out of the larder – Mrs Holroyd ordered far more nor we needed, so she said as we can help usselves.'

Amy saw Minnie's eyes light up in delight, and the smile that spread across her thin face as Mrs Cartwright

152

poured liberal helpings of thick cream over the strawberries. Amy tasted them, and savoured their cool,
sweet juiciness. Minnie gobbled, smacking her lips with
relish. Mrs Cartwright beamed.

'And what's more, tha can both take the evening off
to go and watch the fireworks in the park, the mistress
said. So be off with thee, and don't be late back – I'll
lock the yard door at eleven.'

Minnie was so excited that her normally pale face
was flushed as she prepared in the attic bedroom for
the outing. 'Just think, there's to be a bonfire up on
Castle Hill tonight – we'll get a fine view of that! Come
on, Amy, get ready!'

Amy sat on the edge of the bed, unable to share the
girl's enthusiasm. She was feeling rather strange, dizzy
and with a threatening sensation of nausea. By the
time Minnie had her bonnet and jacket on, Amy felt
decidedly sick.

'It's no use, I can't go, Minnie – I really do feel
rotten. I'd best lie down for a while. You go.'

After Minnie had finally, reluctantly, left, Amy lay
down and eventually she fell asleep. When she awoke
it was to the bang and whine of fireworks in the park.
Through the window she could see them flare and flash.
She sat up, and began to scratch the itch on her elbow.

The irritation did not cease, but seemed to spread.
Her arms, her legs, her body – she felt itchy everywhere. It was when Minnie at last came home, bursting
with excitement, that she discovered the worst.

Minnie stopped prattling in mid-sentence. 'What's
up with thy face, Amy? There's spots all over it. Come
closer to the candle where I can see.'

She frowned as she lifted Amy's chin. 'Hey, I say,
that's bad, that is. Hast any more spots?'

'Yes,' said Amy wearily. 'All over. And I feel sick.'

'Well, I'm not one for bad news, but Mrs Denny had
spots just like them.'

153

'It'll be gone by morning. Hurry up and let's get some sleep,' said Amy.

But when she awoke in the morning she was startled to find Aunt Charlotte peering at her. As Amy sat up her aunt drew back, a hand to her mouth.

'I think Minnie's right – you've got smallpox!' she exclaimed. 'How could you?'

'I'll be all right,' Amy muttered. 'Am I late? I'll get up straight away.'

'That you will – and pack and be off to your own home! You'd be best off with your own folk,' said the mistress. 'Pack and leave at once. I'll send your wages on. Don't waste a second, girl, get off home now, and don't talk to anyone, just go.'

And she swept from the room, her hand still over her mouth. Silly woman, filled with fearful superstition, thought Amy. It was not smallpox, but she'd have to convince the mistress.

Charlotte Holroyd was horrified to see her spotty-faced maidservant enter her study. She waved her hands in protest, refusing to listen.

'Let your own family take the risk, for there's no reason why we should accept the responsibility for nursing you,' she declared. 'Get out this minute, before you infect us all, you thoughtless, selfish girl!'

Amy grew angry, feeling the blood rush to her cheeks. She could not leave in silence. 'Would you talk to one of your own family like that?' she demanded. 'Would you turn your back on Berenice – or Charles?'

Charlotte stared, aghast. 'How dare you! Get out of this house this minute, and don't you ever come back – even if you do recover!'

Amy, so blinded with fury that she dared not trust her tongue, turned and stumbled away. That pompous, self-righteous woman, to deny a creature in need, or so she thought! What a miserable, hypocritical creature she was! Back in her bedroom, Amy found that Minnie's belongings were gone.

She had left Langdenholme well behind her, almost running down the lane with her bundle of belongings, before she cooled enough to consider her position. What if she did have smallpox? She did not feel very ill, just aching and weary, but if she did indeed carry that foul disease it would be uncharitable to take it home to Lionel, and to Mother.

No, she must not go home. Not yet, anyway. She must go away somewhere until she knew for sure, until the danger was past. She trudged slowly down towards the town, debating what to do.

In St George's Square she headed for the porticoed entrance of the railway station. Out of Hawksmoor, away to clean, fresh air until she was assured of recovery – that was the plan.

For the remainder of the morning Charlotte felt ill at ease. It was not her conscience which was troubling her, but the fear that infection still lingered in her home. She ordered Mrs Cartwright to see to it that the bedding of the little attic was burned, and that room and the kitchen and everywhere Amy and Minnie had been in Langdenholme were to be scrubbed with disinfectant. Then all thoughts of her servants vanished from her mind quicker than the smell of disinfectant in the air.

It was three days later, when she was discussing with Percy the possibility of discovering a suitable Holroyd coat-of-arms for their notepaper – and elsewhere, where fitting – that the ill-fated maid's name came up again.

Charlotte looked up as her son and daughter came into the parlour.

'But I can't see what all the fuss is about!' Charles was saying. 'Surely your maid will be back in a day or two.'

'No, she won't,' complained Berenice. 'Mother

dismissed her. It's so difficult doing my hair on my own. Did she offend you, Mother?'

Charlotte saw her son's swift look. 'Yes, why did you send her away?' There was an unaccustomed asperity in his voice, Charlotte thought irritably. It must be the company of his imperious friends in London.

'There's no secret,' she said sternly. 'The girl was carrying a disease. I wanted her out of the house.' Charles opened his mouth to protest. 'No, don't say anything. I did it to protect you all. I always care for your welfare, but then, I don't expect recognition for that.'

'What disease?' asked Berenice, coming to sit beside her mother on the horsehair sofa. Her mother moved her black moire skirts out of the way.

'Smallpox,' she answered equably. 'Minnie and Amy had both been in contact with a case. Amy was covered in spots.'

Charles exploded. 'And you sent her away, perhaps to die?' he cried in indignation. 'How could you?'

'I told you, Charles – to protect you.'

Charles came up close to her, so close his knee touched hers. 'Do you know who she was, Mother? Do you realise who you sent away?'

'What are you talking about, Charles?'

'You didn't know, but I did. She was Amy Mallinson – Aunt Violet's child!'

Charlotte paled. 'What did you say?' She heard Berenice gasp.

'She was our cousin Amy,' Charles said. 'I love her. I want to marry her.'

Charlotte, bereft of words, stared helplessly at her husband. Percy, whose mouth had been opening and closing speechlessly, at last found his voice.

'Good grief, Charles! Now I realise why I sensed something familiar about the child. Of course – she's Violet to the life at her age!'

156

Charles was still glaring at his mother. 'Did you hear me, Mother? I want to marry her. For God's sake tell me where she is!'

Charlotte was flustered. 'I've no idea where she is. I didn't ask where she lives. But Charles, the whole idea is preposterous anyway – one can't marry a first cousin. It's unthinkable! It's obscene! And anyway, she wasn't your class. You couldn't have considered a girl like that – not seriously, anyway!'

'A girl like what, Mother? She is your niece, every bit as good as us.'

'Nonsense,' said Charlotte. 'Tell him, Percy, tell him it's disgusting ever to think of it – why, it's almost incestuous! Tell him, Percy!'

Percy cleared his throat. 'Well, it is rather against church ruling, my dear. The Lateran Council in 1215, I think it was, forbids marriage within the fourth degree of consanguinity.'

'There,' said Charlotte with satisfaction. 'And the Mallinson girl was your first cousin.'

'Is my cousin,' corrected Charles.

'I say was,' rejoined Charlotte, 'for if she had smallpox, she'll undoubtedly be dead by now.'

Charles bent to grip his sister's hands. 'Berenice, you must know where she lives – tell me!'

Berenice shook her head helplessly. 'She never told me. Mother may know – she was to send Amy's wages on.'

'I don't,' said Charlotte smoothly. 'She was insolent, and therefore forfeited her money. I've no idea where my sister went to live. And I've no intention of finding out.'

Charles' face was pale. 'I shall never forgive you for this, Mother,' he said, and there was bitterness in his tone. 'The only woman I ever met that I could love – and you sent her away to die!'

Charlotte folded her hands in her lap. 'There are other young ladies—'

'Don't speak to me of them! I found the one I wanted – a girl you disowned, and ignored all these years! A girl forced to live in poverty and work as a maid because of the loathsome way you treated her family! But she was our equal, whatever you say. Our welfare, indeed! What a hypocrite you are, Mother! You killed your sister's child!'

ELEVEN

Tobias Clegg's weather-tanned face betrayed no surprise when he opened his front door and allowed Amy in. All credit to him, he was a man who never showed his emotions readily; a creature of control and sparing words, Amy thought as she lay in the depths of the feather bed – 'down from us own ducks,' he had assured her.

Even at Hawksmoor station she had had no intention of coming to Jericho Farm. It was just that the first train to arrive had been heading for Brockhurst and she had climbed aboard. To go to Cope Bank seemed appropriate, since it was there she had first met Charles.

Her spots and the itching had magically vanished by the time she alighted at the tiny station. But return to Langdenholme was impossible; explanations to Mother would be difficult. Somehow her feet had led her uphill, past Cope Bank and on towards the farm.

'I've no money,' she'd told Tobias.

'No matter. I told thee there was work here. Tha can help Morgan and me.'

The ache for Charles still lingered, but somehow, away from Langdenholme and the smoke of Hawksmoor, he seemed far removed and the pain was less immediate than it might have been. The distance also served to diminish the guilt she felt at not having got in touch with her mother. By now, Amy realised, she'd probably had word from Langdenholme about the smallpox and feared for Amy, even believing her dead. But Amy could not bring herself to make contact with the old world back there in Hawksmoor. Another day, perhaps, but not yet. In the meantime it was best, perhaps, that she was thought dead. Best for all.

After all these weeks, she wondered if Charles pined for her as she did for him – or was it for him only an interlude, one of many, as Mrs Cartwright's gossip had implied. A sweet voice was singing downstairs.

'As I walked out one May summer's morning
For to view the fields and the flowers so gay,
'Twas on the banks of sweet primroses
That I beheld a maid most fair.'

Amy recalled the song and the night she first heard it, at the music hall with Lionel. It seemed another world, a hundred years away.

'What is the cause of all your grief?
I will make you as happy as any lady,
If you will grant me one small relief.'

Was that perhaps, after all, all she had been to Charles that rainy day on the moor?

'Stand off, stand off, you false deceiver,
You are the cause of all my pain.
You have caused my poor heart to wander . . .
I shall go down to some lonely valley
Where no man shall there me find . . .

Maybe Charles was a deceiver, swearing love only to gain his ends, but it was not easy to forget the paroxysm of ecstasy she had experienced that day, sensation such as she had never believed possible. And Charles had seemed to share that ecstasy . . .

With a jerk Amy pulled herself together. If Morgan were up and singing downstairs already, then the hour must be late. She rose and dressed quickly.

Morgan was slicing bread while Tobias sat hunched at the table, his back towards the narrow stairs. They evidently had not heard her footsteps on the stairs for as Amy reached the bottom step Morgan spoke.

'I'd have liked to go down and stay while Mrs Pilling's that bad, but I can't.'

'Whyever not?'

She shrugged. 'Folk'd talk if tha were alone here with her.'

Amy saw Tobias' broad shoulders stiffen. 'Let 'em,' he said gruffly. 'Any road, there's Uncle Ben.'

'Aye,' said Morgan then, catching sight of Amy, she hurried on. 'And happen tha could fetch me some ribbon when tha's in Hawksmoor, love, pink or blue, don't matter which. Let me pour thee some tea, Amy – it's still hot on the hob.'

Amy watched as the girl limped towards the fire, and for the hundredth time she felt a stab of pity for the girl. So pretty, with her dimpled chin, her glossy black hair and green eyes, and yet blighted by that dreadful club foot – it was tragic. She could recall her horror the first time she had seen it – the day she came to Jericho Farm – and Tobias' moody brown eyes as he saw her look of alarm.

'Club-foot,' he'd said briefly. 'She were born with it.'

'Can't it be cured? Operated on?'

'Happen. If we had the brass.'

160

Many times since Amy had seen his gaze rest sorrowfully on his sister. Morgan was a shy, gentle creature who clearly loved her brother above everything else in the world. It was not that they spoke affectionately either to or about each other, but it was clear in their mutual concern. Amy could sense Tobias' frustration, that in all likelihood he would never in a thousand years earn enough money to cure Morgan. One day, as she followed the girl back into the farmhouse across the muddy yard she had observed the footprints left by the limp, like a full stop and a comma. Amy had reflected, and swore to herself that if ever the day came when she had money, she would see to it that Morgan walked with two full stops. It would be only a small recompense for the kindness they had shown to her.

Tobias' black and white collie shuffled in at the open door from the yard, lifted its nose and sniffed, then came across to where Morgan was stirring a pan at the range.

'Here, Gyp, come here, girl,' Tobias called.

The dog came obediently and sat at his feet, but kept glancing back at Morgan. Amy laughed.

'She's hungry, poor thing. But she does everything you tell her, Tobias. I've never seen such a good dog.'

He regarded her soberly. 'Sheepdogs have to be obedient. She'll do well in the trials, will Gyp. Never a paw out of place.'

He bent to stroke her head, and the movement stirred Amy. He was a kindly, appreciative man.

'About Uncle Ben,' said Morgan without looking round. 'Tha'd best talk to him, Tobias. He's getting old and a bit touchy.'

Tobias grunted. 'Tha'll go to Pillings' then?'

'If tha can manage without me.'

He looked at Amy. She came to life. 'Of course, if you have to go away I'd be glad to fill in – cook and feed the chickens and everything. That's if you'll let me . . .'

161

Tobias got up from the table, scraping the chair noisily on the flagstoned floor, and went out without a word. Amy looked at Morgan, who must have read the question in her eyes.

'It's all right. He's grateful to thee, but he says little. I'd be that glad if tha'd take over – just for a day or so. Mrs Pilling's having her fourth, and she always has a bad time. She's nearly due, dost see?'

'Don't worry – I'll see to everything.'

'Aye, well, it could be more nor just cooking. One of our cows is due to calve and I usually give Tobias a hand.'

Amy took a deep breath. 'I reckon I can manage whatever turns up.'

Morgan smiled. 'I'd be that grateful. And as to Uncle Ben – well, just let him have his say. He means nowt by it, whatever he says. He's just an old fellow, but he can't stand being argued with.'

'I'll humour him, don't worry,' said Amy.

But it wasn't that easy. The old man arrived before Morgan left, settled himself in the rocking chair, and gave his orders with the help of his walking-stick, which he waved to emphasise his words. He poked Amy with it as she passed.

'It'd fair suit our Tobias to wed a lass like thee,' he muttered. 'I mun tell him.'

Amy blushed and was about to protest – until she remembered Morgan's warning, and held her tongue.

The old man's bright eyes followed Amy as she moved about the kitchen, his head cocked on one side like an inquisitive sparrow.

'Aye, tha'rt a bit narrow in the hips for child-bearing, but tha's young yet. How old art tha?'

'Eighteen.'

'Young enough to learn. Our Tobias is twenty-five. High time he were wed. Dost come from hereabouts?'

'From Hawksmoor.'

162

'Oh, a townie. Know owt about country ways, dost tha?'

'I can cook and sew,' Amy replied, 'and I've learnt to feed chickens and collect eggs and pack them for market.'

'There's a lot more to farming nor that, but tha'll learn. Art honest, lass?'

Amy looked up, startled. 'How do you mean?'

'Tha's had no truck with young lads, hast tha?'

Her cheeks burning, Amy clattered dishes in the stone sink in an effort to avoid conversation, but Uncle Ben was not to be diverted.

'Tha doesn't cheat like many a townie, I hope. I'd a cousin once as worked in a warehouse down in Hawksmoor. He told me his gaffer, the fellow as made the cloth, used to have him soak the bales with water before the market, so as to make 'em weigh heavy. Townies are like that. Can't trust 'em no farther nor tha could throw 'em. Now country folk . . . I wish tha'd come from Honley or Holmfirth.'

Tobias came in for dinner just as the beef and onion pie in the range-oven reached its golden peak of perfection. He watched in silence as she spooned vegetables and potatoes alongside the crusty pie. Picking up his knife and fork he began eating. The old man smacked his lips in relish but Tobias made no comment.

'I mun get back up to the top field,' he said as he finished. 'Give Gyp more practice before the trials. Come on, girl.'

The collie crawled out from under the table, where she'd been scavenging for fallen morsels, and followed him outside, eagerness in her quick step and waving tail. Amy hurried out into the sunlit cobbled yard after him.

'Tobias, can I come and watch?'

He was striding away across the yard and did not look back. 'If tha wants.'

She went back inside to clear away and wash up,

163

paying scant attention to Uncle Ben's continued interrogation.

'Canst store apples in autumn and brew ale? Canst make preserves and turn a sheet? Knit stockings? Help when lambing-time comes? There's a lot to learn to be a farmer's wife. Now my Hannah – she were a treasure, she were.'

He paused to rise stiffly from his chair, reach down a spill from the mantleshelf, and light it from the fire. Then, applying the flare to his clay pipe, he went on reminiscing.

'Aye, no man could want better. Not as I ever told her, like. It does no good to fill a woman's head with praise, but she knew, for all that. She always had a roof over her head and food in her belly. She never wanted for nowt, did my Hannah.'

The sun had gone in and there was a breeze blowing. Amy took down one of Morgan's shawls from the peg behind the door and threw it about her shoulders. She made her way up the rutted lane towards the top field, climbing the stile set in the drystone wall. From there she could see Tobias at the top end of the field and the dozen or so sheep he was watching intently.

Not wanting to distract him, Amy moved slowly and soundlessly over the wiry grass spattered with clover, along the edge of the field. Nearer to him, she seated herself on the drystone wall. For the next half-hour she watched him. He spoke no word to the dog. She saw him raise a whistle to his mouth but she heard no sound. It was clear, however, that the dog heard, for she crouched on her stomach, waiting, then wriggled forward on her belly, crouching again, then suddenly started careering around the field. Surely and confidently she rounded up the sheep, harrying gently and persuading any nervous ewe that broke free to return to the flock. Not one eluded her. She split the flock evenly into two, driving half into the far pen before shepherding the remainder into the other. Not once did she falter.

Amy turned her attention to the shepherd. Tobias was rather shorter than Charles but broader in the shoulder, though the appearance of shortness might be due, she reflected, to the short rough jacket he wore over his shirt and thick corduroys. Then she reproached herself for letting Charles inside her thoughts again. Despite her hunger for him, recently she had managed to keep him out of her mind far more. She was beginning to recover, especially since the thought had come to her that perhaps it was not, after all, the man she hungered for, but the wanton delight he had conjured up in her. With determination she concentrated on Tobias.

At last he stowed the whistle away in his pocket and patted his thigh. Gyp came bounding to him, leaping up in anticipation of praise. He knelt to pat her and stroke her head. The dog licked his cheek. He rose and strode down the field towards Amy.

'She did well,' Amy remarked. 'She seemed to do everything you wanted of her.'

He nodded. 'Aye, not bad. She'll do.'

'When are the trials?'

'Saturday next, Holmfirth.'

Amy turned and walked alongside him down to the stile. He made no move to help her as she bunched up her skirts to climb over.

'Heard owt from Morgan?' he asked.

'No, there can't be any news yet.'

Back in the kitchen there was no sign of Uncle Ben. Tobias pulled off his boots at the doorway and crossed, stocking-footed, to the rocking chair. The kettle was singing on the hob. Amy began to brew tea.

'Morgan's an unusual name,' she remarked as she swilled the earthenware pot with hot water, then emptied it down the sink. 'How did she come by it?'

For seconds there was silence. She glanced back at

him. He was frowning, staring at the flagged floor. 'Her father's name,' he muttered.

'Morgan? Morgan Clegg?'

'Nay – I'm Clegg, she's my half-sister.'

'I see.' But Amy was puzzled. Perhaps she was intruding too far.

After a moment Tobias went on. 'There's nowt to hide – nowt as folks don't know already. Her father were a passing gypsy, come with the fair and left with it. My mother only knew he were called Morgan, nowt else. She never saw him again.'

So that was it. Poor little Morgan – no father to call her own. Tobias took the mug of hot tea from Amy's hand.

'Me mother read a lot. She said there were a fairy-woman in a story called Morgan le Fay. Our Morgan were like a fairy, she said. Magic, she were, club-foot or no.'

Uncle Ben, seeming to scent fresh tea, stumbled in from the yard, patting his pockets.

'Hast seen my pipe anywhere, Toby lad? It were here a while back – now it's just mizzled.'

'Nay, it's thee as forgets where tha's put things.' Tobias rose and lifted down the pipe from behind one of the many pictures on the mantelshelf.

The old man grinned a toothless smile and seated himself in the chair Tobias had just vacated.

'Tha should get shut of that thing,' said Tobias. 'I'll get thee another when I go down to the cattle market.'

'There's no call – thissun's good for a while yet,' complained the old man. Tobias compressed his lips, and Amy knew him well enough by now to recognise the sign. Whatever Uncle Ben said, Tobias would have his way.

The dark eyes suddenly turned on her. 'Hast ever driven a horse and cart?' he demanded. Amy shook her head. 'Then come with me to market tomorrow – I'll show thee.'

166

'Into Hawksmoor?' she asked dubiously. She had no wish to be seen and recognised.

'Tha'd be doing me a favour.'

'I would?' she brightened.

'Buying ribbons is woman's work. Be up and ready betimes.'

That night Tobias was out late – down at the barn, Uncle Ben said. Amy washed her hair with water from the rain-butt outside the door, and sat by the fire brushing it dry.

'Like a yard of pump-water, thy hair,' the old man chuckled. 'And black as coal too, like our Morgan's. Reckon it's all but long enough for thee to sit on. My Hannah's hair were red as sunset, it were – not latterly, but when she were a lass. Eh, but I liked brushing it till it shone. Art off to bed, then?'

'In a minute or two. I'll wait to say goodnight to Tobias first – if he's not too long.'

'Art comfortable up there – strange bed and all?'

'Very, thank you.'

'Snug as a bug in a rug, as Hannah used to say. Eh, I miss her most at nights.' His eyes grew watery as he stared into the fire. Amy could guess that he was conjuring up in the flames pictures of a happier past. A black soot-flake trembled on the fire-bars.

'See that – there's a stranger on the bars,' murmured the old man. 'Stranger coming to the house.'

The yard door opened, admitting a cold draught and Tobias' broad figure. Gyp raced ahead of him and crouched by the fire. There was a smell of wet dog-fur, and droplets glistened on Tobias' dark head.

'I need help,' he said brusquely from the doorway. 'Cow's having difficulty. Calf's got stuck. It's a breech.'

Amy looked quickly at Uncle Ben. He was sitting open-mouthed and made no move to rise. Amy got up.

'Can I help?'

'Tha'll have to. Come on.'

Snatching up the shawl she hurried out into the night after him. The barn smelt warm and musty. The cow lay on its side on the straw, panting and heaving. A lantern stood nearby. Tobias knelt, and Amy could see the calf's hind legs protruding.

'Is it dead?' she asked fearfully.

Tobias scowled. 'It will be if we don't make shift. Take hold of its legs and pull when I tell thee.'

Gripping the little legs Amy closed her eyes. *Don't let the calf die, or the cow*, she prayed. *Every penny is vital to Tobias, and he can't afford to lose either.*

'Pull!' commanded Tobias. She pulled with all her might, but the little body did not budge. 'Pull!' shouted Tobias again, and this time there seemed to be an infinitesimal movement. The cow groaned, doing her best to co-operate.

For what seemed like hours Amy pulled on command, hearing Tobias' laboured breathing and feeling the sweat beginning to bead her forehead. Her arms ached and her knees were sore, but she could not give in.

'Keep going,' Tobias ordered. 'We'll win yet.'

At last the cow gave a mighty shudder and Amy opened her eyes. Tobias, his arm plunged deep inside the cow, gave a shout.

'It's coming, Amy! Pull for all tha'rt worth!'

There was a sudden gush of warm liquid all over her arms and the calf seemed to slide out on the tide. Tobias held it up triumphantly.

'We did it, lass! He's all right! The head nearly always comes off in a breech, but we did it!'

The glow in his dark eyes was all the reward Amy needed. He sat at supper with an unwonted smile on his face, and Amy realised with a start that he was a handsome man. Uncle Ben was already abed. The clock on the mantel chimed midnight.

'Off to bed, lass, tha's earned it.'

Tobias patted her arm as he passed her chair, and

for the first time in weeks Amy felt a glow of contentment. It was good to be alive when one had a feeling of achievement.

Charlotte Holroyd took off her rings and added them to those already on the china ring-stand on her dressing table, then toyed idly with the array of hat-pins stuck in the velvet pin cushion. In the mirror she could see her husband behind her, already in his night-gown, arranging his trousers over the valet stand. Moving the box of shaving-papers aside she drew forward a pot of face-cream and began to apply it to her cheeks, turning her head this way and that to survey herself in the triple mirrors.

'Oh, by the way, Percy,' she said, as if it had only just occurred to her, 'I suppose you heard what happened today.'

She saw him straighten, baffled, then yawn and make for the bed. 'Oh, you mean about Charles? Well, yes, I knew he'd get over his sulks in time. It's been three weeks now. He'll come round to your way of thinking very shortly, my dear, I'm sure of it. He's down at the Adega tonight, isn't he?'

Charlotte clicked her tongue. 'Of course he will. That's not what I meant. Did Mrs Cartwright tell you who called this afternoon while you were out?'

Percy looked surprised. 'Well, no, dear. I hardly ever talk to the housekeeper. She's your department. Why? Did she have some titbit of gossip?'

Charlotte unclasped the necklace about her thick neck and laid it in the velvet-lined jewellery casket alongside the garnets and the seed pearls. 'You might call it that,' she said drily. 'Edwin Glover called.'

'Glover?' repeated Percy, obviously mentally running through his list of parishoners. 'Is that the chap—'

'Yes,' interrupted Charlotte. 'The man Father expected Violet to marry. She didn't – the Lord knows

169

why – but it seems they've been keeping company again recently.'

'That's splendid! It will be nice to see Violet married again. A good, reliable sort of fellow, as I recall.'

Charlotte sighed and swung round on the stool, unaware of the blob of white cream on her left cheek. 'Edwin called here on Violet's behalf,' she explained patiently. 'It seems she hasn't seen her daughter for some weeks.'

'That's odd,' said Percy. 'You sent her home.'

'But apparently she never arrived. Violet sent to find out if she was still here.'

'Good Lord! Did you tell her what happened?'

'Of course I did – well, Mrs Cartwright told Edwin, anyway. But don't you see, Percy – Violet sent Edwin rather than come herself. He said she wasn't well, but I know the truth is she just won't acknowledge us.'

'That's hardly surprising, dear, since we haven't acknowledged her in all these years.'

'For heaven's sake, Percy! She claims to be worried about her child, and yet she can't even make the effort to come herself. I mean, fancy sending an intermediary – it's bad form, on private family business too, it really is.'

'But he said Violet wasn't well.'

'So he said. He said she'd been poorly for quite a time, and the anxiety was making her worse. That's his story, but my guess is she just wouldn't lower her pride to come back to Langdenholme. Pride was always her undoing. She's never learnt, it seems. Well, if she won't come here, I certainly won't go to her.'

Percy, sitting up in bed, spread his hands. 'But surely the point is that the girl left here sick – very sick. If she hasn't arrived home, then where is she?'

Charlotte swung back to face the mirror. She noticed the blob of cream on her cheek, and began rubbing it in vigorously. 'How should I know? If she died somewhere of smallpox, she's probably buried somewhere

170

in an unmarked pauper's grave. Pity. She was a pretty baby. But she's not my responsibility now, Percy – my responsibility is to my family, and I did what I thought was right to protect you all.'

Percy sighed and lay down. 'Poor Violet,' he muttered. 'Poor, poor Violet.'

'It's perhaps as well I wasn't in when Edwin Glover called,' Charlotte remarked to the mirror. 'I should have been obliged to tell him that I could not discuss family business with a stranger. Bad form, that's what it is, but then Violet never was one for the niceties. And as to Charles,' she added, rising from the stool and tying the ribbon at the neck of her nightgown, 'you need have no concern over him. He's agreed to accompany Florence Chadwick to the Summer Ball at Langley Hall next week.'

'Chadwick?' repeated Percy sleepily.

'Yes, of Chadwick's Spinning Mill. You'll see, we'll have no problems with Charles. Now as to Berenice and this piano tutor of hers . . .'

Violet Mallinson lay back in the chair beside the dying fire, her eyes closed. Edwin Glover, sitting opposite her, eased himself tentatively forward to the edge of the chair. He felt helpless. He guessed there were tears under Violet's lowered eyelids and he was powerless to help.

'Look, love, I shall have to go. It's getting very late. The neighbours'll be talking if I stay any longer. You wouldn't want that.'

She neither moved nor opened her eyes, and for a moment he wondered whether she was sleeping. It would do no harm, he thought, for she'd slept very little this past week, what with the pain and the worry. He fetched his hat, then stood awkwardly before her.

'Violet, love, I'm sorry to be the bearer of such bad news. I wouldn't have had that job for the world, but be glad Lionel at least is well and happy again with

171

Maggie. Now let's see about getting you well. I'll make an appointment for you to see the doctor tomorrow.'

She stirred and opened her eyes. He was right – there were tears welling. 'My daughter had smallpox and Charlotte never thought to tell me. She let her go, ill and alone. Oh, Edwin! She's probably dead and buried now, and I'll never know where! It's not fair, Edwin! Life isn't fair! A girl that – so good and loyal. Oh, God! I loved her more than life itself. Life is so cruel, Edwin. Charlotte's cruel. How could she do such a thing?'

There was unfathomable desolation in her voice. Edwin, unable to find words, put a hand over hers where it lay, white-knuckled, along the arm of the chair, and squeezed it gently.

'I'll be round first thing in the morning. Try and sleep, love.'

She looked up at him, eyes ravaged by grief and despair. 'Do you think I care what happens to me now? There's nothing left for me. Life's never been easy, but this is just too cruel.'

He dropped to his knees, taking both her hands and squeezing them in her lap, then bent to touch his forehead against them. 'Violet,' he muttered indistinctly, 'I need you, love. Don't give up.'

She made no answer, just withdrew one hand and laid it on his greying head, then she sighed deeply and made to get up. He sat back on his haunches. He saw her work-worn left hand fall to her side as it often did, and saw her knuckles grinding in the hollow of her hip.

'I'll not sleep tonight,' she murmured. 'Not tonight nor any night so long as I remember. My Amy could be alive now, but for my sister. She could have got her to hospital—'

'Violet, love, it's no use now. It's too late.' He rose and held out his arms. Violet, unable to resist comfort any longer, moved to him and bent her face against his shoulder. He put his arms uncomfortably about her, feeling her body tremble. She was weeping at last. He patted her back.

'There, there,' he soothed. 'You'll feel stronger after a bit of sleep.'

She drew away, dabbing her eyes and turning to glance at the clock. 'You're right, Edwin, it is late. It's time you went. Thank you, for everything.'

Edwin Glover was thoughtful as he walked away along the glistening wet cobblestones of Reed Street. Violet Mallinson had precious little to thank him for, he reflected, considering the terrible news he had been obliged to fling, totally unexpectedly, into her lap. That Charlotte Holroyd deserved a dreadful punishment for her inhumanity.

TWELVE

Amy sat on a stool in the cobbled yard outside the front door of the farm. On her lap lay a bowl containing the peas she had already shelled for dinner. At her feet lay the heap of emptied peapods. She was cracking yet another and sliding her finger inside when a shadow fell across her. She looked up, shading her eyes against the early-morning sun. Tobias stood there, a quizzical expression on his dark face and a spade slung over his shoulder.

'Any word from Morgan?'

Amy smiled. 'She's in the kitchen with Uncle Ben. Delivered the baby yesterday – a little boy, and he's fine.'

He nodded. 'She'll be glad. Job well done. Like thee – I'd have had a job with that cow but for thee.'

He leaned the spade against the house wall and strode inside. He'd said little, but Amy was proud of implied gratitude. For a townie, she'd acquitted herself well enough.

How different he was from Charles, she reflected, so sparing of words and making no effort to make himself agreeable. It was almost as if he expected effort only where it brought some return. Necessity, perhaps, made country folk more economical with words than townsfolk were.

Charles. She could visualise him, his golden hair and beard gleaming in this glorious sunshine, but his brocade waistcoat and fancy shoes would be ridiculously out-of-place here at Jericho Farm. She pushed the thought aside, irritated with herself for finding fault, however slight, with her Adonis. But this had been happening more and more lately. A disconsolate mood fell upon her whenever she remembered that night in his room.

'I shall meet you as an equal, I swear, or my name's not Amy Mallinson.'

He had not even noticed her slip. Defiantly she had flung out the proud vow, realising too late what she had said. The 'Mallinson' had tripped off her tongue before she could swallow it – and he hadn't even noticed.

Still, it had been a wonderful day, that day in the rain, in the lodge near the tarn. They had met as equals, just as she had vowed, and the wild fire in her blood had met its equal in his ardour. Closing her eyes, she listened inwardly once again to his protestations of love, jerked out between moaning and ecstasy.

'I love you, little Amy, oh, God, how I love you!'

But it had been terrible disappointment when he went off to London just after, for the Jubilee with his smart friends, with never a word to her. Not that he

174

owed her any apology, any explanation even, but a word – even a gesture – to show he remembered, and was glad . . . It would have softened the disappointment.

'Art ready?'

The voice behind her startled her. Tobias was holding his jacket over his arm.

'Oh – the market! Are you ready to go now?' She jumped up, scattering peapods. 'I'll just take these in to Morgan, and I'm ready.'

He was sitting on the driving bench of the wagon when she came out again. Several piglets squealed in the back. Their wild-eyed look disturbed her; they were clearly frightened at being wrenched from their mother. Tobias saw her look as she climbed up.

'Selling the pigs. Buying a cow,' he explained briefly, then cracked the reins and drove off out of the yard. Chickens clucked and scattered.

For most of the journey Tobias drove in silence, his brow furrowed as if he were deep in thought. Only once did Amy interrupt his concentration.

'Did you say you'd let me drive, Tobias?'

Without looking at her, he cracked the reins again. 'Not now. We're late,' he said tersely. Crestfallen, Amy fell silent and, as if he sensed her disappointment, he muttered, 'On the way home, happen.'

The streets of the town were thronged with people and carts and wagons clattering about their business, and in the open cobbled space where the cattle market was held the air vibrated to the sound of shrill voices, rumbling carts and the squeals of nervous animals. The air smelt sulphurous and dirty, and Amy realised with a start how clear and pure the air was up at Jericho Farm in contrast. Tobias descended from the wagon and began unloading the pigs. Then he came back to the footboard, reaching up and putting a hand on Amy's foot.

'Thee wait here. I'll be back.'

175

For some time she sat there, watching the moving sea of faces and gestures. When Tobias at last returned he climbed up and sat beside her.

'Pigs are sold. I've seen the cow I want.'

'Have you bought it?'

'Not yet.'

'Why not?'

'Can't be seen too eager. I can bide me time.' He reached into his pocket and pulled out a shilling. 'Stalls are up that side street. Go get Morgan's ribbons.'

By the time Amy had found the stall, selected the ribbons, paid for them and retraced her steps to the wagon, Tobias had gone again. When he returned his face wore a set, determined expression. He reached into his pocket again, drew out some coins and counted them. Then he looked at Amy, his dark head cocked to one side.

'Art a good business woman?' he asked.

She shrugged. 'I reckon so. I usually get a bargain when I go to market – you learn to, when money's always short.'

'I wonder,' he murmured, then held out his hand, the sunlight glinting on the coins in his outstretched palm. 'Here's the top figure I'll pay for yon cow. See if tha can get it for that – or less. Yon's the beast – that brindle over there.'

Amy followed his finger to where the creature stood amongst others in the pen, then she nodded. 'I'll do my best,' she said, taking the coins and lifting her skirts to climb down.

As she moved away Tobias called out, 'Nah then, think on to get thy luck-penny, lass. It'll bring us no good fortune else.'

The farmer, a slack-bodied man with bright eyes set in grizzled, weather-beaten features, was standing by the pen earnestly bartering with another man in a cloth cap who, evidently dissatisfied, shook his head and shambled away, muttering. Amy accosted the farmer.

'That your cow?' He nodded. 'How much?'

He sized her up for a moment, his fingers jingling the coins in his pocket, then named his price. Amy was conscious of Tobias, across the square on the wagon, his eyes on her back, and she made a mental resolve to meet his challenge. Townie she might be, but she was no fool. She made an offer.

It took several minutes to clinch the deal, but when at last the old farmer begrudgingly agreed to a compromise figure some shillings below what Tobias had given her, Amy felt elated. She handed over the money, and turned to go, to tell Tobias he could come and fetch the animal.

'Hold on, lass, dost want thy luck-penny?'

She turned back. The old farmer's eyes held a gleam.

'Luck-penny – oh yes, of course.'

The old fellow pressed it into her palm, and held her hand in his for a second. 'Know what they say, lass – accept my penny, means tha'll come back.'

'Come back – to be sure I will.' She smiled, and hurried away. Tobias showed no surprise as he took the change she offered him.

'And here's your luck-penny too,' she added. He took it, looked at it briefly, then tucked it into his pocket along with the other coins. 'Thanks.' After he had coaxed the cow into the wagon and climbed on the running board he nodded to her.

'Tha's not a bad lass, Amy,' he muttered. 'Tha might almost be taken for a country lass.'

Praise indeed from Tobias, she reflected, and when at last, on the lane nearing Jericho Farm, he allowed her to take the reins, she felt almost happy.

His arm was about her waist, holding the reins either side of her. As they turned into the farm gates he suddenly spoke.

'Why didst come to Jericho?'

She felt her heart flutter. 'How do you mean? I

177

didn't like being in service. You once told me there was work for me here—'

'I did that,' he interrupted. 'But there's more to it nor that. There were a reason tha came here.'

'No – truly. You offered me work. I needed it.'

'Aye, well, if tha says so.'

She climbed down and hurried across the yard to the house, leaving him to see to the wagon and the animals. The alarm she felt at his questions dissipated quickly when she came into the warmth of the kitchen. A flushed Morgan was taking crusty loaves out of the oven and the air was rich with their scent. Uncle Ben was dozing in his chair by the fire. After a moment Tobias came in.

Morgan looked at him with affection. 'Tha got us another cow, Toby?'

'Aye. And Amy has thy ribbons.'

She smiled, pleasure lighting her pretty face. 'Lay the table, Amy. Supper's ready, and tha can show me the ribbons after.'

Tobias stood by the window. 'Rain clouds blowing up,' he commented. 'I mun mend that chicken coop tomorrow.'

'Aye, and I wish tha'd fix the roof at the same time afore it teems with rain again,' said Morgan as she dolloped ladlesful of stew on to plates on the dresser. 'That wet stain's creeping further down my bedroom wall. It'll reach the bed next.'

Tobias grunted, turning to pull out a chair. 'Reckon I'll have to fix it. Landlord ought to, but I reckon as we'll be a long time waiting of them. Tha can't expect owt from them Holroyds.'

Amy started, a fork poised as she was about to lay it for Uncle Ben's place. 'Holroyds?' she repeated.

'That's right,' said Morgan, thumping a plate down in front of Tobias. 'Tha knows Reverend Holroyd, well, it's his wife really who's landlord. It were her father, mayor as was, who used to be landlord.'

178

'Cedric Moorhouse?'

'That's him. Holroyds never come here, never see what wants doing. Never inspect any of their property, so other tenants say.' Morgan's lips were tight. 'Just send someone to collect rent, that's all they do.'

'Sit and eat,' said Tobias. 'I'll do it soon, don't fret.'

'Better get it done soon, lad, or we'll have harvest time on us hands. Uncle Ben! Supper's ready – come on now, wake up.'

The old man staggered to the table, smacking his lips. 'By heck, that smells good,' he crooned, 'and I'm fair clemmed. I'll do justice to thy stew, Morgan, that I will.'

Conversation was desultory during the meal, and while the other three ate with healthy appetites Amy mulled over this new piece of information. It was somehow ironic to realise she had left Aunt Charlotte's place at Langdenholme only to move into another property she owned. But it was a relief to know she never came here. Nor would Charles be likely to come.

'*Holroyds never come here.*' She was uncertain whether she was glad or sorry. Uncle Ben pushed his plate away at last.

'That were fair grand, Morgan, a right tasty bit of stew.'

'Wilt have a bit more, Uncle Ben?' Morgan half-rose.

He waved his hands. 'Nay, nay, I'm thrussen. Couldn't eat another mouthful.'

'Tha'll have a bit of apple pie, like as not,' said Tobias.

'Nay, I'll not, or I'll end up fat as a mole. I'll just have a read of the paper, and then I'll make tracks for bed.' The old man rose and returned to his chair by the fire, picking up the newspaper which had fallen down by the side.

Rain was pattering on the window by the time Tobias finished his meal, pulled on his jacket again and went out into the yard. Morgan began washing the dishes in the stone sink and Amy picked up a cloth to dry them. The old man cleared his throat.

'Nay, these are terrible times we live in. There's a man got attacked down by the cut and robbed of all his money. Name of Dyson, from Peter Street.'

'Dreadful,' said Amy.

'It were all he had – he'd just sold his shop, and had all the brass in his pocket. He's done for now.'

'He was a fool to be carrying all that,' said Morgan.

The old man clicked his tongue. 'Daft, isn't it? There's wicked folk like that thief, and there's good 'uns like them Co-op people. It says here they've got a women's guild now.'

'Aye, they've done a good job for us ordinary folk, them Co-op people,' agreed Morgan. 'A good idea, having a women's branch.'

'They had a meeting, and the speaker were Mrs J. S. Pearson, it says here. That's old James Stott's grandson, tha knows – well, his wife. I knew old James Stott when he were mayor, a long time back. Grand fellow he were. Says here, Mrs Pearson gave an illuminating talk on *The Function of Women in the Co-operative Movement* and a vote of thanks was ably proposed by Mrs Violet Mallinson. The meeting concluded with afternoon tea.'

A dish clattered to the stone floor and broke. Morgan looked at Amy in surprise. Amy coloured. 'I'm sorry. Butter-fingers.' She bent to pick up the pieces.

'No matter,' said Morgan. 'It were an old one.'

Later that night, alone in the bedroom she shared with Morgan, Amy watched through the window the thin veil of cloud trailing across the moon. Mother, it seemed, was well, well enough to be giving votes of thanks at a meeting. She wasn't pining, then, for her lost daughter. All the same, Amy felt homesick. Life here at Jericho Farm was pleasant, and she missed

Charles desperately – but most of all she longed to see her mother. Mother and Lionel. Funny how much one could miss people one had taken for granted all one's life.

She must get in touch, and soon. It was cruel of her, plunged in self-pity, to leave them to fret for so long, wondering why she hadn't come home.

In their cosy living room James Stott Pearson pushed several letters across the chenille-covered table to his wife.

'There, Annie, I've dealt with these. The only one left now is this one from Edwin Glover. Perhaps you could deal with that. Tomorrow, though, not now. It's time we were in bed.'

His wife twisted the letter round to read it. 'Oh, yes. I was so sorry to hear about Mrs Mallinson. Such a nice lady – gave a splendid vote of thanks for me, she did. I do hope it's not serious.'

He rose and stretched. 'Well, folks don't usually get taken to hospital for trivial reasons. He says she collapsed with kidney trouble.'

'We'd best send her a letter too – I'll find out what ward she's in.' Annie shook her head sadly. 'Such a nice lady. Such a pity.'

'Now remember, don't stay too long, Mr Glover. She's very tired.'

Edwin Glover watched the ward sister's erect back as she retreated down the ward, then turned to the figure in the bed. Violet looked pale and drawn, her body appearing shrunken under the starched sheets. She seemed to have lost a lot of weight of late. She must have been sickening for some time, he realised, but she'd never let on. Her thin hand reached to cover his.

'Don't look so worried, Edwin. I'll be all right.' She smiled, a sad, resigned smile which touched him to the heart. He covered her hand with his.

181

'To be sure tha will, lass. We'll have thee out of here in no time. Doctors'll see thee right.'

She sighed deeply and her gaze wandered around the room. 'My father died here in the Infirmary.'

He looked at her anxiously. 'We'll have no talk of dying, Violet Mallinson,' he heard himself saying with false heartiness. 'Tha's not going to die. Just think on, more folk come out of here cured than die here.'

'That may well be, but I'd still like you to write to those London solicitors for me. I want my affairs set in order, just in case . . .'

'I will, love, I will. I'll do it tomorrow.'

'Not that there's much,' she said wearily, 'only bits and pieces, really. But I should make a will, I reckon. It's hard to know what to do, with Amy gone.'

'Now come on, Violet,' Edwin interrupted. 'There's no call to be talking of such things as wills.'

'Let me be, Edwin. Let me have my say.'

He fell silent. She deserved peace of mind – after all, she'd had little enough of that all these years. 'Go on, then, lass.'

She took a deep breath. 'Ask about the shares my father left me. They're probably still not worth much, but I'd like to know for Lionel's sake. There could be something for him to get wed on.'

The nurse came pattering back up the ward. She stood by the bed, taking Violet's hand and pressing a finger to her pulse. She looked at Edwin.

'I think you'd best go now, Mr Glover. Mrs Mallinson is really very tired.'

He rose reluctantly. 'Aye, very well.' He bent to brush his lips against Violet's forehead. 'I'll come see thee again tomorrow, love, never fret, and I'll do what tha wants first thing in the morning. Sleep well now.'

She smiled, a weak smile of gratitude. 'I know. Goodnight, Edwin.'

He strode away, emotion tightening his throat. At the doorway he glanced back. She looked so tiny, so fragile in that cold, antiseptic bed. As she raised a slow hand to wave to him, he had the strangest feeling that it might possibly be the last glimpse he would ever have of her. All those wasted years . . .

He rushed away down the corridor, trying to blink away the tears that scalded his eyelids.

The ward sister, seeing that the last visitor had left, took a lozenge from her pocket and popped it into her mouth. For years now she had sworn by the efficacy of Moorhouse's Miracle Cough Drops and was convinced that it was the sanitising effect of their mentholated flavour which had kept her safe from all the infections which daily surrounded her. Trouble was, they were becoming harder to come by these days.

Sucking vigorously, she drew towards her the sheaf of papers on the desk and read the doctor's notes.

'*Mrs Violet Mallinson*,' she read. '*Bright's Disease. Early symptoms of kidney failure. Liquid diet only. Copious blood in urine. Pulse rate falling.*'

The nurse dipped a pen in the inkstand and scratched more words on the notes.

'*Eight p.m. Continued high fever. Pulse slow and erratic. Condition continuing to—*' She paused, uncertain how to spell 'deteriorate', then, making up her mind, she wrote, '*to worsen.*'

THIRTEEN

For days now Amy had not quite been feeling herself. Not sick, she told herself firmly, but a curious sensation of being apart, detached from the rest of the world, seeing events around her as though through a veil. Light-headed, that's how it felt, as Lionel once told her it felt to drink too much ale.

It was hard to summon up interest when Morgan was telling her about the Simpsons one morning as they were changing the bedlinen.

'Funny folk they are, not from hereabouts. Down South they come from, I'm told, but they're not like us. Very quiet, both of 'em. Thought they was a married couple, but they're not. Brother and sister, they are.'

'Are they?' Amy could show no interest, but Morgan did not appear to notice. She limped to the far side of Tobias' bed and held a corner of the mattress.

'Give it a good shake, Amy. Goosedown gets so lumpy. Our own geese, tha knows. Aye, I were telling thee. That Biddy Simpson never speaks, but Clem's not quite so stand-offish. He has spoken once or twice coming out of chapel. Happen we ought to invite them to tea.'

Amy's nose began to itch, tickled by the goose down. She rubbed it vigorously, and Morgan laughed.

'Itchy nose? Know what that means?'

'No – what?'

'A kiss, a curse or meet with a fool, they say. Better watch out, Amy.' Laughing, she fluttered a clean sheet over the bed. In silence Amy tucked in her side and replaced the pillows.

It was when the two women were walking back to the farm from the pump, each carrying a pail of water, that Morgan pointed at Biddy Simpson.

'Here she comes – with that handsome brother of hers,' Morgan whispered, then she nodded to the pretty fair-headed girl in a shawl. Amy saw Morgan's eyes turn instantly to the young man.

'Morning, Biddy. Morning, Clem.'

They both nodded and murmured, 'Morning,' but made no move to stop and talk. The young man's gaze rested on Morgan, and she lowered her eyes until they had passed. Once out of earshot, she spoke excitedly.

'Didst see him? Isn't he handsome?'

Amy agreed. 'And the girl was pretty, too.'

'Oh, her,' Morgan snorted. 'She knows it, too. She won't look at any of the lads – 'cepting our Tobias, that is. I reckon she fancies him.'

Amy was startled. 'Does he know? Does he like her?'

'He never notices lasses. No time for 'em. But I've seen the way she watches him in chapel. She'd cast a spell on him if she could, I'll be bound. Tell thee what, though, Amy, that Clem Simpson could cast a spell on me any time. Not as he's likely to, I fear.'

'He was certainly looking hard at you,' Amy assured her. 'I saw him.'

Morgan flushed. 'I wish tha were right, but what lad would look at someone like me? I'll limp me way to the grave still a spinster, I reckon.'

'That's not true, I'm sure of it. A good man can recognise a beauty, and beauty's not always on the outside, you know.' Amy found herself speaking almost savagely, protectively. Only a fool would look on a girl like Morgan, club-foot or not, with anything but love, she thought.

That Biddy Simpson, now. She was pretty, no doubt of that, but there was a cold air about her, nothing one could find instantly attractive. Amy had seen the way the girl's eyes had travelled critically over her, questioning and cold. Strange, thought Amy, but she had felt hostile herself, rejecting the notion of that girl fancying Tobias. She certainly was not the right woman for him. He deserved better.

Her thoughts then turned to her mother. She must go and see her, reassure her. Tomorrow – yes, tomorrow was Saturday and she would go back to Hawksmoor.

'By all means,' said Morgan. 'I'm off to watch Tobias at the trials anyway.'

Amy bit her lip. 'Oh – I'd forgotten.'

'No harm. I'll be there with him, and happen Uncle Ben and all. Toby has high hopes of Gyp this year.'

'I hope he does well, only – I'd like to see my mother.'

'Course tha would, after all these weeks. I wonder tha didn't speak of her before. Toby and I reckoned tha were probably an orphan, since tha said nowt about family. Father too, hast tha?'

'He died when I was a baby. I've a brother, that's all.'

'Oh, same as me! At least' – Morgan's voice lowered – 'he's my half-brother, but no one ever had a better. He's a real grand fellow, is our Tobias. Everyone thinks the world of him, quiet as he is. I reckon there's not a lass in the village as wouldn't give her eye-teeth to catch him.'

Amy nodded. 'Including that Biddy Simpson?'

Morgan tossed her head. 'Her? She's not for the likes of him. She doesn't even talk like us, her with her south-country voice. Nay, our Toby's in no hurry to wed, and when he does, it'll be to some lass with summat about her, not Biddy Simpson.'

On Saturday morning Amy hurried along Reed Street filled with eagerness to be going home again, and a twinge of guilt at her neglect. She was not prepared for the news the next-door neighbour delivered.

'Nay, there's nobody in, love, because Lionel's at work and thy mam were taken to hospital last week.'

'Hospital? An accident?' The words stuttered from her mouth, her brain numbed by the news.

'Nay, she were poorly. Kidney trouble, thy Lionel said.'

Kidney trouble. That pain which troubled her and she never would discuss; Amy recalled now, flooding

186

with guilt and fear, how often her mother would hold a hand to her side, her mouth set and tiredness etching her face. She had been sicker than she would let on – and Amy had never guessed.

Her feet could not carry her to the Infirmary swiftly enough. The ward was quiet, save for a woman moaning softly in a corner bed and the nurse's footsteps on the wooden floor.

'Mrs Mallinson is rather poorly, dear. Her daughter, you say? Well, just for ten minutes, then. Talking does tire her so.'

Mother lay almost unrecognisable on the pillows, her thinning hair unpinned and outspread around her face. Her eyes were closed, and her skin was yellow as parchment. All the life seemed to have gone from her, and Amy felt the deep pain encircling her heart. She stood by the bedside, reluctant to waken her, and touched gently the workworn hand lying on the sheet.

Mother's eyes opened slowly, remained expressionless for a moment, then brightened into recognition.

'Amy!' The thin voice registered disbelief and joy. Amy pulled a chair close, sat and leaned to kiss her forehead. It was dry and hot.

'Oh, Mother! Forgive me! I should have come back before – I had no idea!'

'Amy, my love. I thought you were dead.' The voice was so fragile it sounded as if a breath of a breeze would have wafted it away. 'They told me you had smallpox.'

'No, no, Mother! Oh, how could they! It was only a rash – strawberries – it was only Aunt Charlotte who panicked and thought it was smallpox. Oh, Mother!'

She bent her head and pressed it against her mother's hand. She felt a gentle touch on her hair.

'No matter, sweetheart. You're alive. A miracle. I'm happy.' The words came slowly, with difficulty and a laboured effort to draw breath between each phrase.

Amy felt fear. Mother was dying. She seized her hand, willing her own life-force into the stricken body.

'Yes, I'm alive. Everything is all right, Mother. I'll come home and care for you. You'll get better soon, you'll see.'

Her mother smiled, a slow, tired smile. She could find no more strength to speak. Amy tried to stem the tears of grief and guilt.

'You *will* get better, Mother, you *must*! We need you, Lionel and I! Oh, God, Mother, I'm sorry.'

There was no stemming the tears now. The nurse came back and tapped her on the shoulder.

'You'd best leave now, Miss Mallinson. It's time for your mother's medication. You can return later today, if the doctor thinks she's up to it.'

One last kiss, one last pressure of hand on shrunken hand, and Amy turned to go. At the doorway she looked back. Mother was no more than a slight mound under starched sheets and counterpane. Choking, she stumbled away down the corridor.

'*A kiss, a curse, or meet with a fool.*'

That night Amy sat alone by the fireside at Jericho Farm, her head sunk on her chest. She was roused from painful reverie by the sound of voices outside in the yard. The kitchen door burst open.

Morgan stood there, her eyes shining as she flung off her shawl. 'Tobias won, Amy! He won first prize with Gyp! Ah, he's that pleased.' Amy looked up at her, but words would not come. Morgan, seeing the stricken look in her eyes, came quickly to her. 'Amy, what's up? What's happened?'

She took hold of Amy's hands and knelt in front of her, her eyes searching the other girl's with concern. Tears blinding her eyes, Amy shook her head.

'My mother – she's dead,' she croaked.

Morgan gasped, then flung her arms around Amy's shoulders. 'Oh, Amy! When did it happen?'

When Amy managed to control herself she sat upright. 'Today. I wasn't with her. When I went back to the hospital, she'd gone.'

There were men's voices outside. Amy sprang to her feet. 'I can't talk tonight. Oh, Morgan! Tell Tobias I'm sorry – I can't!'

She sped upstairs to the safety of her room as she heard the latch click and men's heavy footsteps. She was aware of voices murmuring in the kitchen below and then silence. She stood by the window looking out at the wisps of cloud trailing across the moon and could feel nothing but the leaden weight of grief mingled with anger. She wished she could give vent to the anger and frustration welling inside her with tears, but none would come. She was left with a feeling of grief and guilt.

The moon retreated behind the clouds, and the image heightened her sense of desolation. Soon it would be harvest moon. Harvest. '*As ye sow, so shall ye reap.*'

She was turning away from the window to begin to undress for bed, when there was a tap at the door.

'Amy, can I come in?' It was Tobias' voice.

Slowly she crossed to the door to open it. He stood there, his broad frame filling the doorway. By the light of the candle she could see his uncertain expression.

'Morgan told me. I'm sorry, lass.'

He made no move to come into the room. Dumbly Amy nodded and turned away. For a moment there was uneasy silence. He cleared his throat.

'I brought thee this. Wrong time now, I reckon.'

She glanced back. With an embarrassed look on his dark features he was holding out a small plaster figure, a shepherdess with a crook in her hand, her gaudy gown painted in crimson.

'It's nobbut a fairing,' he muttered. 'A token, I meant it as a gift. I'm sorry.'

He laid it on the dresser and strode quickly out. Amy

189

looked at it without picking it up, and felt touched. A cheap fairing it might be, but it was a gesture that spoke volumes. Violet Mallinson's heart would have been warmed by such a gesture.

Amy flung herself on the bed and wept, sobs shuddering her body until at last, near cock-crow, sleep claimed her exhausted frame.

The heartache and dizzy nausea that remained with Amy over the succeeding days rendered the funeral only a hazy memory in the weeks that followed. Even Lionel seemed too overwhelmed with shock to evince surprise at Amy's reappearance. Between them they had got through all the formalities of death like mindless machines, incapable of logical thought.

'We'll have to let Aunt Charlotte know,' Lionel said, his lip trembling.

'No!' said Amy. 'She wouldn't recognise her living—'

'But we must. I'll send word.'

Edwin Glover proved himself a staunch friend. Desolate though he was, he helped Amy to see to all the essential details.

'And if there's anything I can do for thee, lass, anytime, tha's only to say. I know how much thy mother cared about thee both.'

'You're very kind. Thanks, Mr Glover.'

'Papers to sort out, owt that needs doing, think on. I've to see to the solicitors, any road, so it'll be no bother. I know where to find thee now, so I'll let thee know what happens.'

'Thanks. I can manage the papers.' He was a kindly man, clearly devoted to Mother. Under no circumstances could she let his eyes fall on Mother's diaries. If he did not already know about Frederic Newman, then his memory of her must remain untarnished.

None of the Holroyds came to the funeral. Amy found herself hoping Charles would suddenly appear at the graveside, but he did not. Numbed as she was already, it hardly seemed to matter.

Lionel was reluctant to remain in the house in Reed Street alone.

'If you're going back up to the farm, I'll stay at Maggie's for a bit. Mrs Braithwaite told me I'm welcome. I'll go there while we decide what to do.'

His bag packed, he left with Maggie. It was good to see the girl on his arm – she was a good girl; she'd see him over the worst Amy thought. She sorted her mother's papers alone. Despite the sunshine outside, the little house seemed cold and cheerless without the loving presence of Mother.

The September evening sunlight spilled across the table as she sat reading.

'Oh, my beloved Frederic, however long I live I shall never forget these nights of passion with you! Such torment and yet such delight! Rarely can two creatures have experienced such blissful union, a joy sublime I shall carry with me to the end of my days.'

Amy laid the exercise book down and gazed out through the dusty window on to the street. *Dear Mother, how I misjudged you, how angry and shocked I was to read those words once. But I was ignorant and inexperienced. Now I too have known that passion you spoke of . . .*

Charles. With him she had lived that wild passion her mother knew, experienced for the first time ecstasy such as Mother meant. Charles – the man she had dreamt of and longed for ever since. But he had not sought her. He had not come to the graveyard. It was saddening to feel disappointment in one's idol.

But these days remorse weighed more heavily upon her than pining for her lost love. Again and again she recalled the last meeting, here in this room, with Mother.

'*I'll have you out of that house – I insist on it – or I swear I'll never call you daughter again.*'

'*I'm sorry, Mother. I must lead my own life.*'

The cruelty of life, never to give her the chance to make peace, to make amends. All her days it would haunt and hurt to know that she had left this house in disagreement, in defiance.

A leaden weight lay in the pit of Amy's stomach. Even as she made her way back to Jericho Farm she felt sick and dispirited beyond help from anyone.

Amy stood by the chicken coop, scattering corn from the bowl to the hens squawking and clucking all around her, while Morgan, inside the coop, was filling her basket with eggs. She could hear Morgan singing, '*As I walked out one May morning.*'

The reason for the girl's contentment was clear. After the harvest festival at chapel on Sunday, Clem Simpson had invited her to go with him to the celebration tea and buns that followed. All the villagers were in festive mood now the harvest was safely home. Not that there was much to harvest, in this bleak country where mainly sheep and cattle thrived. But the chapel had been liberally decked with cabbages and apples and home-baked loaves and plaits of bread and pots of home-made jam and jars of fruit preserved to brighten the long, dark days of winter.

As she scattered the last handful of corn she heard the sound of whistling. Tobias was leaning a ladder against the side of the grey stone farmhouse and climbing up, a stack of roof tiles balanced on his shoulder. Morgan stooped to emerge from the coop, her face flushed and her basket filled.

'Here, Amy, take this. I want to catch that old hen there – she'll do fine for the stewpot.'

Handing over the basket, she hobbled after the hen, who seemed to sense danger, fluttering this way and that out of reach before she finally caught it. She carried it up to the farm courtyard, its wings pinioned between her arm and body. Amy watched her sit on the low stool, hold the feathered body firmly in one hand and stretch its neck across her knee with the other. With a swift, deft movement she jerked till the neck cracked. The bird fluttered for a few moments and then lay still. Amy turned away.

'Nay, don't take on,' said Morgan cheerfully. 'Chickens have to be killed, specially when they lay no more eggs. Tha'll enjoy the stew same as the rest of us.'

Amy smiled bleakly, regretting she had let her distaste show. Morgan shielded her eyes against the sun and stared up at the roof. 'I know yon roof needs doing before the bad weather comes but I wish he'd leave it today.'

There was a clatter of boots on the rungs. Tobias lifted more tiles from the next stack at the foot of the ladder.

'Nay, tha could leave that to another day,' Morgan reproved him.

'Tha wanted it doing. Tha's nagged enough,' he replied.

'Tha needs thy strength for tonight.'

He cast her a quick glance and started up the ladder. 'Makes no odds,' he muttered.

Amy looked questioningly at Morgan. 'Wrestling match,' the girl explained. 'He's won every harvest time this last three years. There's not a man in the valley as is stronger nor our Toby. He always wins a gold sovereign – very useful, is that. We could fair make use of it right now.'

She spoke with quiet pride and Amy felt warm towards her, so loving and loyal towards her brother. She was plucking the chicken with swift dexterity that spoke of years of practice. She glanced up at Amy.

'Tha'll come and watch, won't that? Do thee good to get out a bit.'

'I'd like to – if Tobias doesn't mind.'

'Him mind? He'll not even notice! Once our Toby sets his mind to summat, he gets on with it, choose how. He'd not notice if the Queen herself were there.'

Morgan was right, Amy reflected, as she sat that warm evening on the grass near the makeshift wrestling ring on the village green. Firm sturdy stakes driven into the ground surmounted by a thick rope marked out the area where the main bout was to be held. Dusk was thickening, and oil lamps stood ready at each corner of the ring.

It was good to be out and amongst humanity again, mingling with the crowd of eager spectators rather than still brooding at Jericho Farm. There was such enthusiasm and vitality in the air that she could feel her drained senses beginning to recharge. She was glad she'd allowed Morgan to persuade her to come.

Morgan too was excited, she could see, for Clem Simpson stood not far away from them amongst a knot of people. It was clear from his glances in their direction that it would not be long before he found some reason to stroll across to join them. Biddy Simpson stood beside her brother, her demure downcast looks inviting attention from the men in the group.

'Just look at her,' muttered Morgan, 'simpering away with the lads as if butter wouldn't melt in her mouth. Fair makes thee sick, she does.'

Clem broke away from the group and came across.

'I hope your brother's all he's cracked up to be,' he said to Morgan with a cheery smile. 'I've just been persuaded to bet a shilling on him. I hope he doesn't let me down.'

Morgan pouted. 'He'll not do that. Who's he down to fight?'

Sensing invitation, Clem knelt on the grass beside her. 'It's a fellow called Sykes. He's beaten all the others easily, so now he's up against the champion. Big fellow he is, thighs like an ox.'

Morgan nodded. 'I know Jack Sykes. He's a sturdy enough lad, but he'll be hard put to it to beat our Tobias.'

Someone lit the oil lamps and it was as if their glow in the deepening gloom attracted people like moths to the flame. Bodies pressed closer. Morgan and Amy scrambled to their feet so as not to lose their ringside positions. Biddy appeared at Amy's side.

'We've got a shilling on Tobias Clegg. Have you laid a bet on him?'

Amy gave her a quick glance. Her southern voice was as disagreeable as her question. 'No, I haven't.'

The girl shrugged. 'I thought you'd have had faith in him,' she said with a sly smile.

At that moment Amy saw him stepping into the ring. He was naked to the waist and the light from the lamps cast dark shadows on his face, his expression one of deep concentration. On the far side of the ring another man climbed in, also stripped to the waist, a big, bull-like creature with matted fair hair. He clasped his fists together and raised them in the air to the accompaniment of delighted cheers and boos from the crowd. A third man in jacket and corduroy breeches came to the centre of the ring and held up his hands. He waited for the roaring of the crowd to subside.

'Ladies and gents, we now come to the final round of the wrestling championship,' he announced. 'Jack Sykes, having beaten all the other contestants, will now challenge the reigning champion, Tobias Clegg. The best of three falls, or a knock-out to decide.'

Above the cries Amy could hear him admonishing the two men to fight fair, and then he stepped out of the ring. A hand bell clanged, and the two contestants began to move, warily, from their respective corners.

Once more Amy found herself admiring the breadth of Tobias' shoulders and the firm muscle beneath the flesh. His bull-like opponent was even bigger, over six feet tall and massively built. But he moved with surprising speed, closing in with a grunt to lock Tobias in a vicious embrace. The two men strained and heaved, each swaying in the attempt to overbalance the other. Sweat began to glisten on their backs.

Amy, ignorant of the rules of the sport, was aware only that Tobias had his work cut out to defeat this giant. Minute after minute passed, to the roared encouragement of the crowd, and finally the two bodies toppled and rolled across the grass. There was a flailing of limbs, tangling and locking until it became impossible to distinguish which limbs belonged to which man. Amy could only watch for the dark head of Tobias in the mêlée.

She saw Sykes, his chest across Tobias' body, gouging his thumb into Tobias' eyes. The referee could not see; his view was shielded by Sykes' thick body. After what seemed like hours of watching writhing, tangled flesh, Amy heard the bell ring. Both men rose and stumbled to their corners. There was a scent of hot flesh mingled with sweet grass. Someone poured a pail of water over Tobias' head and he shook himself. Amy felt the droplets on her cheek.

She saw him compose himself, waiting for the bell to ring again. He looked magnificent, his shoulders gleaming in the lamplight and his black hair glistening and unkempt. He had an eager, wild look about him, more animal than man, yet there was still control and dignity in his tense body. The bell rang.

During the second round Tobias managed to throw his man and pin his shoulders to the ground. The referee called, 'One-two-three!' The crowd roared its delight as Tobias returned to his corner and the big man scrambled to his feet with a malevolent look in his eyes. Morgan was jumping up and down in excitement.

'Keep it up, lad! Tha can beat him!'

The big man sprang, catching Tobias unawares so

that he fell back against the rope. Sykes pressed his full weight against Tobias, punching at his head. When Tobias, straining hard, at last managed to throw him off and pull himself upright, Amy could see the glaring red weals on his back where the rope had burned the skin. Sykes lunged, kicking Tobias off balance and bringing him crashing to the ground, hurling his massive weight on Tobias' neck and shoulders.

'One-two-three!' called the referee. 'Second fall to Sykes.'

The crowd cheered. It evidently met their approval that the combatants had scored one fall apiece. Everything now hinged on the third fall.

Morgan squeezed Amy's arm. Biddy was watching imperturbably. The bell rang for the third round. The two bodies locked in combat again. Amy held her breath, willing Tobias with all her might to bring the big man down. Her nails dug into the palms of her hands as she watched his sinewy muscles tauten under the skin as he strained, grunting.

Twice the bodies locked, fell, rolled and fought, eluded and rose to their feet again. She could see the men's eyes glinting as they watched each for a sign that might indicate the next move. The crowd, too, seemed to be holding its breath.

'Come on, Toby, tha can do it,' Morgan breathed.

Suddenly, from nowhere, a rock came hurtling into the ring and struck Tobias with a crack on his forehead. She heard him moan and saw him stagger. Blood gushed from the cut near his eye and began to spurt down his face. For a moment he looked bewildered, disbelieving. The other man, seeing his opportunity, rushed in.

Amy could not be certain what happened. There seemed to be a raining of blows from Sykes' fists and Tobias stumbling, staggering, trying vainly to see through the welter of blood pouring down his face and dripping from his chin. Amy heard Morgan's gasp.

197

'Why doesn't the referee stop it?' Amy exclaimed. 'He can't see!'

Morgan shook her head helplessly. Tobias was swinging his arms, blindly trying to find his mark. The next moment the big man hurled his full weight at him, bringing him down with a crash. Then he lay full-length along Tobias' body, pinning his arms above his head.

'One-two-three!'

The referee was back in the ring, holding Sykes' bloodstained arm high in the air. The crowd bellowed, booing and cheering. 'The champion!' shouted the referee.

Tobias was sitting on the grass, blinking and wiping the blood from his eyes with the back of his hand. Amy felt a wave of nausea sweep over her and clutched the rope to steady herself. Morgan ducked under the rope and knelt by Tobias.

Someone brought water in a pail and a cloth. Morgan began cleaning the blood and filth from her brother's face. Vaguely Amy was aware of the clink as money changed hands around her, and then the crowd began to melt away. Anger surged through her; anger that Tobias had been robbed of a fair fight, and anger at her own weakness.

Clem and Biddy Simpson lingered nearby.

'Well, that's my shilling down the drain,' said Clem.

Tobias was leaning against a corner-post, pale, and the blood still running from his temple. Biddy went up to him.

'Well, I don't think too badly of you, Tobias Clegg,' she said, giving him an arch smile and, taking her brother's arm, she walked away.

Amy flared. 'It's not his fault – somebody threw a rock – you must have seen it!'

Biddy cast her brother an amused smile. 'So that's your story, is it? At least you lost nothing on him,' she added deliberately. The blood thundered in Amy's head, and the next moment darkness closed about her.

Next morning Morgan came into the bedroom and drew back the curtains, letting in a stream of sunlight.

'I don't know who's the worse patient, thee or Tobias,' she said, turning to the bed. 'Tha were both in a bit of a state last night.'

Amy struggled to sit up. 'How is Tobias?'

'Middling. That cut of his were hard work to staunch. I tried marigold leaves and then bruised nettles – never been known to fail before. I'd have tried cobwebs but there were none in the house as I could see. Took me half the night to make it stop bleeding. But what with thee passing out and all—'

'I'm sorry, Morgan. I don't know what came over me.'

'Doesn't tha? Well I do. It's as plain as the nose on thy face. No wonder tha left home.'

Amy looked up sharply. 'What do you mean?'

Morgan laughed. 'Now come on, I'm not daft, nor is Tobias. It were clear what were wrong with thee. Tha's expecting – that's it, isn't it?'

FOURTEEN

Amy swallowed hard. 'Well, I was beginning to suspect—'

'Suspect? It's as clear as day. I thought as much when tha acted strange over that chicken yesterday. Last night I knew for sure.'

Amy hung her head. 'I'm sorry, Morgan.'

'Nay, tha's no need to be sorry – not to me.'

Shame was burning Amy's cheeks. She hadn't

wanted to admit what she suspected, even to herself. But now Morgan had put it into words, there was no escaping it.

'Art going to wed?' asked Morgan.

Amy shook her head. 'I can't.'

Morgan cocked her dark head on one side. 'Can't? Why ever not? Oh – he's not wed already, is he? Oh, Amy!'

'No, it's not that. It's just – oh, it's impossible, that's all.'

'Tha'll tell him, though, surely.'

'No.' There was no hesitation. Charles must never know, she decided. If he'd loved her as he swore he did, he'd have moved heaven and earth to find her before now – she would have done, in his place. No. Whatever pain and difficulty lay ahead, she would undertake it alone. Oh, God, if only Mother were still alive! She got up out of bed.

'Can I stay here a while, Morgan, until I find somewhere to go? I can't go back to my mother's house. I'll try to find something soon, I promise.'

'That tha won't,' replied Morgan emphatically. 'Tha'll stay here. Who better to give thee a hand nor me? I've had plenty of practice at bringing bairns into the world, and I'll see thine in – that's if tha'll let me.'

She held out her arms, and Amy felt them close warmly about her. If ever she had needed affection and reassurance, it was now.

Over the next few weeks only once did Tobias refer, indirectly, to Amy's condition.

'There's no question of tha leaving here, lass, dost understand? This is thy home for as long as tha wants to stay.'

Amy felt humbled. Neither brother nor sister reproached or questioned her over her behaviour or the disgrace she might bring upon them. Instead they accepted her without reserve, showing her all the concern and affection she might have expected from

200

her own family. Life continued as usual in Jericho Farm, except for one thing. It became clear that Uncle Ben was dying slowly.

Ben Clegg had been an amiable, uncomplaining man all his life and he saw no reason to have any fuss about his dying. He knew he was going, for he grew daily weaker and less capable and finally he was forced to take to his bed.

'I'm nobbut running down,' he said, 'like yon grandfather clock in the living room – only difference being as tha can't pull the weights and get the pendulum swinging again with me. But I'm not complaining – I've had a good innings.'

Uncle Ben was near enough eighty, Tobias reckoned. He was in fact their great-uncle. 'It's a good age,' Tobias said. 'Like most Cleggs, they can survive owt!'

As the golden-brown leaves of October changed in November to black-lacquered tracery on the cobblestones, Uncle Ben's face grew cadaverous, for he refused to eat. Night and day he could be heard talking to his Hannah.

'It'll not be long now, lass. Tha won't have to wait long. I'll be that glad to be back with thee.'

Amy, busy about the work on the farm, was relieved that Morgan and Tobias' attention was diverted from her. Clem Simpson called one Sunday to ask if he could accompany Morgan to chapel, and Amy saw how eagerly the girl whipped off her apron and prepared to go. She hobbled out of the door with him, her pretty face aglow. He took to calling regularly, and sometimes his sister came with him.

Her gaze always lingered on Tobias but he seemed to take little notice. Nor did he ever accompany them to chapel, and Amy welcomed the hour she spent alone with him. Never questioning, never forcing conversation, his presence was sufficient to give her a sense of peace and safety. Even when she sat reading again the letter from Edwin Glover, Tobias asked no questions.

'My dear Amy, I have now concluded the correspondence with your dear mother's solicitors in London. It was her will that what she possessed be divided between you and your brother Lionel – he to inherit the house and furniture and fifty pounds, yourself to acquire her shares and an equal sum.

'I have not yet been able to ascertain the exact value of the shares, but your mother did tell me they had very little value. The choice is yours, whether you wish to retain them in the hope of improvement, or to sell them. I will be happy to deal with the matter on your behalf. Sincere good wishes, your friend, Edwin Glover.'

He might as well sell them, Amy reflected. There was a new life on the way, and she must plan. She must put all thought of Charles out of her mind, however painful it might be, and think only of the coming child. The fifty pounds from Mother's will, and whatever the shares might fetch, would be invaluable.

Lionel must be told about the child. She wrote to him, telling him all except the name of the father of her child. His reply came swiftly.

'Dear Amy. I'm so sorry, but there's no point crying over spilt milk. We must plan. Maggie and I intend to marry in the spring. I see no reason why we shouldn't all set up home at Reed Street. You and the baby will both be welcome. It's always been your home as well as mine. Maggie and me don't give a toss what the neighbours might think. Your loving brother, Lionel.'

She smiled as she read. Dear Lionel, she thought; no question, no complaint, just down-to-earth proposals.

He had more than a streak of Mother in him. She considered. There would be comfort in the familiarity of Reed Street but she was loth to intrude upon Lionel's wedded life. It would be no good for him and Maggie, and in time they might well have a family of their own and then the little house would be overcrowded. How much better it would be for a baby to be brought up here, in the clean, fresh air of the countryside, far away from the filth and smoke of Hawksmoor.

She sighed and went out into the misty yard to fetch the washing from the line. By the time she came in, her fingers were numb with cold. She hung the peg-bag on the hook near the scullery sink and then began folding the damp washing. Morgan was beating up the batter for Yorkshire pudding.

'Uncle Ben's asking for thee,' she said. 'He wants thee to go up.'

The washing folded, Amy went up to his room. The old man lay in bed, his face as pale as the pillow but his eyes bright.

'Eh, lass, how hast bin? I've not seen thee this last day or two.'

'I'm well, Uncle Ben. I've been busy.'

'Aye, tha'rt a good lass. Tha'll make someone a good wife. I told Tobias he could do worse.'

Amy blushed. 'Oh, Uncle Ben.'

'I mean it, lass. I said he'd do well if he could persuade thee. Tha's well brought up – anyone can see – but there's no airs and graces about thee for all that.'

He laboured to draw another breath. 'Tha's got a gentle nature too, and that counts for summat. My Hannah were like thee, and we had fifty years' happiness. There's nowt so bad for a man as having a scold for a wife. And what's more' – he wagged an approving finger – 'it's plain as day that tha's an honest lass, and that's to be prized above all else – virtue in a woman. I told him.'

Amy, her eyes downcast, could not bring herself to look the old man in the face. 'And what did Tobias say?' she murmured.

'Him? Nowt – but that's Tobias all over. He never says what he's thinking.'

And well he might not, thought Amy, but it must have been hard for him to listen to praise of her virtue when he knew otherwise.

The old man sighed. 'I grow weary, lass. Let me sleep a bit. Promise me, though, if our Tobias gets round to it, tha won't turn him down out of hand. Tha could do worse thisself than have him. He's a good lad, as loyal and honest a man as ever tha'll find.'

'I know,' said Amy. 'Sleep now, and I'll bring your supper up later.'

By the time she reached the door and turned, Uncle Ben's eyes were already closed. From the kitchen below rose the smell of hot fat. Morgan's Yorkshire puddings were already in the oven and it would not be long before Tobias came down from the hill meadows for his supper.

Amy was climbing uphill over the field of stubble where the last haymaking had robbed it of its lush summer grass. She was panting, conscious of her thickening weight. Climbing the hill back to Jericho Farm was far harder now than it used to be after delivering eggs to the inn in the valley.

A figure came striding down towards her. It was Tobias, his hair blowing in the damp breeze. He must have left in a hurry, not to be wearing his cap. His dark face, the white scar prominent on his temple, wore a look of distraction. She felt a sudden presentiment.

'He's gone, Amy. Get back up to Morgan.'

She frowned, bewildered. 'What? Who?'

'Uncle Ben. In his sleep. I'm off down to the undertaker's.' He was about to go on downhill, then stopped. 'Oh – he left this for thee.'

Thrusting a hand in his pocket he pulled out something, which he offered to Amy. Wondering, she took it, then raised questioning eyes to Tobias. 'A penny? For me?'

'Luck-penny, he said, to make sure tha'd come back.'

'I don't understand—'

Tobias was fidgeting. 'I told him about thee and thy love-child, and tha were probably going home.'

'I see.' She looked down at the coin. This was no time to tell Tobias she would much rather stay here.

'I mun go,' said Tobias, and rushed away.

Amy continued to climb uphill, her heart heavy. She had been about to write to Lionel, to explain that she would not be coming back to Reed Street, but now . . . The last thing in the world she would do was to stay and embarrass Tobias if he would prefer her gone. It saddened her also that Uncle Ben's faith in her had been shattered at the end, for it had clearly been a dream he cherished, to see her and Tobias make a match of it. It had not occurred to him that Tobias might be glad to see the back of her.

She would leave Jericho Farm. There'd be no need then for Morgan and Tobias to have to make up a tale about her being a widow lady to explain her condition. With luck she'd be gone before it became evident.

She ran a hand down over her belly. *Ah, child, we must shift to fend for ourselves, you and I.* The last thing in the world she wanted was to leave Jericho Farm. Apart from the longing for Charles, she had never known such peace as in the last four months.

Charles. Oh, my love, I little knew what I was inviting that night by the tarn when, in the heat of passion, I cried out to you 'Fill me!' Ah, my love, you did that, with a vengeance – and look where it's got me.

The kitchen seemed unnaturally quiet without Uncle Ben. It was natural enough that brother and sister and their guest should talk in subdued tones until after the funeral, but even the kettle seemed to sing on the hob less joyfully, the fire to crackle and hiss less energetically, and when Gyp came in from the yard she lay despondently on the rag rug with her ears laid back and her eyes mournful. No one seemed inclined to occupy Uncle Ben's chair. His clay pipe and tobacco still lay on the mantelshelf alongside the clock, where they had lain since before he took to his bed.

Though they had not voiced their affection for him while he lived, all three missed him sorely. One night Tobias sat at the kitchen table after the supper dishes had been cleared away, writing replies to the letters of condolence they had received. From time to time he sighed as he wrote. It was clear to Amy that he found it hard to express his appreciation; a man of few words in speech, it was not easy to find them now to write of his feelings.

Morgan limped across the room and around his chair, trailing a hand across his shoulders. 'Shall I reply to some of them, Toby? It's only fair I should do some.'

'I mun do it meself.'

Amy cleared her throat. 'I must write a letter too – to my brother, to arrange to go home. When would it suit you both that I should go?'

'I'd rather tha didn't,' said Tobias.

'Not write?'

'Not go home.' His dark eyes met hers. Amy's eyebrows rose. Morgan hobbled round the table to her.

'He's right, tha knows, Amy – tha'd be best off here. I doubt thy new sister-in-law knows much about childbirth.'

Amy was overcome. 'I confess, I'd rather stay here, but are you both sure?'

'Aye,' said Tobias shortly then, throwing down the

206

pen, he stood up. 'I've had enough. I'll do the rest tomorrow. Get the cards out, Morgan, and we'll have a game of cribbage.'

When Amy went to bed she was almost content. *If only Charles were here*. The need for love whispered in the wind outside the window. Ah well, in the meantime she could be content with the affection and concern of the brother and sister downstairs in the kitchen playing cards together. She could account herself a very lucky woman.

Amy wrote to Lionel, and then became absorbed again in the day-to-day life of the farm. Edwin Glover, true to his word, saw to Mother's will and in due time sent Amy her fifty pounds bequest.

That would be more than sufficient for the baby's needs, Amy decided, and she gave no instructions for the sale of the shares. Morgan, eager for life to return to normal, plunged into the preparations for Christmas.

'It's stir-up Sunday this week,' she said. 'It's high time the plum puddings and the fruit cake were made else they'll never be matured in time. Sooner the cake's made, moister it'll be.'

Tobias too kept busy. Now the days were growing shorter there were hardly enough daylight hours, and Amy saw little of him except when he came in briefly at midday to snatch some food. One afternoon he came in, startling Amy by dumping a cabbage sharply on the table and sitting down to pull off his boots.

'Women!' he exclaimed irritably.

Morgan, who had followed him in from the yard, took off her shawl with a thoughtful expression. She smiled wryly. 'Not thee, Amy. It's that Biddy Simpson who's riled him.'

'Why? What's she done?'

Morgan laughed. 'She's done nowt, only hang about our Toby and keep on moithering about Christmas and sending cards and all that. She fancies him. She's as good as told him she's sending him a card, and she expects one from him.'

'Cards is expensive,' muttered Tobias. 'I can't afford 'em. What does she want hanging about our pigsty for, any road?'

'Never heed,' soothed Morgan. 'Tha can slaughter the old sow in the morning.'

'Well, keep that woman away from me, that's all,' muttered Tobias. 'She sets me nerves on edge.'

Morgan took hold of the bowl on the dresser. 'Here, we've been mixing the plum pudding,' she told him. 'We've been waiting of thee to have a stir, then I can put in the threepenny bit and the ring and the thimble.' She smiled impishly. 'I'll make certain Biddy Simpson doesn't get that ring. If right were done, Toby should get the coin, me the thimble, and thee the ring. Ah well, we shall see.'

No ring for me, thought Amy. *My child will have to carry the stigma of being a bastard all his life.* But she held her tongue, conscious that she could not voice the thought, for Morgan herself had had to live down the same slur.

The next morning Morgan was down in the village. Towards midday the kitchen door opened suddenly, admitting a blast of cold, sleety air as Tobias entered. He came across to the table, his dark eyes probing Amy's.

'I mun talk to thee.' The urgency in his tone made Amy look away from the trail of muddy footmarks which would be sure to excite Morgan's anger. The look in Tobias' eyes disturbed her. It was hard to tell whether it was anger or anxiety.

'Will you have some soup? It's ready.'

'Nay, listen!' he exclaimed, peeling off his jacket and draping it over a chair. She could see a stain of blood on his sleeve. 'Just sit down and listen.'

She pulled out a chair and sat at the table. Tobias

sat too, leaning forward on his elbows. 'I've been thinking,' he said. 'Wilt tha marry me?'

Amy gasped. 'Tobias! Oh, no! I can't!'

His eyes darkened. 'Nay, listen,' he said urgently. 'I know tha loves someone else, but I've give the matter a lot of thought. I want thee to wed me.'

She stared, conscious that she must look stupid with her mouth agape, but she was bereft of words. She could only shake her head dumbly.

'Look,' he said earnestly, 'I'm not fooling meself. I just reckon it would be best – for both of us.'

She found her voice at last. 'Tobias, you're very kind, but you don't have to do this, just because it was Uncle Ben's wish.'

He jumped up and strode round the table, seizing her by the shoulders. 'Nay, not his wish – mine! I know tha loves that other fellow, but I want to look after thee. Let me wed thee and care for thee.' He swallowed hard, then went on, 'And it would give thy bairn a name.'

Amy's heart swelled. Clumsy he might be, but his heart was full of generosity. His work-roughened hands still lay on her shoulders, and there was reassurance in their grip. She could not bring herself to look him directly in the face. The bloodstain on his sleeve was level with her eyes.

Seeing where her gaze rested, he let go of her suddenly. 'Tha doesn't have to decide this minute,' he said roughly. 'But don't take too long – for the babby's sake. It would be best done before Christmas.'

He hesitated, waiting for a reaction. When no word came he added awkwardly, 'It'd fair please our Morgan to have thee for a sister. And I'd reckon it an honour.'

He snatched up his jacket and made for the door. Amy did not move. 'I mun get back to the pigsty,' he muttered.

'Tobias.'

He turned as she spoke his name. 'Aye?'

She rose slowly, gathering all her dignity with effort. 'Tobias, I am grateful to you. Your uncle was right – you are an honourable man, but you deserve better than a woman who – who—'

'Don't say it!' He jerked the words out with a savagery that surprised her. 'I won't have it! However it came about, it makes no odds to me! I know thee for an honest lass.'

She felt humbled by his faith in her. 'Listen, Tobias,' she said gently. 'I can't be less than honest with you. I can never love you – not the way a wife should love a husband, that is—'

'Fiddlesticks!' he snapped. 'I'm offering to wed thee because I want to. And what's more' – he took a half-step towards her, then stopped – 'tha doesn't have to be a wife – not that way, any road – oh hell! What I mean is, tha can do as tha likes – have thy own room. I just want thee to stay here so I can see to thee and thy bairn can have the Clegg name.'

Jerking the door open, he rushed out and slammed it behind him before Amy could reply. She sank down again on to the chair, laid her arms on the table and rested her forehead on her hands, overcome. Dear Tobias, so kind and concerned, he deserved better than she could offer him, she thought. Her heart would forever remain with the man who had stirred such ecstasy; she was sure she would never experience it again.

Oh, Mother, I understand only too well now what you wrote in your diary. Amy began to sob unrestrainedly.

By the time Morgan came home Amy had managed to compose herself. If her eyes were still red from weeping, Morgan, lost in her own thoughts, did not appear to notice. At last she sighed.

'I can't make up my mind what I should do,' she confided. 'Clem Simpson wants us to walk out together, regular like, but I can tell our Toby's not keen. I reckon it's because he can't stand that Biddy. She's a fool unto herself, is that one; always making sheep's eyes at him. All the folk in the village are talking.'

As Amy made no comment, she went on. 'I know it's time he were thinking of getting wed, but she's not the one for him, and that's for sure.'

It was clear she knew nothing of Tobias' proposal. Amy felt obliged to speak.

'Tobias has asked me to marry him.'

She saw the delight that sprang into Morgan's black eyes. 'Oh, Amy! That's wonderful! Oh, tha will have him, won't tha?'

She flung her arms around Amy, hugging her close. Amy felt a lump in the throat. What dear creatures they both were, brother and sister. Their love afforded her a sense of security – the answer was clear.

After supper Morgan cleared the dishes from the table. Tobias sat in the chair by the fire and struck a lucifer to light his pipe. Amy came to stand before him.

'I've thought it over, Tobias. If you're still of the same mind, I will marry you.'

He looked up at her, the match still burning. For long seconds he gazed at her until the match burned down to his fingertips. He shook it and spoke quietly as he tossed it into the fire.

'Aye, well, that's settled then.'

Morgan turned from the sink. 'I'm that glad,' she said contentedly. 'Now the pair of thee can get off to see the vicar in the morning and see about calling the banns. We can just get the wedding in before Christmas.'

As she lay in bed that night Amy thought again about Mother's diary.

'My beloved Frederic, I have never known such rapture as when I lay with you!'

211

Mother was right. There came only one man in a woman's life who could bring such ecstasy.

Suddenly she felt a distinct flutter, and put a hand to her belly, filled with a sense of wonder. There was a child there, moving, eager for life.

Oh, Charles! Forgive me! I shall love you till the end of my days, but I have no choice. The die is cast.

FIFTEEN

Once the banns were read the news was out. Amy was conscious of wondering stares when she walked down to the village, but no one commented. Even Biddy Simpson looked away quickly when she saw her coming. It must have taken a great effort on her part not to let her disappointment show, thought Amy.

She must get in touch with Lionel, and quickly. He would be very surprised to learn that his sister was to be married even before his own wedding, but she longed to have him come to the wedding service. Few would be there, but Lionel must be among them.

He wrote back quickly.

'You know you were welcome to have a home with us, but if this is what you really want, I'm happy for you. Of course I'll come.

'By the way, I had a letter from Aunt Charlotte. I don't know why, but she wrote asking me to visit her. I wasn't going to go, but Maggie insists – she says she's flesh and blood, after all, and I should see what

212

she wants. So I'm going up to Langdenholme Saturday afternoon.'

Amy was startled. Aunt Charlotte actually recognising the Mallinsons she hated? There must be a good reason, for that woman never did anything without a calculated motive. Immediately Amy repented of the thought. It was uncharitable. Perhaps Aunt Charlotte was remorseful now that her sister was dead, and anxious to do right by the nephew she had cheated. In any event, Amy found a new state of serenity creeping over her, a sensation of peace and being at one with the world, and it was disquieting to have unkind thoughts. Far better to give Aunt Charlotte the benefit of the doubt. Even the thought of Lionel possibly coming face-to-face with cousin Charles at last did not fill her with anxiety, as it might once have done.

No, in her new-found peace of mind, Amy realised that the deepest sentiment she could summon up about Aunt Charlotte was curiosity. And a week later another letter from Lionel satisfied it.

'I saw Aunt Charlotte on Saturday. I understand now why Mother didn't like her, or you either.

'She didn't tell much, asking questions about Mother and you most of the time. She did say she had been quite poorly lately and that's why she hadn't been able to come to Mother's funeral.'

Amy snorted. Even if that were true, she could have sent a letter of condolence, a floral tribute, or one of the family in her place.

'She said Uncle Percy was busy conducting a funeral service himself that day, and Charles and Berenice were away in London – Berenice was visiting her fiancé's family.'

213

So Berenice had become engaged – was it to Elliot Benson, her piano tutor she was so infatuated with?

'She asked about Mother. I said we didn't even know she was ill until she went into hospital and we learnt she had Bright's Disease. I told her how grateful we were to Mr Glover for all his help in settling Mother's affairs.

'She asked what I was doing. I told her I planned to get wed soon if I could get enough brass together. Then I told her about trying to get into textiles, but I couldn't get the scholarship I needed. She went very quiet at that. She only said that life has a way of frustrating our most cherished ambitions and we had to learn to come to terms with it. It made me mad, but I said nothing. It's too late now.

'She mentioned you too, Amy, but I thought it odd that she said nothing about you working at Langden-holme. She just asked where you were. I said I didn't know. I didn't want her bothering you, not the way things are.'

Dear Lionel, she thought. With him and Tobias both so protective towards her, she was very fortunate. She wondered how Aunt Charlotte might have reacted if she had learnt that her niece was soon to give birth to her grandchild. Not that Lionel could have told her, since he knew nothing of Charles' part in this. Aunt Charlotte, Charles and Lionel – they must all be kept in ignorance. She read on.

'Aunt Charlotte was pretty quiet for a long time. It started thundering and I said I'd best get back home. She said I must call again sometime. She also said she'd see to getting flowers put on the grave every month, like she used to when Grandfather first died.'

The least she could do in the circumstances, thought

Amy, but come the summertime, let it not be roses. She had never been able to fathom out why, but Mother had always hated roses.

'She's a funny woman. I couldn't make her out at all. I shan't go there again. I bet she'd have a fit if I took my wife and Aunt Charlotte found out it was a girl who was once her maid. Hoping this finds you as it leaves me. Your loving brother, Lionel.'

Amy smiled, amused by Lionel's impish humour. Aunt Charlotte's invitation to him had evidently been born of nothing more than idle curiosity. By now she undoubtedly believed Amy to be dead. It was difficult to remember without rancour the way she had dismissed Amy and Minnie from her household, believing them to have smallpox. For all she knew, Amy was dead and her mother and brother none the wiser.

Ah well, if remorse and even penitence were now beginning to seep into Aunt Charlotte's hardened soul, it was not before time.

'Who are you writing to, dear?' Percy Holroyd's mild blue eyes peered curiously over the top of his spectacles. His wife, seated at the writing desk, clicked her tongue in annoyance.

'You mean to whom am I writing, I presume,' she snapped. 'Well, if you must know, it's a firm of solicitors in London.'

'Oh.' Percy thought for a moment. 'But why in London, dear? Our solicitors are in Hawksmoor – can't they deal with the matter, whatever it is?'

'No. Now wait until I've finished.'

Percy sighed and turned back to his newspaper. At last Charlotte finished writing, blotted the paper dry, folded it and put it in an envelope.

'There,' she said. 'That's that done. Now perhaps we can get somewhere.' She rang the bell.

Her husband lowered the paper, inspecting her expression to determine whether it was wise to question further. The maid entered. Charlotte held out the letter.

'Take this and see it gets into the post at once,' she said, and as the maid withdrew she turned to Percy. 'You remember I told you I heard Mr Roebuck talking the other night, Percy – the meeting of the Technical Governors?'

'Oh, yes.' He didn't, but it was necessary for domestic peace to say the right words.

'I thought you would – about those shares. Mr Roebuck is a shrewd little fellow, never misses a trick. So I thought it best to find out about those my father used to have.'

'Which shares was that, dear?'

'Oh, Percy! The Messel ones – you remember. Father left them to Violet in his will.'

It was coming back to him now. 'Ah, yes. You were quite happy about it, as I recall – they had very little value, you said.'

'Yes, but that was years ago. Now, if Mr Roebuck's information was correct, they've leapt in value. I wondered if Violet still had them.'

Percy considered. 'She could have sold them years ago.'

'Not if she had any sense.'

'Well, she was hard-up. And now she's gone, they'll be Lionel's, anyway.'

'That's what I want to find out,' Charlotte pronounced. 'I contacted Edwin Glover – Lionel said he was handling all Violet's business. He didn't tell me much, of course – he's a very discreet man – but he did give me the solicitor's address. So I've written to ask them the terms of my sister's will. I've a right to know, being her closest relative.'

Percy forbore to point out that perhaps Lionel had a better claim to that title. 'But I fail to see why the shares should interest you, my dear,' he said amiably. 'If they're sold, it's too late to worry, and if they've passed to Lionel—'

'He might be willing to sell them. To me. After all, they're pharmaceutical shares, they should be kept in the family, Percy. They could go to Charles as a wedding gift.'

'Oh?' said Percy in surprise. 'Has he decided to marry that Chadwick girl, then? I know they've been keeping company, but—'

'Not yet,' interrupted Charlotte, 'but if he's got any sense he very soon will.'

Percy disappeared behind his newspaper to contemplate the prospect. If she was right, then with Charles gone and Berenice married to that young Benson fellow, Charlotte would have to direct all her plans and conversation at him. The prospect was bleak. Heart fluttering at his own temerity, he ventured to point out possible disappointment.

'The boy might not want to sell.'

'He wants to get married. He will.'

A slight pause, then he tried again. 'If he finds out the value has soared—'

'He won't. He's not the sort to take advice from solicitors or anyone. If I offer a good price – attractive enough – he'll jump at it.' There was such conviction in his wife's tone that Percy realised, after years of experience, that now was the time to stop. He turned his attention to the obituary column.

Charlotte shut the lid of the writing desk. 'I think I've got one of my sick headaches coming on. It's probably from having to explain all this to you. Oh, why couldn't I have a husband who could deal with all the business, like other women do!'

Pressing a lace-edged handkerchief to her brow she went out, leaving a trail of lavender in her wake.

Percy's lips compressed in an ironic smile. A business-minded husband would have robbed Charlotte of her sole pleasure – wielding power and influence. And if she did it with more than a touch of bitterness these days, one must remember that she was continually plagued with rheumatism – and those sick headaches. She wasn't young any more.

He forced his attention back to the *In Memoriam* column.

'In memory of Emily Dyson. One year ago today.
No need for words, except to say
Still remembered, in every way,
Gone, but never forgotten.'

The banns had been read twice. It had been arranged with the vicar at the village church that the marriage should take place immediately after the third reading. They had all agreed that it should be a quiet wedding with Lionel and Maggie as their only guests. They would witness the ceremony and come home to the farm for tea afterwards.

Morgan began to prepare the big bedroom with its double bed, which had been unused since Uncle Ben's death. 'There's two big wardrobes, so there's plenty of space for thy things and Toby's,' she told Amy. 'Lovely room, that. Gets all the morning sun.'

Rather than have to explain her arrangement with Tobias, Amy remained silent. She saw Tobias' quick look, and knew he would honour his word.

Strange that I should feel disloyal to you, Charles, when you have given no thought to me. I have loved no other man but you, I carry your child, yet I am about to share another man's bed. Though the ecstasy is ended, security begins.

It was true, she thought. Tobias might lack polish and the social graces, but he was steady and reliable – more than that, his reassuring strength and protectiveness gave her comfort. Thoughts of Charles brought nostalgia and regret, but no longer rending heartache. She could contemplate her forthcoming marriage with equanimity.

Morgan was beginning to grow excited. 'Even if we can't afford a wedding feast and fine new gown for thee, Amy, let me at least trim up thy best dress. Tell thee what – I've a set of pearl buttons in my box, and Mrs Pilling has a pretty bit of lace she cut off a gown. I'll pop down and see if she'll let me have it.'

She came back later, the lace in her hand and her black eyes flashing.

'That bloody Simpson girl!' She exploded. 'There she were, gossiping by the pumps when I came past. She saw me coming – she made sure I could overhear her, catty bitch.'

'What's up?' asked Amy. 'What did she say?'

Morgan hobbled to the cupboard in the corner, wrenched open the door and took out her sewing box. 'She's jealous, that's what it is, but she's no call to talk like that! She had her eye on our Toby, I know, and she's fair mad because she's got no chance! But she's no right to go talking like that. Trouble-maker, that's what she is! But I told her.'

'Told her what?'

'I told her she was a pig, and she could keep her snout out of our business. I told her to button her lip, or I'd shut her mouth for her. Foul-mouthed bitch!'

'Morgan! Whatever did she say?' Amy could not help looking down at the girl's twisted foot. If that malicious Biddy Simpson had said anything to hurt Morgan . . .

Morgan was searching through the box for the needle and thread. 'She were having a go at thee. She were telling the others it were as plain as day that tha'd a bun in the oven. It were the only way tha could get Tobias Clegg to wed thee, she said. Tha'd have never gotten him else.'

'I see.' Amy was thoughtful. Titillating gossip in a small village spread like wildfire. It could cause Morgan and Tobias much disquiet. Her new-found sense of peace was beginning to trickle away.

'Take no heed of her,' muttered Morgan, jabbing a rejected needle back into the pincushion. 'She's just trying to ill-wish thee, out of jealousy, calling thee a whore. She knows she's lost Toby now – not as she ever stood a chance. She wants to make things bad for thee, but I'll not let her. She's wasting her time, take no heed, let her prattle and cast her spells, she'll do nowt as can harm us.'

'Sticks and stones
May break my bones
But names will never hurt me?'

Whatever the girl said, Amy thought, she could do no harm so long as Morgan and Tobias weren't hurt. Ill-wishing? Casting spells? It must be Morgan's gypsy blood that made her believe such superstition.

'There's them buttons,' said Morgan. 'Go fetch that dress and I'll do it before supper.' The anger was gone from her eyes. Amy looked at her with affection. Like a summer storm, she was, all flash and fire one moment, all sunny and sweet the next. She wouldn't keep up a quarrel with Biddy Simpson for long; she was growing far too friendly with Clem Simpson for that.

Morgan finished sewing, biting off the thread with her teeth, just as Tobias came in from the yard. He flung off his jacket and came to stand by the fire, rubbing his hands together.

'Any tea brewed, lass? It's perishing out.'

'I'll get it,' said Amy, drawing the kettle over the hob.

Morgan held up the dress. 'There, see, I've put them

buttons of me mam's on,' she said with satisfaction. 'Makes a world of difference, with that bit of lace too.'

'It's lovely,' said Amy. 'Thanks, Morgan.'

Tobias lifted a finger. 'That reminds me – while I think on . . .' He went to a sideboard drawer and took out a ring. 'Me mam's wedding ring,' he said. 'Dost mind, Morgan, if I give it Amy, or dost tha want to—'

'Nay,' cut in Morgan. 'It's only right. Give it Amy.'

He turned to Amy. 'Try it on, lass. See if it fits.'

In silence she held out her left hand. He took it and, with difficulty, slid the ring on to the third finger. For a moment he stared down at the small white hand lying in his palm, then took the ring off abruptly. 'It'll do,' he said.

For the rest of the evening Amy could still sense the touch of his hand on hers. Despite the size and roughness of that hand, it had been remarkably gentle . . .

As the mantel clock struck ten Morgan rose, stretched and said she was off to bed. Tobias remained sitting by the fire, gazing into the coals. Amy watched him, unobserved, and her conscience troubled her.

'Tobias,' she said uncertainly, 'I can't decide . . .'

He started up out of his reverie, then stood up. 'What?'

'I don't think I can marry you.' She rose too, and stood before him. Gyp's body lay outstretched between them. She saw the bewilderment in his eyes deepen. She looked away, studying her feet.

'What art saying, lass?'

'I can't, Tobias. People are talking—'

'Let 'em.' His voice sounded rough. 'Us getting wed makes it all respectable. They can't talk then.'

'It's not that, Tobias—'

'What then? Respectability matters to thee, doesn't it? Or is it that I'm not good enough—'

'No, of course not.'

'Because I know tha's educated and better nor me in every way, but tha'd not regret it, lass, marrying a

221

common fellow like me. I'd not cheat thee, like thy fellow did, I promise thee. I'll treat thee like a duchess, not like he did.'

Amy looked up at him. There was fire in his dark eyes. 'No, it wasn't like that, Tobias.'

'He abandoned thee, when tha needed him.'

'He doesn't know.'

He was staring down into her upturned face, clearly at a loss to understand. Then he shook his head. 'I reckon tha hast thy reasons and I'll not question. I want to care for thee.'

'And another man's child?'

'I could make a better job of it nor he could. I want thee. Tha's a brave lass, Amy Mallinson.'

She felt the tears start to prick. 'I'm not, but I don't want to be only a half-wife to you – you deserve better. Oh, Tobias, you're so kind, and I've so many faults!'

'We all have faults, lass. There'd be no need for love and understanding and forgiveness else.'

'I'm trying to say I don't think I'm good enough for you, Tobias Clegg. I can't love you – but I need you.'

The bewilderment fled from his dark eyes, and his mouth lifted at the corners. 'Aye, well, then that's settled,' he said tersely then snapped his fingers at the dog. 'Come on, lass.'

The dog leapt to her feet and followed him outside.

It was a bright, cold day a week before Christmas when Amy and Tobias were married. Lionel and Maggie were already waiting at the door of the village church when they arrived. Most of the villagers were at work and only a few curious heads turned to watch as Amy walked by with Tobias and Morgan.

The vicar seemed oblivious to the fact that his church was almost deserted and spoke the words of the marriage service with the same solemnity as his Sunday sermon.

'Wilt thou, Tobias take this woman . . . Wilt thou,

Amy, take this man . . . Wilt thou promise to love, honour and obey, till death do you part?'

Amy heard the words as if in a dream, watching the pools of colour cast at their feet by the high stained-glass windows. When Tobias murmured 'With this body I thee worship,' she felt her cheeks redden. At last the vicar pronounced them man and wife, and Tobias bent his head to kiss her fleetingly.

The rest of the day maintained the air of unreality, the walk back up to the farm, sipping tea and eating carraway-seed cake. It gave Amy pleasure to see Morgan and Maggie exchanging recipes, evidently warming quickly to each other.

And even greater pleasure to see Lionel standing by Tobias, deep in conversation in the yard by the drystone wall. Tobias was pointing down towards the valley, and Lionel followed the direction of his finger, nodding. The two dark heads inclined towards each other, Tobias the taller by inches and his breadth making Lionel seem slight and stoop-shouldered. It was also noticeable how pale her brother was compared to Tobias' weatherbeaten complexion.

When at last the couple left, arm in arm, to walk down to the station, life seemed to revert nearer to normality. Tobias, uncomfortable in Sunday-best suit and starched collar and tight new boots, changed into his familiar jersey and corduroys.

He sat at ease by the fire until the clock struck ten. As always Morgan rose and stretched. Tobias looked across at Amy.

'Thee go up, lass,' he murmured. 'I'll come up when tha's abed.'

In the big, strange bedroom she pulled on her flannelette nightgown and crawled between the cold sheets. She lay there, watching the flickering shadows cast by the candlelight on the walls, and after a time she heard Tobias come into the room. He nipped out the candle flame and in the darkness she heard the sounds as he undressed. Moments later he climbed into bed and lay still and unmoving, well away from her.

Amy felt strange. The last time, the only time she had lain so close to a man's body . . .

'Art all right, lass?' came Tobias' voice in the darkness.

'Yes,' she murmured.

'Goodnight then. God bless.'

The strangeness melted. There was comfort in his nearness, even if his back was turned towards her.

When the maid brought the bedtime hot chocolate into the dining room at Langdenholme, Charlotte and Percy had reached the closing stages of their game of cribbage. Charlotte was in charge of the score board. She did not look up as the maid placed the tray on the table beside her.

'Let's see, I'm ninety-five and you're ninety-six,' she told her husband. 'Pretty close, but I think I can pip you at the post. I've got fifteen-two, fifteen-four, and two for a pair. Six. That makes me a hundred and one. There, I've done it again!'

Triumph glowing in her voice, she turned to pick up a cup of chocolate. Percy sighed, deeming it wiser not to point out that as she had dealt, it should have been his first count. With that seven of spades she'd turned up, he had a total of twelve points and should have won the game.

She was sipping her chocolate contentedly. 'I'm glad Charles has seen sense at last,' she remarked. 'It did him good to have a fling in London – he's been so restless ever since last summer. Now Robert Chadwick's as good as offered him a junior partnership—'

'If he marries Florence,' pointed out Percy.

'The deed's as good as done,' his wife replied sharply. 'He knows job and marriage go together – he's no fool. He's bringing Florence here for Christmas, isn't he? All we have to do now is decide what to give them as a wedding gift. I've been thinking—'

'You did mention those shares, my dear. Did you find out what you wanted to know?'

Charlotte clattered the cup down on the saucer. 'That came to nothing. No, I thought we might give Charles those outlying cottages and the farm that my father bought. He could collect the rents then – it would save having to use the agent.'

'Good idea,' agreed Percy. 'But what happened about the shares?' He could not resist impish inquisitiveness.

Charlotte turned aside to put the cup and saucer on the tray. 'Very likely Violet sold them – she always needed money.'

Percy refrained from remarking that he had suggested the same thought himself recently. 'I take it you heard from the London solicitors then, dear. What did they say?'

'Not very much. Only that my name did not occur in Violet's will, and so in the interest of confidentiality they did not feel they could disclose any of its terms.'

Percy picked up the pack of cards, shuffled them and put them back in their box. A smile hovered about his lips. At long last someone had as good as told Charlotte to mind her own business, and he felt a small glow of satisfaction.

SIXTEEN

Christmas, though cold and damp, was not without its happy moments despite the sadness that still overhung the farm after Uncle Ben's death. As they ate plum pudding following the Christmas goose, Morgan found the silver ring in her portion and was clearly delighted.

'I've got the threepenny bit,' said Amy.

Tobias held up the thimble, and they all laughed. 'Nay,' said Morgan, 'I can't see thee darning thy own socks or turning a collar. Amy getting the joey means she'll come into some brass.'

'Then I'll give the thimble to my wife,' said Tobias, and handed it to Amy with a smile.

Morgan's next moment of happiness came when Clem Simpson called to take her to evening service. He stood, tall and laughing, under the circular kissing bough she had painstakingly woven from holly and ivy and misletoe and persuaded Tobias to hang from the rafters. The macassar oil on Clem's hair gleamed under the light of the candles in the kissing bough.

'I'll not miss this chance, Morgan,' he laughed and, sweeping her up in his arms, he kissed her, at length and clearly with great enjoyment.

'Now, thee kiss Amy,' Morgan ordered her brother, and for the second time Amy felt his lips on hers. This time his kiss was not so swift and diffident as it had been in the church.

He was a good man, she reflected, and true to his word.

When the new year brought deep snows and foot-long icicles hanging from the farmhouse eaves, she was glad of his warm presence in the big double bed. But though he often lay close, sometimes in his sleep curving his body behind hers and even laying an arm across her, he never once made any demand upon her, and she was grateful.

She was conscious that her body was becoming grotesque. Seven months gone, she was unwieldy and clumsy. Tobias seemed always to be watching her and anticipating her needs. If she dropped her thimble he would start from his chair to retrieve it before she could move. Without a word he would unfasten her shoes for her.

'Thy toe-nails need cutting. I'll do 'em for thee.'

She felt like a child again; it put her in mind of the days long gone when Mother would soap and bathe her in the big tin bath before the fire, towel her down with laughs and hugs, and then take her on her knee and cut her nails.

One windy night he sat at the table, shaping a piece of wood for the cradle he was preparing. Woodshavings lay all around him on the flagged floor. Amy hummed a tune as she brushed out her long hair.

'If I washed me hands, would tha let me do that for thee?' His tone was shy, awkward, even. She held out the brush. Morgan looked on fondly.

Amy closed her eyes and revelled in the sensuous pleasure of the brush strokes, light and tentative as though he feared she might break. There was a warm sense of intimacy, the three of them close in a warm room on a cold night when the wind howled out on the moor.

But if Amy felt clumsy and unappealing then, she felt even more so at eight months. She smiled ruefully across the hearth at Tobias.

'I feel like a sweet dumpling,' she said. 'I shall be glad to shed this load.'

He snorted. 'I'm very fond of sweet dumpling,' and there was a smile on his lips.

Then, unexpectedly, with snow still falling and temperature well below freezing, some of the ewes began lambing. Tobias was out at all hours, down in the barn tending to them. The big double bed seemed vast and cheerless without his warm presence. It was often nearing dawn before she felt him crawl into bed and sink at once into an exhausted sleep. His concern, not only for her but for the newborn lambs too, touched her.

He sat by the fire, cradling a lamb in his arms and coaxing it to drink from a bottle with a teat.

'He'll make a good father, will Toby,' said Morgan.

Amy felt a sudden rush of feeling for him. *Hold on, it's only maternal feelings, Amy Clegg, but your own little one is only a month away . . .*

It was late March and the snows had melted from the valley, leaving only scattered patches on the high moors when Amy's baby was born, a week early. Reality fled, and for what seemed like eternity she endured a haze of pain and sweat. At last the fog cleared and she saw Morgan bending over her, beads of sweat on her forehead and her hair in untidy wisps all about her face. She wore a rapturous smile.

'Tha's got a son, Amy – thee and Tobias, tha's got a son!'

She laid a bundle down beside Amy on the bed. A wrinkled little face and a thin cry – it was for all the world like one of Tobias' baby lambs.

'Rest a bit now,' said Morgan, 'and I'll fetch Tobias up presently. I'll go tell him the news.'

Amy lay bemused, unable to believe it was all over. In a while Tobias came. He stood by the bed, dark eyes wide, searching her face.

'Art all right, lass?'

'I'm fine, and so is the baby.'

His gaze slid to the child. For a time he stood in silence.

'What are you thinking, Tobias?'

'Nay, only that it's spring, there's buds on the trees. It's Easter, time of the resurrection and all that—'

He turned away and looked out of the window across the fields. For a moment Amy feared he was thinking that this new life was not his child. He would be glad it was all over safely, for her sake, but for the baby he could feel nothing. The thought saddened her. She looked down at the red-faced little creature, and felt protective. There was nothing about the tiny face that reminded her of Charles, nothing at all.

'I think I'll call him Joel,' she said softly.

Tobias turned from the window and came back to the bed, kneeling suddenly and placing a kiss on Amy's forehead.

'Aye, I like that,' he muttered. 'My son Joel.' He gripped Amy's hand and said no more, but she could feel the intensity of emotion that stirred him.

'*My son, my son Joel.*' If ever there was a sign of acceptance, proof of his love for her, that was it. Amy felt a lump in her throat.

He got up suddenly from his knees. 'Tha'd best sleep now, lass. Morgan said I wasn't to tire thee.' He stroked the hair back out of her eyes with slow, caressing movement. 'Tha's done well, lass. I always said tha were a clever lass.'

From the time of the christening of baby Joel at Easter the weather took a sudden turn for the better. It gave Amy great pleasure to sit outside with the baby in her arms, watching Tobias at work. The muscles in his back rippled as he swung the axe to chop firewood, and she recalled that it was the sight of those muscles which had first drawn her attention to him, that day at the Cope Bank fair with Cissie. Was it only last summer? Somehow it seemed a lifetime away, part of another world which was more and more receding from her memory.

One afternoon she came into the kitchen. Tobias was bending over the crib, a look of tenderness on his dark face and the baby's tiny fist clutched tightly about his forefinger. He straightened.

'Has Morgan told thee of the barn dance?'

'Barn dance?' She pricked up her ears with interest. She would never have associated dancing with him. 'No.'

'We have one this time every year. It's for all the

village folk. It's been going since me grandfather's time.'

'I look forward to that. It sounds fun.'

Luck was with them and the weather remained fine and warm. On the evening of the dance Amy could see from the bedroom window people climbing the hill in their Sunday best as she was putting the baby to bed. Once she was satisfied that Joel was settled, she changed out of her apron and working dress into her prettiest cotton gown, brushed out her long hair and went downstairs.

Tobias was nowhere to be seen. Morgan was gathering up jugs of ale and lemonade. Amy picked up the basket of currant teacakes and scones she and Morgan had spent all afternoon baking.

The barn was cosy with the mellow light of lanterns and bales of hay around the walls, the trestle table at one end laden with food brought by the village women, and a group of fiddlers tuning up at the far end. Knots of villagers stood chatting and greeting each other, and there was an air of anticipation of the evening's pleasure ahead.

Having rearranged the food and drink on the table to Morgan's satisfaction, Amy stood for a time watching as the fiddlers struck up and dancers moved on to the floor. She felt content. The furthest thought from her mind was the old way of life down there in Hawksmoor, but suddenly, without warning, she was brought face to face with it. Framed in the open doorway of the barn stood a couple, a tall young man and a pretty young woman by his side, both far more elegantly dressed than the rest of the company. With a lurch of disbelief Amy recognised Charles Holroyd.

She stood, her breath caught in her throat and her head beginning to swim. It could not be true! He could not really be here – it must be her imagination playing her tricks. Yet she had barely given him a thought in months.

She saw Morgan detach herself from a laughing group near the table and limp across to the couple. She saw Charles nod and smile and engage her in conversation for a few moments before taking the arm of the pretty young woman at his side and leading her into the dance. Their steps led them eventually to pass the spot where she stood, and she saw Charles' sudden look of disbelief as he caught sight of her. She saw his lips part and his eyes widen, but he continued to dance, and in a moment he was lost to view amongst the swirl of bodies.

Amy hurried to where Morgan stood. 'You were talking to that fair-headed young man,' she said awkwardly.

'Oh, yes – that's Mr Holroyd, Mr Charles, that is.' replied Morgan. 'They're our landlords, tha knows, though they never come to the dance as a rule. Nice of him to come, and bring his young lady and all. I've heard tell of Miss Chadwick, though I've never set eyes on her till now.'

Morgan limped away to pour beer for two young men standing holding out their mugs and teasing. Amy looked back at the dancers. The fiddlers crashed to the climax of their tune and there was a burst of applause as the dancers moved to the side of the barn to await the next dance. The music started up again and bodies began to fill the floor.

Amy was startled to hear a once-familiar voice at her side.

'May I have this dance, Amy?'

She looked up into Charles' handsome face. He held out his hand, and without thinking, she took it and allowed him to lead her out. As his arm encircled her, he spoke quietly. 'I can't believe my eyes. I thought you dead, Amy.'

She did not answer, surprised at her own lack of reaction. She might have expected her feelings to turn topsy-turvy at the sight of him, the touch of his hand

231

to make her senses reel, yet here he was, his arm about her and his slim fingers interlaced with hers, and it meant no more than dancing with a complete stranger.

As they reached the barn door he stopped dancing abruptly, taking her hand and leading her outside. The night air was cool, heavy with the scent of warm hay drifting from the barn. He spoke jerkily, without looking at her.

'It gave me a terrible shock seeing you, Amy. I honestly believed you were dead.'

She looked up at him. 'Did you mourn for me, Charles?'

He looked round then, his eyes searching hers curiously. 'Of course – I loved you, Amy! I was besotted with you!'

'But you didn't try to find me.'

He spread his elegant hands helplessly. 'What use would that have been? My mother told me you left with smallpox.'

Strange how cold she felt, how perfectly in control of herself. 'But you never sent to find out whether I had survived or not.'

'People don't usually survive smallpox,' he said testily, and then he peered at her closely. 'It didn't even mark you – there's no scars on your face, Amy. You're just as beautiful – if anything, more so.'

Ah, there it is – the charm I remember so well, but it's too late now, she thought.

'Amy, it's not too late. Say it's not too late. I could never get you out of my mind. You're so different – so lively and independent – there's never been another girl like you, Amy. Let's meet again.'

She nodded towards the barn. 'And what of your young lady, Miss Chadwick?'

'Ah, you know about her. Yes – we're engaged, to be married in two weeks' time. But she won't know, Amy. I can arrange things—'

She looked up at him coldly. 'I see. You would like

her as your wife and me as a plaything, is that it? I'm sorry, Charles. I'm your cousin, no more and no less.'

She turned away and began retracing her footsteps towards the barn. He moved quickly, seizing her by the elbow.

'Amy, please! Don't go! I need you! But don't ask me to marry you – I can't, it's all arranged. Florence's father has plans for me – I can't back out. But oh, Amy, I can't lose you again! That would be too cruel! Oh, life has been hard for me—'

She stared up at him in disbelief. 'Hard? For you?'

The gloomy look came over his handsome face again. 'Ah, you've no idea. Having to marry whether I like it or not, but I'm up to my ears in debt. I'll have to sell this farm – my mother's only just made it over to me as a wedding gift. I've no choice.'

Amy's scorn was quickly replaced by curiosity. 'This farm? Do you mean to say you are the owner of Jericho Farm?'

He nodded moodily. 'Mother would have a fit if she knew I was getting rid of it, but I see no other way. I shall give instructions to the solicitor in the morning to find a buyer for me. You can see what a run of bad luck I've been having, Amy. Don't turn your back on me now. I need you! I won't let you go!'

She shook her head. 'You are not my master – or my gaoler, Charles. I am a free woman.'

'Amy, listen to me! There's no escape from reality!'

There was such pleading in his eyes that for a moment she felt herself beginning to weaken. He looked so wistful, so forlorn. Then she pulled herself together.

'I'm not your wife, Charles, nor ever will be. Go to that girl in there – she has a right to know your problems, and it's her duty to help you, not mine. Reality for me is here – with my husband.' She turned to go.

'Amy, please!'

She turned to look back at him, icy disdain in her

233

heart. All that love, all that longing she had expended on this vain, self-indulgent creature! Now every trace of it was gone. Fate had been kind, after all, sparing her from this weak man.

He stepped closer, hunger in his eyes. 'Kiss me, Amy. One last kiss, at least.'

Poised, cool, confident, she looked at him with pride. 'No, I will not. I'm married, Charles, to a man far finer and nobler than you will ever be. I wish you well, you and your betrothed, and I hope some day you may find the contentment I have found.'

As she turned to walk up to the farmhouse he took a few tentative steps to follow her.

'Is that your last word, Amy?'

Without answering, she walked on. When she reached the farmhouse door and looked back, he was gone. Poor Charles, she thought with compassion. Whatever his wealth and privileges, he would never know the peace of mind that she had found.

Musing, surprised still that he no longer had the power to excite her, Amy did not realise the full significance of what he had told her. It was bewildering, not to say disappointing, that she felt nothing now, not even outrage, for the father of the baby lying peacefully asleep in his cradle. She looked down at Joel with love. It seemed far more natural, somehow, that Tobias should be his father, not Charles.

It was only when she lay in bed waiting for Tobias that she suddenly recalled Charles' words. '*I'll have to sell this farm – I've no choice.*' That would mean a new owner for Jericho Farm – and, by rights, it should be Tobias. The only obstacle was money. Her mind began to race . . .

By the time Tobias came up, nipped out the candle and began to undress, she was barely aware of him.

'Tha looked very pretty tonight,' he murmured in the darkness. 'And I reckon Mr Holroyd thought so and all – I saw him talking to thee.'

234

'Yes,' she murmured, but she wasn't listening. Mentally she was already composing the letter she would write to Edwin Glover first thing in the morning.

Edwin Glover's reply was prompt.

'I am delighted that Lionel is soon to be married, and if you are coming down to Reed Street to clear out the last of your mother's belongings, I shall be delighted to meet you there. I shall look into the matters you spoke of, and tell you what I discover. If convenient, I shall call at Reed Street at two on Friday. I remain, your sincere friend, Edwin Glover.'

Amy began to grow excited. Now she had only to get away from Jericho Farm for a couple of days without arousing suspicion.

Morgan was happy. 'I'll be glad to have little Joel all to meself. Now tha's no longer feeding him, I can manage the bottle well enough.'

Tobias, too, seemed equable. 'Of course tha mun tidy up the house if thy Lionel and Maggie's to move in soon. Take thy time, lass – make a right job of it. Here, take this.'

He dug in his pocket and pulled out a coin.

Amy took it, wonderingly. 'What's this? A penny?'

'Luck-penny,' he grunted. 'Make sure tha'll come back.'

She could hardly wait for Friday, but when at last she stood alone in the dusty living room at Reed Street the excitement began to yield a feeling of nostalgia. The room brought back so many memories of childhood. The big black range now wore a distinctly rusty tinge; it sadly lacked Mother's weekly application of a generous coating of black lead, she thought. Amy fetched the Zebo from the cupboard under the scullery sink and knelt before the range.

She brushed vigorously, recalling the nights on this

hearth, the weekly bath in the zinc tub before the fire, feeling the heat on one's face and the cold draught from the scullery door on one's back. In imagination she could feel again the caress of soft towels, the delicious sensation of climbing into a clean night-gown and being taken up on Mother's knee to have her hair twisted into rag curlers, before the bedtime prayers.

The grate gleaming again, she washed her hands with the bar of cracked soap still lying in the soap-dish. It was going to take time to tidy everything and burn the rubbish, she realised. Better start before Edwin Glover came. She lit the fire and set the kettle on the hob.

He arrived on the dot of two o'clock, brushing aside Amy's apologies for the ashes in the hearth.

'Tha can't expect to get rid of all that paper without making a mess.'

Amy brewed tea and fetched her mother's best china cups. 'Mr Glover, I'm sorry I asked you to go to so much trouble,' she began, but he cut in quickly.

'No trouble, I assure thee. I've found out who the solicitors are, and I've taken the liberty of having a word with them.'

'Not mentioning my name?'

'Nay, have no fear, I can keep a confidence. I was most discreet, believe me.'

'I'm sure you were. And how much was it, Mr Glover?' She looked up from pouring the tea.

Edwin Glover sat back, slapping his hands on his thighs in satisfaction. 'There's no difficulty – with the money from the Messel shares there's enough to buy Jericho Farm three times over. Thy grandfather invested well – those shares have made thee a wealthy young woman, Amy Clegg.'

She set the teapot down, turning to him, her eyes shining. 'We could do it, then? Have you sold the shares?'

He nodded, beaming broadly. 'I have, and the money's lodged in an account in thy name.'

236

'Oh, That's wonderful!'

'And I've done more – I've told the Holroyds' solicitor as my client might be interested in the farm, and made a tentative appointment to see him this afternoon.'

Amy clasped her hands together. 'Oh, Mr Glover! I'm so grateful! Will you do it for me? Pay the full price – don't quibble, or we might lose it.'

'I don't reckon as there's any fear of that. The price is fair enough, not unreasonable at all. I reckon that cousin of thine must be in need of brass in a hurry. He could have got more.'

Amy was ecstatic. 'Then please, please go back and settle the bargain for me – but, remember, don't let them know my name, or it could all go wrong.'

Edwin Glover's smile faded. 'But I have to give a name for the title deeds, Amy.'

'Then give my husband's name – the name on the deeds must be Tobias Clegg.'

He shook his head and lifted his cup of tea. 'Eh, but tha'art a good lass, Amy, just like your mother. I drink to thee – and her.'

In silence Amy lifted her cup and drank, but inwardly she was eager for him to be gone, to get to the solicitor's office and secure Jericho Farm before any of the Holroyds got wind of her scheme. More than anything, she would have liked to go with him, to settle the deal in person, but she knew she must endure the frustration and lie low until the farm was safely in her hands. Charles might not care who bought it, so long as he got his money, but Aunt Charlotte was another kettle of fish. Never again must that woman have the chance to destroy the happiness of others.

The maid entered the drawing room at Langdenholme and laid the tray of tea and muffins on the table beside her mistress.

'I've brought tea for two, madam. Mr Charles hasn't come back yet.'

Charlotte clicked her tongue, signalling the maid to leave. 'Really, Percy, this is too much,' she complained. 'Charles promised to bring Florence to tea at four, and here it is almost five already. Where in heaven's name can he be?'

Percy Holroyd rose from the table in the window where he had been composing his sermon for Sunday, and crossed to the sofa. 'I really don't know, my dear. Taking advantage of this beautiful weather to walk with Florence in the park, perhaps.'

Charlotte frowned, inspecting the cup closely before pouring tea into it. 'Well, it's really not good enough, Percy. How can we possibly discuss the wedding if he doesn't even bother to show up? He really needs taking in hand, that boy. He's far too wilful.'

Percy restrained from remarking that it was a little late now for that. 'Those muffins look delicious. I think I'll have one.'

She handed him a cup of tea and put a muffin on her own plate, splitting it and spreading it liberally with butter. 'Yes, he really does need a firm hand to control him. I rather think that Florence Chadwick is the girl to do it – I hope so, for her own sake. She's a girl after my own heart, is Florence. She doesn't suffer fools gladly.'

'That's so, dear.'

'Did you hear her at the George when we all had dinner there last week? She ticked the waiter off good and proper.'

'I heard her, dear.'

'And well she might. He did spill gravy on her lap, the clumsy fool. So you see, she's the right kind of woman for Charles, quite apart from the fact that she comes of a very good family and is educated – she speaks a little French and Italian, you know. Oh, where on earth are they? It really is too trying! I shall speak severely to Charles about this.'

She split another muffin, piling it high with cream and raspberry jam and scowling at Percy. He watched with relief as she split and stuffed the third muffin with yet more cream and jam. As long as she was filling her mouth with delicacies, she could not continue to scold.

Edwin Glover returned to Reed Street to report that all that was needed now was Amy's signature for the release of the money. Amy went to bed, hugging the delicious secret to herself, full of joy and anticipation at the prospect of laying before Tobias the gift he most wanted in the whole world.

She crawled between the sheets of Mother's bed, still damp despite the hot bricks she had been placing between them all afternoon. Though she missed Tobias' nearness in bed she reflected that if he had been there she would have found it impossible to contain herself. But she must – for one more day, until it was in the bag, but after that . . . It gave her joy to visualise the disbelief, followed by the pleasure on his face.

And that was not all. There would be more than enough money left to wipe away all the fears of the past; security was theirs. And the price of an operation for Morgan. Though Morgan never spoke of it, it was clear she hated her deformity and wished herself beautiful for Clem Simpson's sake. Morgan could not go on believing herself unworthy of him, loving him as she did, Amy decided. The club-foot cured, the full stop and comma replaced by two glorious full stops, there would no longer be that blight on her life . . .

Violet Mallinson's favourite book of poems lay, covered in dust, on top of the bookshelves. Amy picked it up lovingly, noted the protruding piece of paper and opened the book at that place. She might

239

have guessed; it marked Mother's favourite poem by Christina Rossetti.

'Remember me when I am gone away,
Gone far away into the silent land;
When you can no more hold me by the hand,
Nor I half turn to go yet turning stay.'

The thought of Mother now in that silent land brought tears, and it was some time before Amy's blurred vision cleared. When at last it did, she noticed the sheet of paper and the handwriting, and the small envelope.

'If anything should ever happen to me, see that this envelope is delivered to my sister, by hand, so that she is sure to receive it.'

The envelope was addressed *'Mrs Charlotte Holroyd, Langdenholme, Greenhead Lane, Hawksmoor.'*

Curious, thought Amy – but then, perhaps not. Mother must have recognised that death was imminent to want to speak to Charlotte again. She must have been ill then – the note must have been written just before she was taken to hospital, for it was unfinished and the envelope still unsealed.

Amy hesitated; then opened the envelope and slid out the single sheet of paper. As she read the careful writing in her mother's neat hand, she could hear the gentle voice speaking the words.

'My dear sister, we have not spoken in many years and yet I cannot leave this world without trying to heal the breach. I do not have long, I know, and it grieves me to think how remorseful you may feel when you hear I am gone.

'So let me tell you, whatever has passed between us, and despite the many times I swore I would never forgive you for the misfortunes you caused my Tom

and my Lionel, I will remember only the good things. You cared for my baby Amy when I could not. For that I thank you, and for the rest I forgive you, with all my heart. I pray my maker will forgive me as whole-heartedly. Your loving sister, Violet.'

Amy sighed and put the letter back into the envelope. It clearly meant much to her mother that Charlotte should read her words and, thought Amy, it might mellow the wretched woman's heart and teach her a lesson in loving-kindness. She must deliver the letter herself, by hand, as Mother had requested. She would get it over and done with today, just as soon as she had been to the Hawksmoor and District Bank with Edwin Glover to sign those papers.

SEVENTEEN

Edwin Glover emerged from the gloomy interior of the solicitor's office into the brilliant sunlight of Westgate and walked briskly up to the corner of Market Street, where Amy stood waiting. He took hold of her elbow.

'There now, lass,' he beamed. 'It's all done and settled. I've handed over the cheque and everything's complete. Jericho Farm belongs to Tobias. Now, how about me taking thee to the Pack Horse for a bit of dinner? Just to celebrate, eh? Thy mother would be fair proud if she could be with us now.'

Amy glowed. 'I'm deeply grateful to you, Mr Glover, but I won't come to dinner, thanks. I've some errands still to do and the house to finish and, you see, I want to get back to the farm tonight.'

He smiled and nodded. 'I understand – want to break the good news, of course you do. Eh, but that lad's lucky to have a wife like thee. Well, I'll be off and have a pint to celebrate, anyway. Goodbye, Amy, and good luck.'

It didn't take long to walk up the cobbled road to Trinity Street and then off down the leafy lane round the lower side of the park. The sun was warm on her back as she turned into the pillared gateway of Langdenholme and walked up the laurel-bordered drive to the front door.

This time she did not hesitate. This time she came as an equal, not as a servant. She rang the bell.

The maid looked surprised. 'Mrs Holroyd doesn't usually receive at this time of day – she's in the conservatory. Dost have a card?'

'No,' said Amy, 'but I think she'll see me. Tell her it's her niece Amy.'

The maid returned quickly and led her through the flock-wallpapered vestibule and out through the French windows into the chokingly hot, damp atmosphere of the conservatory. She could see her aunt's corpulent figure seated in a basket chair by the window, almost obscured by the dense foliage of the palms. For a fleeting second she had a strange sensation of having lived through this scene before as she walked quietly towards the seated figure.

Charlotte looked up. 'Well?' she demanded. 'I must confess, I was very surprised to learn from my son that you were still alive.'

Amy studied her haughty features. 'Did you feel no remorse, Aunt, when you learnt it was your niece you had dismissed?'

Her aunt snorted. 'Why should I? You inveigled your way into my house, furtively, like a burglar, without letting on who you really were – why should I trust or care about you? And why did you do it, I'd like to know?'

'A burglar comes to steal, Aunt. I stole nothing.'

'But there must have been something here you wanted, or wanted to find out, or you wouldn't have gone to such lengths.'

Amy spoke quietly. 'If ever there was something here I wanted, I certainly don't now.'

'Then what was the meaning of all that charade?'

'It doesn't matter now. I didn't want to humiliate you – I came today only to deliver this.' She reached into her pocket and took out the letter. Charlotte made no move to take it, so she laid it in the ample lap. The older woman looked down at it with suspicion.

'What is it?'

'Only a letter, Aunt, from my mother. I've only just found it.'

The older woman's eyes widened. 'From Violet? For me?'

Podgy fingers tore the envelope open and Amy saw the sunlight sparkling on her rings. She was holding the letter at arm's length, adjusting it into focus. At length she laid the letter down again on her lap.

'It was written just before she died,' Amy said. 'She was anxious to make her peace with you.'

For a moment Charlotte sat silent, then, without looking up, she murmured, 'Very noble of her to forgive me, I'm sure. I thought she might have mentioned those shares.'

Amy gasped. 'The Messel shares?'

Charlotte looked up. 'You know of them?'

'They're gone – sold.'

Charlotte sighed. 'I might have guessed. She never asks whether I forgive her.'

'Forgive her? What did she ever do to you?' Amy could hardly contain herself. 'It was you who always wronged her!'

'Hold your tongue, girl!'

'You told Grandfather she was going to elope with my father – she told me!'

'She still married him, just the same.'

'It was no business of yours who she married! Between you and Grandfather, you saw to it my father could get no work in Hawksmoor – I know, I've heard!'

'So your mother bleated to you. I would have credited Violet with more guts than that.'

'She did nothing of the sort! Hints – that's all. You have nothing to be proud of, Aunt Charlotte, doing her down whatever way you could. Greed – that's what it was!'

'I took care of you, my girl, when your mother abandoned you. Don't forget that, young woman.'

'Because my grandfather took me in, and my mother had to go away! I'm not ungrateful, but I do remember what you did to Lionel too – making sure he didn't get his scholarship.'

Charlotte's ruddy face turned pale. 'College minutes are confidential matters,' she muttered. 'If somebody's been telling tales—'

'Unfair to Mother, unfair to Lionel, and you certainly didn't treat me with humanity when I came here as a maid.'

'I didn't know you were my niece then.'

'As if that mattered! You lavish more care on – on' – Amy looked around wildly, then pointed down the garden – 'on those roses down there than you do on your servants and family! People are unimportant to you! You're a selfish, hypocritical woman, Aunt Charlotte! After today, I hope I never clap eyes on you again! I only came for Mother's sake.'

Charlotte's eyes glittered. 'How dare you! How dare you speak to me like that! Who do you think you are? I'll have you know I'm a highly respected person in this town, a governor of the College—'

'I don't care!' Amy burst in. 'You're no better than

244

I am! We're of the same family, you and I, and you have no right to treat people the way you do.'

Charlotte lifted her head, looking at her with supercilious disdain. 'I'm only glad my sister is not alive to see you make such a spectacle of yourself, Amy. She would be ashamed. Thank God my children would never disgrace me as you do Violet.'

Amy burned with fury. It was on the tip of her tongue to fling the truth at this cold, sneering woman, tell her of the illegitimate grandson she did not know. But no – it would achieve nothing to destroy a mother's illusions about her son. And Joel must remain hers, hers and Tobias'; the Holroyds must never lay claim to him, she resolved.

'I could tell you things – but I won't,' she said quietly. 'You would not be so proud. But I'll hold my tongue.'

Charlotte's face purpled. 'What are you hinting, miss? Is blackmail your game? Is that it? If so, you're wasting your time—'

'You're right – I am. My place is at home, not here.'

'You're no better than a trollop, coming here to cause trouble. You're a disgrace to your husband, whoever he is.'

'He's a fine man,' said Amy softly, 'and I'm proud of him. But let me tell you, before I go – my mother may forgive you, but I do not. Some day, I hope, you will be punished for what you have done.'

She turned to leave. 'Wait a minute.' Charlotte rose stiffly to her feet, the chair creaking under her weight. 'I remember now. Charles mentioned your husband – a tenant of one of our farms, isn't he? That's right. I remember now. Well,' she paused, relishing her words, 'let me tell you this, my girl, your husband will be out of that farm before his feet can touch the ground. He will that – I'll see to it. Now get out of here before I have the dog set on you. And don't ever come back here again.'

Amy drew herself upright, jutting her chin in the air.

'Don't worry, Aunt Charlotte – I vow I will never come back. There's just one thing I must tell you before I leave—'

Her aunt waved a dismissive hand. 'Don't bother. Just get out.'

'You're wasting your time threatening my husband, Aunt. He's safe, and there's not a thing you can do about it.'

Aunt Charlotte sneered. 'He's our tenant, isn't he? Or was, because this very afternoon—'

'Too late, Aunt Charlotte. The farm is his. I bought it.'

Amy turned and swept triumphantly out of the conservatory, leaving her aunt bereft of speech.

Edwin Glover stood, bare-headed, in the sunlit grave-yard looking down at the headstone. '*Violet Mallinson. 1860–1898. Rest in peace.*'

In his hand he held a small spray of flowers. Laying aside his hat and cane, he knelt with difficulty, and placed the spray on the grave.

'There, Violet, love. From me to thee, with love. I remembered tha never did care for roses, so I've brought all else but roses.'

He bent his greying head, and for a moment remained silent. Opening his eyes again, he smiled at her name carved in the stone. 'I've seen thy lass again, love, and I reckon tha'd be fair proud of her now. Fine husband she has, a bouncing son tha'd be proud to own. She's done well, has the lass, and she'll do all right for herself from now on. She loves her husband, that's plain, whether she had to wed him or not. She's a fighter, is that one, just like thee. Yon Tobias Clegg has done all right for himself, getting her for a wife.

'I wish I'd done the same with thee, Vi – I should have tried harder. But I feel as close to thee as if we had been wed. No couple were closer, I reckon.'

He rose stiffly and stood looking down at the flowers

on the earth. 'Aye,' he murmured, 'I wish I'd have made you Violet Glover before tha went. Ah, well—'

He put his hat on and turned away slowly. Young Amy would be away from Hawksmoor again by now, he told himself, her life beginning to shape itself at last. It was sad to have to go back to his empty house and make tea for one . . . Still, he'd done his best for Amy in the way he knew Violet would have wanted, and he would always be ready to help as a good friend should. Life wasn't without purpose . . . At the lychgate he paused, looking back and shaking his head.

'Eh, she's a grand lass, yon Amy. I didn't think there could be another like you, lass, but your daughter is you all over again, God bless her.'

That evening the doctor's expression was inscrutable as he emerged from the bedroom and walked downstairs with Percy Holroyd. In the privacy of the drawing room he spoke, at last.

'It would seem your wife has had a stroke, I fear, Reverend Holroyd,' he said. 'Brought on by some undue excitement, I imagine, although I have been advising her for some time that she was carrying rather too much weight. I do not think she has been following the diet I recommended.'

Percy, still bewildered by shock, stared at him. 'She's not going to die, is she, doctor?'

The doctor shook his head. 'I think we can safely say there is no danger of that, though she will have to lead a rather quieter life from now on. And some of the damage occasioned by the stroke will remain, I fear. Some paralysis will undoubtedly persist.'

'She'll be able to walk again, won't she?'

'Oh yes, I think so – the paralysis does not appear to have affected the limbs. Fortunately, it seems to have been restricted to the upper area, but there, I'm afraid the prognosis is not promising. I can call in a second opinion, if you so wish.'

'No, no, doctor. I trust your judgement. Does that mean her face will stay like that?'

The doctor nodded. 'Such contortion of the facial muscles is unlikely to recede, I'm afraid. You'll soon grow accustomed to it, I'm sure. But what is likely to prove far more intractable is the paralysis of the vocal chords and muscles. In my opinion, it is unlikely Mrs Holroyd will ever regain the power of speech.'

Percy was bewildered. He was relieved that Charlotte would recover and be able to walk and function as before, but it took some effort to come to terms with the rest of the prospect.

'Dear me,' he murmured. 'We must make sure to do all possible to make her comfortable.'

But for the rest of the day he mused. Charlotte silent for the rest of her life was hard to credit, but with that smile fixed to her face for ever – that was too unbelievable. '*God moves in mysterious ways, his wonders to perform.*'

Amy was exultant. She had robbed Aunt Charlotte of her bid to play her trump card and had spent the rest of the afternoon back at Reed Street polishing and dusting till the house was neat as a new pin for the newly-weds to enter. Now she was going home to Jericho Farm to lay her gift before Tobias.

It was later than she had realised. As she turned off the village street and climbed the rutted lane towards the farm the sun was already beginning to set, filling the western horizon with a golden glow that gave promise of yet another glorious day tomorrow. All her tomorrows would be glorious now, with Tobias and baby Joel and a home they could call their own. All the disappointments and frustrations of the past could be forgotten, buried down there under the pall of smoke that overhung Hawksmoor.

She was singing softly to herself as she climbed the last stretch of the lane.

> *'As I walked out one May summer's morning,*
> *For to view the fields and the flowers so gay—'*

She stopped suddenly and her breath caught in her throat. Tobias was standing on the high ridge, his back towards her, and the sunset spreading out all around him like a glorious sunburst. He looked magnificent, haloed like some Greek god just descended to earth from Olympus. Emotion flooded her, a great, welling surge of love and pride.

He had not seen her. He stood watching the sunset, hands thrust deep in pockets. She would not disturb him now, she decided. He was a deep man, a quiet, private person and he needed his moments of solitude. Her news could wait a little longer.

Morgan was sitting in the rocking chair crooning to the baby in her arms. She started up as Amy entered.

'He were crying so I brought him down. He's got his wind up now. I'll put him back to bed.'

Amy crossed to her and turned back a corner of the baby's blanket to see his face.

'Goodnight, sweetheart. Sleep well, my baby.'

'I'll take him up, then supper's to lay out before I take the swill down to the sty.' Morgan limped to the staircase, then looked back uncertainly. 'Toby's had me make up the bed in the little room for him. He says he can't be doing with the big bed any more.'

'Oh?' Amy was startled.

'Happen it's Joel as disturbs him. He needs his sleep, having to be up betimes in the morning.' Morgan clumped upstairs.

More likely he couldn't be doing with a half-wife, thought Amy. It was asking too much of any man, and he'd been uncommonly forbearing. She had been unfair. She began laying the table for supper.

After a moment Tobias came in. He nodded to her and hung his jacket up on the doorpeg.

'Tha's back, then. Everything all right?'

'Yes, thanks. And Tobias, there's something I have to tell you—'

'And there's summat I want to tell thee – I can't keep it in any longer. I love thee.'

The sudden declaration startled her. She looked at the floor. 'You don't have to say that, Tobias.'

'I know I don't have to,' he growled. 'I need to. I love thee, Amy. I'm going in the little room tonight.'

'There's no need, Tobias—'

'Of course there's need! Dammit, I'm a man of flesh and blood, tha knows, not a saint!' He walked around the far side of the table, avoiding her gaze. For a moment there was silence, then he spoke, gruffly. 'I had them bring the boar up today to service the sow.'

She looked at him intently, trying to search his dark eyes, but he did not meet her gaze. She wondered at his meaning – an effort to change the subject, or had the sight of animals coupling made him realise only too well what was missing in his own life?

She jerked her mind back to the news she had been longing to tell him. She walked round the table and turned him gently to face her. 'Tobias – I have a gift for you.'

She saw the light that leapt into his eyes. 'A gift? Dost mean – what I said – ?'

She stared, uncomprehending, and saw the look of hope in those black eyes. 'What you said?'

The hope vanished, and he looked away. 'Aye – just afore we were wed. Never heed, it doesn't matter.'

Then it came back to her. '*I shall ask nothing of thee, Amy, till tha comes to me of thy own free will.*' A blush reddened her cheeks. He had misunderstood, and she had dashed him down unwittingly. How could she explain that he'd leapt to the wrong conclusion without hurting him? Morgan reappeared, smiling broadly.

'Come on, sit down and we'll have us supper now.'

Amy could see Tobias' eyes fixed upon her as they

ate, and she made an effort to make conversation. Morgan talked on contentedly, seemingly unaware of the tension between husband and wife.

After supper she picked up the swill bucket. 'I'm off down to the pigsty. Won't be long.' The door closed behind her, and there was silence in the kitchen. Then came a low, soft whistle. Tobias jerked a thumb towards the door.

'Yon's Clem Simpson, waiting for our Morgan again. She'll be happy, any road.'

Amy moved behind him. He still sat at the table, his hands lying on the white cloth. The breadth of his back, the sight of his broad, roughened fingers made her tremble. She longed to caress that back, reassure him, lift those fingers to her lips and kiss them . . .

'I'm glad tha came back,' he muttered.

'Did you ever doubt it, Tobias? This is where I belong.' Remembering, she reached into her pocket. 'Here's your luck-penny. You take it, love – you need good fortune.'

'Nay, thee keep it.' He pushed her hand away, and his touch made her shiver.

'Let's go up to bed, Tobias. I'm weary.'

She could see the uncertainty in his eyes. 'Nay.'

'Please. Just one more night. I missed you last night.' She touched his shoulder and felt it stiffen, but he rose slowly.

'Aye, well, for tonight. Thee go up first.'

She was lying in bed when he came, and she watched him as he entered. 'No, don't blow out the candle yet. Leave it a bit.'

There was awkwardness in his every movement as he undressed. She tried to ease it by talking.

'I'll keep your luck-penny, Tobias, but I don't need a token to come back. Nothing would keep me here unless I wanted to be here.'

'Tha mun keep it, any road up. Not to fetter thee,

for I know better. Tha's like a bird, thee, and only a fool would try to tether thee.'

She laughed softly and he climbed into bed, taking care to lie well away from her.

'I know what I'm talking about. Tha's free to come and go as tha wish. The blackbird wouldn't come back every spring to delight us with his song if we was soft enough to try and cage him. Tha's free, lass, and I hope tha'll keep coming back too.'

His hands lay on the counterpane and she watched those strong fingers again – not long and tapered like Charles' but broad and capable and promising security. There was honesty and reliability, loyalty and protectiveness in those hands. She needed those hands, as she needed the man.

'Touch me, Tobias,' she murmured.

For a second he looked startled, then lifted a hand and put a finger gently on her cheek. She closed her eyes and lay still, unmoving. The finger traced the outline of her cheek and chin, as lightly and delicately as if she were a piece of fragile china. She surrendered to the sheer pleasure of his touch, savouring it and allowing herself the luxury of feeling completely vulnerable and yet safe.

'Hold me,' she murmured.

The fingers stopped moving. She felt him lean across to the side table and heard him blow out the candle, then turn to her and hesitate. She wriggled across the gap between them and cradled close to the warmth of his body. She heard him take a deep breath, feeling her skin against his. In the warm peace of the darkness she felt him shiver, and then he pulled her close and wrapped his arms around her. In her own body stirred a joyful expectation.

'I come of my own free will,' she murmured. 'I love you, Tobias.' She felt his arms tighten.

He breathed into her ear. 'Is this thy gift, lass? If it

be so, there's no happier man alive, for I love thee with all my heart.'

'It is,' she whispered. The deeds could wait till tomorrow.

He moved with sureness now; a dexterity born of confidence and love. Words flashed through Amy's mind, unbidden.

'Such passion I have never known till now, and I thank God that he brought my beloved Frederic into my life just when I believed I could never love again.'

Ah, Mother, I too have now learnt the truth. My beloved Tobias. Love and frenzy swelled until she heard her own voice moaning in a culminating cry, echoing around the low rafters.

'Fill me!'

And then there was peace.

BESTSELLING FICTION FROM ARROW

All these books are available from your bookshop or newsagent or you can order them direct. Just tick the titles you want and complete the form below.

☐	THE COMPANY OF SAINTS	Evelyn Anthony	£1.95
☐	HESTER DARK	Emma Blair	£1.95
☐	1985	Anthony Burgess	£1.75
☐	2001: A SPACE ODYSSEY	Arthur C. Clarke	£1.75
☐	NILE	Laurie Devine	£2.75
☐	THE BILLION DOLLAR KILLING	Paul Erdman	£1.75
☐	THE YEAR OF THE FRENCH	Thomas Flanagan	£2.50
☐	LISA LOGAN	Marie Joseph	£1.95
☐	SCORPION	Andrew Kaplan	£2.50
☐	SUCCESS TO THE BRAVE	Alexander Kent	£1.95
☐	STRUMPET CITY	James Plunkett	£2.95
☐	FAMILY CHORUS	Claire Rayner	£2.50
☐	BADGE OF GLORY	Douglas Reeman	£1.95
☐	THE KILLING DOLL	Ruth Rendell	£1.95
☐	SCENT OF FEAR	Margaret Yorke	£1.75

Postage _____

Total _____

ARROW BOOKS, BOOKSERVICE BY POST, PO BOX 29, DOUGLAS, ISLE OF MAN, BRITISH ISLES

Please enclose a cheque or postal order made out to Arrow Books Limited for the amount due including 15p per book for postage and packing both for orders within the UK and for overseas orders.

Please print clearly

NAME...

ADDRESS..

....

Whilst every effort is made to keep prices down and to keep popular books in print, Arrow Books cannot guarantee that prices will be the same as those advertised here or that the books will be available.